BOOKS BY NE

Sex, Lies & Lingerie

SEX

Lies & Lingerie

New York Times & *USA Today* Bestselling Author

NELLE L'AMOUR

To join my mailing list for new releases, sales, and giveaways, please sign up here:
NEWSLETTER: nellelamour.com/newsletter

NICHOLS CANYON PRESS
Los Angeles, CA USA

Sex, Lies & Lingerie

Cover by Arijana Karčic, Cover It! Designs
Formatting by BB eBooks

To all my wonderful readers.
You rock my world.

NOTE FROM NELLE

Dearest Reader~

I'm thrilled to bring you this updated version of my *Gloria's Secret Trilogy*. I have added dual POV throughout, and while the story essentially remains the same, you will now get so much more insight into Jaime Zander's complex mind as well as the challenges and jeopardy he faced while pursuing Gloria. Plus, a whole lot more of his yummy alpha hotness!

Be sure to have a fan nearby. Happy Reading!

MWAH!~Nelle ♥

*"The only lie I ever told you is I liked you
when I already knew I loved you."*

—WRDSMIT71

PROLOGUE
Gloria

Fifteen years earlier . . .

Darkness shrouds us. We prowl like two cats, my eyes darting left and right, my ears attuned to even the slightest sound.

I nervously tap my partner in crime's shoulder. Like me, he's clad in black sweats and a hoodie, along with black gloves and athletic shoes. Identical black ski masks cover our faces. We blend into the thick opaque air, only the whites of our eyes visible.

"Kev, I'm scared. Maybe we should back out," I whisper. My heart's thudding in my ears, and I can feel sweat beads clustering on my flesh.

He squeezes my hand. It's cold and clammy beneath my gloves. "Glorious, we've come this far. There's no turning back."

Something scuttles across my shoes. I jump. Kevin beams the flashlight he's holding onto the floor. Phew! It's only a mouse.

The seconds feel like hours. The safe, Kevin assures me, is only steps away. It feels like miles. Kevin swings the flashlight until it lands on the huge vault in front of us. All slick, polished steel, it's bigger than I imagined—a massive, towering fortress.

"Hold this." Kevin hands me the flashlight. I try hard to calm my trembling hands as I watch Kevin rotate the fist-sized combination lock.

Right. *Click*. Right again. *Click*. Left. *Click*. Right. *Click*.

"Bingo!"

My thundering heart practically leaps out of my chest when the heavy door springs open. My eyes grow round, filling the apertures of the ski mask. Bundles of one hundred dollar bills are stashed inside, stuffing the safe to the hilt.

Kevin instantly starts shoveling them into his large satchel. I'm paralyzed with shock and fear.

"Glorious, what are you waiting for?"

No matter how much I will them, I can't get my hands to move. The stacks of green bills beckon me, but this feels wrong. So, so wrong. *What am I doing here?*

Kevin continues to shovel handfuls of the neatly tied up green bundles into his canvas bag.

"C'mon, we've gotta work fast." His voice sounds frantic.

Reluctantly, I crouch down and extend a trembling hand into the safe. The touch of the raw money burns my fingertips. *I can't do this! I can't!*

An ear-deafening siren sounds. Hot infrared lights flash. The effect is dizzying. An inner panic button goes off inside me as all the air leaves my lungs.

"Fuck!" shouts Kevin. "We've gotta get out of here."

"Leave the money," I plead.

"No. It's ours. *Yours.*"

No choice. Each grabbing a handle of the heavy, money-laden satchel, we sprint toward the exit.

Heavy footsteps. Not ours. The glaring ray of a flashlight beams into my eyes, blinding me. "What the fuck are you doing here?" The booming, accented voice echoes in the chamber. We're doomed!

"Nobody steals from Boris Borofsky."

"Fuck you," Kevin shouts back.

A powerful arm grips my neck. I open my mouth to scream, but no sound comes out. The other hand rips off my ski mask. My platinum tresses tumble out.

He fists a handful of my hair, yanking my head back. His wretched pink eyes clash with mine, one blue and the other brown.

"You little cunt!" growls the accented voice. "You're going to pay for this, *seka!*

"And so are you, bitch," spits Kevin.

Something hard presses into my chest, just above my heart.

Kevin wrenches me free from my assailant but not before a deafening boom explodes in my ear. A scorching white fire shoots through my body. *Oh the pain!*

"You motherfucker." My Kevin.

I feel my body sag as another shot is fired.

"FUUUUUUCK!" A roar like a wounded lion, not mine.

"Oh, Glorious!" cries Kevin as he lifts me in his arms.

The world inside my head fades to black.

CHAPTER 1

Gloria

I was running late. I was never late. "Late" wasn't part of my vocabulary. Damn that breakfast meeting. My guest, the stiff-lipped head of a major Madison Avenue ad agency, showed up forty-five minutes late. There'd been a cab accident en route that had caused a traffic jam. The unexpected had no place in my life. To make matters worse, I had to run back up to my hotel room because I'd carelessly left my cell phone in a different handbag. As the CEO of Gloria's Secret, one of the largest retail emporiums in the world, I couldn't be without my lifeline for the rest of the day.

Clutching my briefcase in my right hand, I anxiously pressed the elevator "Down" button several times with the other. I was staying in New York City at The Walden, a recently renovated five-star, twenty-one story Park Avenue hotel that dated back to the fifties. Unfortunately, my favorite hotel, The Ritz-Carlton, was booked up so I had decided to give this new, highly-rated venue a chance. So far, I hadn't been disappointed. The accommodations were outstanding as was the service.

The elevator, to my relief, arrived quickly. I dashed inside the sleek car, which still retained some of its mid-century charm, and hit the "L" button for the lobby. The polished metal doors slid closed. Just before they met in the middle, a manicured masculine hand flashed between them, preventing them from closing.

In a panic, I fumbled to press the "Open" button, fearing that the doors would slam shut on the hand and crush it. I'd seen this uncanny thing happen once before as a child and had never forgotten the gory scene. Flustered, I lost grip of my stuffed briefcase, and it tumbled onto the floor. In my haste to make it to my next meeting on time, I'd forgotten to zip it. This was just not my day. The contents—dozens of photos of gorgeous supermodels clad in skimpy under-wear—scattered around my black stilettos. My teeth clenched. I just didn't need this right now. I crouched down to gather up the spillage—no easy task in my tight pencil skirt and six-inch heels. As I began to frantically collect the photos, two loafer-clad feet appeared before my eyes.

"Let me help you." The voice was virile, velvety, and deep.

Before I could blink an eye, I was facing the intruder who had caused me to drop my briefcase. He had bent down to help me gather the loose photos. Our eyes stayed locked on one another. Mine shooting daggers his way. His deflecting every one of my visual assaults. Just a palm's width apart, I felt his warm breath heat my cheeks and could smell a hint of his deliciously spicy cologne. I recognized it immediately. *Homme,* which means "man" in French. It was part of our newly launched men's line of fragrances. The perfect gift for a woman to give to her man this coming Valentine's Day.

I studied his face and what I could glean of his body. Let's put it this way: I had seen a lot of male models, but this guy was something else. Manly. Built. Mid to late thirties. He was one hundred percent pure gorgeousness with his broad shoulders, intense denim blue eyes, mop of silky chestnut hair, and strong dimpled chin. A fine layer of stubble laced his olive complexion. Along with sockless suede loafers, he was wearing a battered leather bomber jacket over a white cotton T-shirt that showed off his taut chest, and faded designer jeans that revealed a ridge of muscles along his thighs. I assumed his legs were long, but it was hard to tell in his squatting position. What I could tell for sure was that there was a sizeable package between them. My gaze shifted quickly back to the floor.

"Interesting photos," my companion mused, his eyes lingering on a particularly sexy one of a D-cup model fondling her lace-encased breasts. A wry smile twisted his lips. "Hmm. I think I fucked her once." He picked up another. "She looks familiar too."

"Give me those!" I snatched the photos from him and slipped them into my briefcase.

"Are you a photographer?" he asked, not the least bit intimidated by me.

"Hardly."

"So, you're some kind of pervert who collects photos of beautiful semi-naked women with big tits."

"And you're some kind of pervert who sleeps with them." I shot him my dirtiest look and continued collecting the scattered photos. We both reached for the last one, and my hand brushed up against his. God, his hand was beautiful! Large, long-fingered, and so, so soft. Even the violet veins that splayed across them were works of art.

Caught in the moment, I suddenly realized we weren't moving. The elevator doors were still open. In my flustered state, I'd forgotten to hit the "Close" button.

"Would you mind hitting the "Close" button?" My voice was edgy.

"Good idea. Places to go; people to meet." He rose to his feet. My eyes roamed up his long, athletic legs. He was easily six foot three. A magnificent pillar of leanness and muscle.

With his elegant forefinger, he pushed the button, and the doors glided together. The elevator descended, but before I could stand up, it came to a jolting halt. I felt the onset of a mini panic attack. My heart raced and sweat pooled behind my knees. I hated being out of control.

"Are you okay?" asked the mysterious stranger, crouching down again.

I gulped. Unable to find my voice, I nodded like one of those bobble head dolls. The truth: I was losing it, and I wasn't sure if it was the effect his gorgeousness was having on me or that of the erratic elevator.

He brushed my chin with the wispy tip of my long platinum braid. "Don't worry. This happens all the time with this elevator."

Without warning, the elevator jerked and began to free-fall. I gasped while the breathtaking man beside me grinned smugly as if he was enjoying every minute of this situation.

"Hey, we're moving again. This is an express elevator, so we'll be down in no time."

My heart dropped to my stomach even faster. This man was having a very uncomfortable effect on me. I felt my cheeks heat and my heart tick like a metronome.

In no time, the elevator reached our destination, and the doors opened wide. My companion lifted me to my feet. His firm grip around my shoulders sent a parade of goosebumps down my arms. We stood face-to-face. My five foot nine frame in six-inch heels confirmed his estimated height. Standing erect, his body was even more imposing than I'd imagined. His shoulders were square, his hips narrow, and his legs long and solid.

"Ladies, first," he said with a sexy wink.

With my briefcase in hand, I shot out of the elevator and

walked briskly through the bustling mid-century themed lobby to the entrance of the hotel. The clickety-clack of my heels across the marble floor echoed in my ears. Mr. Infuriating strode next to me, keeping up with my pace with ease.

Outside the tall steel and glass building, we stood side by side. The early morning rush of New York pedestrians and cabs passed us by. The weather was picture-postcard perfect and surprisingly mild for a mid-February day. I was glad that I didn't wear a coat.

"Can I give you a ride?" he asked. "My driver will be here any minute."

"I have my own driver," I replied without looking his way.

"Impressive." I didn't miss the playful sarcasm in his voice.

His driver, in a sleek black Ranger Rover, pulled up first. A hotel valet raced to open the back door for my companion.

"See ya." He winked at me again.

Bastard!

With an irritating smirk, he slid into the Rover. His eyes lingered on mine before the passenger door closed. My deadpan face didn't move a muscle as the SUV pulled away.

Two minutes later, my black Town Car pulled up. My driver stepped out and escorted me into the back seat.

"Good morning, Miss Long."

"Good morning, Nigel," I said brightly as I sidled gracefully into the car. Trusty Nigel was always my driver when I came to New York for business. I could always count on the jovial, silver-haired Brit to get me anywhere. And there on time.

"Where to this morning?"

I gave him the address of ZAP! It was located in the

heart of Soho.

I leaned back against the comfy leather seat and let out a sigh. This was the tenth—and last ad agency—I was visiting. Since the beginning of the week, I had met with all of the top Madison Avenue agencies. It had been a draining, whirlwind tour.

Truthfully, none of them had impressed me. As CEO of Gloria's Secret, the largest lingerie retail chain in the world, I was looking for a creative team to help me bring my empire to a new level of sensuality and sales. With the insane popularity of books like *Fifty Shades of Grey,* I was convinced women were looking for a new way to express themselves. A way that consensually communicated: *Take me—I'm yours.* If we were going to stay ahead of the competition, then I had to be the first to tap into this hot, new erotic trend. We were already developing a line of provocative products.

The car cruised down Fifth Avenue, Nigel expertly weaving in and out of the maddening mid-town traffic. In the back seat, I mused about my upcoming meeting.

Unlike the other ad agencies I'd visited, ZAP! was a relatively new kid on the block. What was called a "boutique agency." My partner Kevin had heard about their cutting-edge work and had urged me to meet with them. My heart set on a big agency, I reluctantly agreed to his request, but after researching it a bit, I was glad I'd trusted Kevin's instincts.

Several things I'd read online about the agency had impressed me. First, they had created a campaign for a new Japanese minivan that made the word "minivan" sexy. The campaign's tagline: *"And the mommy goes "mmmmmmm."* Anyone who could turn an oppressive minivan into a sexy beast scored points with me.

Secondly, the founder and CCO (Chief Creative Officer)

of the agency was a woman. Jaime Zander. Our new ad campaign needed the touch of a woman. Someone who had insight into women's sexual desires and fantasies. Someone who had read *Fifty Shades of Grey* and understood its phenomenal success. I, too, was drawn to the sexy, enigmatic Christian Grey and believed that our new BDSM-inspired undergarments would give a woman a better chance at landing her own Mr. Grey. Or, at least, let her fantasize she could.

Lastly, I was drawn to the ZAP! website. It was innovative and creative rather than corporate and boastful. I especially liked the key personnel profile photos—all adorable baby pictures, including CCO Jaime, with her head full of chestnut curls, sweet dimpled chin, and checkered overalls.

Nigel dropped me off in front of a brick townhouse on Spring Street. I double-checked the address on my cell phone, thinking that ZAP! might be housed in slightly more corporate headquarters. But sure enough, this was where the agency was located. My courteous driver opened the passenger door for me. Hopping out, I told him I would text him after the meeting was over.

Once inside the building, I stepped into the reception area. Unlike the stark, leather and chrome waiting areas of the Madison Avenue *Madmen* agencies I'd met with, this one was warm and funky, filled with eccentric mid-century furnishings and a shag carpet that reminded me a little of the hotel I was staying at. The blazing orange letters—ZAP!— were hung like giant puzzle pieces on the bright yellow wall behind the receptionist's console. She was an artsy-looking girl in her early twenties who sported a graphic Jim Morrison tee and several tattoos on her arms. She was a far cry from the impeccably groomed young women who manned the front desk at those other ad agencies I'd visited.

"I have a ten o'clock meeting with Jaime Zander," I told her.

She glanced at her computer screen and asked me if I was Gloria Long.

"Yes."

"Cool."

She dialed an extension, announcing my arrival to whomever was on the receiving end. I assumed it was Jaime's assistant. "Someone will be right out to bring you back to Jaime's office. Make yourself comfy."

Before I could take a seat on the curvy couch, a twenty-something man with inky blue hair and an earring sashayed into the reception area to fetch me. He was very attractive, very stylish, and very gay. He smiled brightly at me, revealing a set of perfect white teeth. "I'm Ray, Jaime's assistant. Jaime is so looking forward to meeting you. Follow me."

Though younger, he reminded me a lot of my best friend and head of Public Relations, Kevin Riley, who was at the Lexington Avenue Armory preparing for the highly anticipated pre-Valentine's Day Gloria's Secret Fashion Show. My assistant, Vivien Holden, was there too. Right after this meeting, I would be rushing uptown to join them. As always on one of these business trips to New York, we had a hell of a lot going on. In fact, too much. The sooner I got out of New York, the better. Boris Borofsky was lurking out there somewhere. Inwardly, I shuddered.

With my briefcase in hand, I followed Ray through a gutted space to the end office. I liked the way everyone sat in the open and was immersed in their work. My eyes took in the posters for various ad campaigns that lined the walls. Most of them were familiar and indeed quite memorable.

"Jaime had to run down the hall to check out a spot we just produced for one of our clients and will be right back.

Can I get you anything to drink?"

"I'm fine, thank you," I said, surveying my surroundings and deciding where to sit. I chose a Scandinavian armchair over the couch. Sitting tall and cross-legged in a chair was always more empowering than sinking into a cushion. I liked to be in control of a meeting, especially when it was with someone I didn't know.

My eyes toured the expansive office. Like the reception area, it was warm and funky, filled with eccentric, colorful, artsy furnishings. Intriguing abstract portraits and landscapes dotted the walls, all signed PAZ; one of the portraits was of a blue-eyed baby girl that looked a lot like the photo I'd seen online. My favorite piece of furniture was Jaime's desk, which was shaped like a large kidney bean. For a busy CCO, she had few things on it. Just a stack of neatly arranged bright-colored files, a state-of-the-art Apple computer, and a single framed photo. Behind the desk was a credenza that displayed the many awards the small advertising agency had garnered. From what I'd gleaned of Jaime's taste so far, she must be quite a creative and interesting woman. I was looking forward to meeting her and getting down to business.

With a few minutes to spare, I used the time to my advantage. Pulling out my phone from my handbag, I checked my emails. There were easily a hundred new ones from people who reported to me around the world. From store managers to subcontractors. Why did everyone have to bother me with their silly problems? But that was my job. To run the company. There were only two that I urgently needed to read. The first, from Kevin, who was likely updating me about the status of this afternoon's annual Gloria's Secret Fashion Show. I opened it and sucked in a deep breath. So far everything was on schedule and moving forward. The other one was good news too. It was from one of my product managers informing me that the first prototype of the sex toys we were developing had been shipped to our Los Angeles headquarters. A smile spread across my face. We were about to expand our business, which now included intimate apparel, active wear, and beauty products with a collection of BDSM-inspired lingerie and a complementary line of fun, innovative sex toys. Our consumer research with focus groups had strongly indicated that this could be a breakout piece of business for us—women believed that vibrators, dildoes, and bondage accessories like lace masks and silk handcuffs were a natural extension of our already sexy product line. And that Gloria's Secret was a store where they would feel comfortable purchasing these provocative items. We had indeed evolved into a major "lifestyle" brand. As I was about to hit reply, an email with the word "Update" in the subject line came in from Kevin.

G~

The run-through was HOT! Except the lead model tripped on her heels and sprained her ankle. Looking for a replacement. Challenging as all models are working Fashion Week. Will keep you posted.

~xoK

I replied to his email with a smiley-faced emoticon. Among the many things I loved about Kevin was that he was a problem solver. He had once saved my life. If it weren't for him, I wouldn't be who I am; there would be no Gloria's Secret. I was confident he would find a replacement, and the show would go on.

As I began to reply to the remaining emails, the sound of sprite footsteps diverted my attention. I swiveled my head to the doorway. Before I could take my next breath, my jaw dropped to the floor and my phone slipped out of my hand.

Oh. My. God. It was him! That pompous asshole who had caused me to drop my briefcase in the elevator and then played head games with me. What the hell was he doing here? Maybe he worked for Ms. Zander?

He took long confident steps in my direction. I hesitantly stood up. He took my hand in his and shook it. His grip was firm, the touch warm. My body stiffened and my heartbeat quickened.

"Ms. Long, a pleasure to meet you officially."

My mouth frozen open, I was speechless. Finally, I found my voice. "And you're . . ."

"Jaime Zander."

Holy, holy crap! In a state of borderline shock, I collapsed back into my chair. He shot me a devilish smile. Damn him. He knew I was caught off guard. Big time.

Wordlessly, I gazed up at his face. The baby photo that I'd seen online flashed into my head. It was him all right. Though maybe thirty-five years older, he had the same baby blues with that thick fan of lashes, silky chestnut hair, and that distinct dimpled chin. He had been one of those babies that old ladies would look at and say, "Oh, he's pretty enough to be a girl."

Mortification struck me like a lightning bolt. I was not easily rattled, but Mr. Zander had succeeded. I suddenly didn't want to do the meeting or give him my business.

Paralyzed, my eyes stayed locked on him as he lowered himself into the chair catty-cornered to mine. We were in such close proximity I could inhale the intoxicating scent of him and feel his warm breath on my cheeks.

"Are you sure I can't get you something? A coffee? Water? Tea perhaps?"

A fan?

"No, thank you," I said, nervously tugging on the thick, platinum braid that wrapped around my shoulder and cascaded over my breasts. The sooner we got down to business the better. His presence was making me bristle. *Get a grip, Gloria. You're one of Forbes's One Hundred Most Powerful Women in the World!*

Composing myself, I began by telling him that I was seeking an outside agency to bring my company, Gloria's Secret, to a new level of sales and sensuality.

Listening, he folded one long, muscled leg over the other and relaxed back in his chair with his sculpted arms casually crossed over his crotch—I mean, lap. "Gloria's Secret. The #1 lingerie retailer in the world. Two thousand forty-five stores worldwide. Estimated annual sales revenue: 6.2 billion dollars."

He had indeed done his homework. But there was no way in hell I was going to let him know that I was impressed. My expression remained impassive while I responded.

"Yes. We've enjoyed phenomenal success. But we can't stop here. Imitators are springing up. We've got to stay on the cutting edge, ahead of the competition." I paused. Okay, now the test. "Did you read *Fifty Shades of Grey*?"

He grinned. "Of course."

Ha! I didn't believe him. He was bullshitting me. I could tell by the wry look on his face.

"Okay, then what's the full name of Christian Grey's adoptive mother?"

"Are you testing me, Gloria?"

"It's Ms. Long, and yes, I am . . . Well?"

Without wasting a second, he blurted, "Grace Trevelyn Grey. And she's a pediatrician."

I mentally screwed up my face. Score one for him. Except for one feminist copywriter who pooh-poohed the book for demeaning women, none of the Madison Avenue suits had read it. I had to hand it to him. But exam time wasn't over yet. "Mr. Zander—"

"Please call me Jaime."

Ironically, his first name was the same as the swoon-worthy actor who was playing Christian Grey in the movie version. Jamie Dornan, though they spelled it differently. But in terms of sex appeal, they were neck to neck. Muscle to muscle. *Organ to organ?*

"All right, *Jai-me*, tell me, what, in your opinion, has made the book so popular with women?"

He leaned into me, looking straight into my eyes. His gaze penetrated me. As much as I wanted to turn away, my vision stayed fixed on him.

"Truthfully, while the sex is hot, I believe women fall for the romance."

"What do you mean?" I was all ears.

"Well, *Ms. Long*, wouldn't you like me to scoop you up in my arms . . . tell you that 'I want you, body and soul, forever' and make insane love to you on the couch?"

Inwardly, I gasped. He had actually quoted Christian Grey. My eyes took in his mountainous biceps and then traveled down to his crotch. Holy shit. It was tented. My temperature instantly rose ten degrees. A hot flash. Confession: I had the burning urge to shrug off more than just my suit jacket.

He leaned in closer and growled in my ear. "Or would you prefer me to throw you over my desk . . . or perhaps carry you away and devour you on the conference room table down the hall?"

I squeezed my inner thighs together and could not stop my crossed leg from swinging like a pendulum—a behavior so not in my repertoire. I jerked away from him and found my voice. "You seem to know women rather well."

He sat back in the chair. "Yes, I do." His tone was confident, almost cocky.

"In my experience, the only men who understand women are gay. Are you, by chance, gay, Jaime?"

He let out a deep, sexy chortle. "Hardly. I could have several hundred stunning women give you a stellar recommendation."

"Oh, so you have them review you like you're a book on Amazon?" My deadpan sarcasm camouflaged my shock at the number of women he'd likely fucked.

He laughed again. "You're quite witty, Ms. Long. I have to say I like you."

Again, I was speechless and growing more heated by the second.

He moved in again closer to me and snagged my braid, coiling it around his exquisite, long-fingered hand. "So, what will it take to win your account?"

The hair play was distracting me. Sending a barrage of sparks to my core. This was likely some form of sexual harassment, but while my brain was whispering stop, my body was clamoring for more. Why did something so wrong feel so right? Battling my physical sensations, I forced myself to remove his hand from my tresses and composed myself once more. "I've asked every agency I've met with to come up with a pitch by Friday. Do you think your agency could do that?"

"Not a problem. I'll put my best person on the job right away."

"And who might that be?" I asked, my voice dripping with a mix of curiosity and sarcasm.

He grinned wickedly. "Yours truly." With that, he rose and escorted me to the door. Before I could step over the threshold, he barricaded it with his body and outstretched arms. His biceps flexed as he pressed his hands against the framework. We were face-to-face again, only a breath away.

His eyes burnt into mine. "I meant to tell you, Ms. Long,

I find your eyes fascinating."

Most people did. My right eye was blue; my left one brown. I had a rare genetic condition known as heterochromia. In press releases and on the Internet, both eyes appeared to be brown thanks to Photoshop. But because I suffered from dry eye syndrome, I was unable to use contacts to conceal my idiosyncrasy the rest of the time.

Jaime continued to study my mismatched eyes. "They're contradictions just like the rest of you."

That I hadn't heard before. "What do you mean?"

"Your mind says one thing, your body says another."

His words spurred another rush of head-to-toe tingles and sent my heart into a gallop. My breath hitched. He was unhinging me again. "Mr. Zander, can I please leave?" I spluttered.

With a smirk, he pivoted so that he was leaning against the doorway. He gave my braid a little tug as I hurried past him. "Ms. Long, I look forward to the *pleasure* of seeing you again."

"The same." *Bastard!*

As I stomped down the hallway, I could feel his fiery eyes on my backside. His voice traveled down the corridor. "Oh, by the way, I find your black lace push-up bra and matching thong very sexy. And that garter . . ."

Cringing, I just kept moving. How the hell did he know what I was wearing under my suit?

CHAPTER 2

Jaime

Leaning back in my desk chair, I folded my hands behind my head and chortled out loud. That meeting was priceless. Especially the expression on her face when she found out that I was the one and only Jaime Zander. Mentally, I gave myself a round of applause for not giving myself away during our unexpected elevator encounter or revealing that I recognized her immediately from the many photos I'd seen of her online. Though I had to admit she was far more stunning in person. And far more intriguing. *And* challenging.

She's something that Gloria Long, I mused. Thank fuck, I did my research and knew all I could about her. The information about her past was sparse, but there was an endless number of entries about her as a businesswoman. My takeaway: she was tough cookie, but I could make her crumble. And not just in the boardroom.

With a content smile, I closed my eyes. Jesus fucking Christ. That ass. That gorgeous ass. It was imprinted on my brain. No matter how much I tried, I couldn't get it out of my head.

I bet it was perfectly round and sat high. Her cheeks, firm but supple, as smooth and white as porcelain. My twitchy cock flexed beneath my desk. In my mind's eye, I fantasized bending her over my desk, squeezing those scrumptious cheeks apart, and then fucking her from behind. Pummeling her with my dick as she shrieked, those beautiful big tits bouncing in rhythm, threatening to fall out of the cups of her lace bra, as she rocked backward to meet my thrusts. Hearing her yelp as I tugged hard on her long platinum braid, tilting her head back, as I brought her to the point of no return. No pain, no gain. I bet she was a screamer. Yeah, for sure and if she wasn't, all of Manhattan would hear her come by the time I was done with her.

My hand involuntarily jumped to my spiraling cock when a ping from my computer intercepted my fantasy. An email. My eyes snapped open and my attention leaped to the screen. As I read whom it was from, my cock deflated and my spine tightened. How the fuck did she get my address? What the hell does she want? *She* was one of the last people I ever wanted to see or hear from.

Subject: SURPRISE!

Against my better judgment, I read the rest of the email. How ironic. An invite. Fine, I'd go. It would just be another opportunity to fuck with her mind.

Gloria's.

CHAPTER 3

Gloria

Insanity. Utter insanity. That was the only way to describe the electrifying pre-show atmosphere at the Lexington Avenue Armory. Production personnel were running around like banshees getting it together. They were talking into headsets and cell phones and frantically jotting down notes on clipboards and in notebooks. The look of stress and panic was etched on everyone's faces. Adrenaline was flying. The much-anticipated Gloria's Secret Fashion Show was scheduled to start in an hour, but it seemed like we'd never get there.

It was always like this even though this was our tenth show. This one, however, was more ambitious because it was celebrating our first decade of putting them on. For the first time, the show was being broadcast on a major television network in addition to being shown live on our website. Every fashion journalist and blogger in the world was going to be here including reporters from *Entertainment Tonight* . . . *Vogue* . . . *TMZ* . . . just to name a few. And the celebrity list was endless.

"Glorious! Thank God, you're here!" a familiar breathless voice called out. It was my trusted head of PR and Special Events, Kevin Riley. Kevin and I had been best friends forever. Since childhood. We knew everything about each other and shared a dark secret that bonded us eternally. We had been through a lot, and never for a minute did I forget that I owed so much of my success to him. In fact, my life. I loved him like a brother. We even had nicknames for one and other. I called him Kev, and he called me Glorious. We'd built Gloria's Secret from the ground up together.

"What's going on?" I asked as he jogged up to me. While Kev could be an outrageous dresser, today he was dressed for functionality in perfectly shredded black jeans, a tight T-shirt, and high-top Keds. With his spiky, dark-haired good looks, svelte toned body, and charismatic smile, he could easily make women melt, but that was not his preference. The diamond ear stud he proudly wore said it all. It had been a birthday gift from me.

With a flutter of his deep-set hazel eyes, he sighed, "The usual. The models are having meltdowns over who's wearing what . . . Kim Kardashian's people just called saying she's miffed because she's not in the front row . . . and Rihanna's limo is stuck in traffic."

I rolled my eyes. There was no need to freak. All these hiccups were routine for this show. Business as usual. I trusted Kevin implicitly with my heart and soul. He'd make sure things worked out. They always did.

His cell phone rang. He put it to his ear and said, "Great." Smiling, he ended the call. "Rihanna's here! Gotta go." He gave me a peck on my cheek. "Glorious, this show is going to rock!"

God, I loved Kev! He brought good luck and sunshine even in the darkest times. As he scurried off, my eyes drank in everything. This show *was* going to rock! The set designer that Kevin had hired had created an outrageous fantasy of a sexed up heaven. Dry smoke emanated from the stage floor and rose up to the high ceiling where virtual clouds were projected. The plan was for dozens of gorgeous Gloria's

Secret models, clad in outrageous angel wings and the barest of bare undergarments, to float down from the ceiling via invisible ropes onto the runway. Some would even be entwined with sexy male angels in hot embraces. We were selling sex—fantasies and wet dreams. I so loved it! If the televised show went off without a hitch and got high ratings, tomorrow—Valentine's Day—would be our stores' busiest day of the year and lead to record first quarter earnings.

While I took in everything and contemplated my mandatory end-walk down the runway, another familiar, this time shrill feminine voice, sounded in my ear.

"If you don't do it my way, I'm going to have you fired." It was Vivien Holden, my assistant, arguing with a tired, overworked production assistant. I didn't need to spin around because she was already in my face.

She was clad in a purple mini skirt that barely covered her ass, a tight white blouse opened far enough to reveal her eye-worthy cleavage, and six-inch black patent stilettos that made her compact busty body rise to almost five foot six. I had to admit Vivien was stunning; she was younger than me by four years. I was thirty-three, she, twenty-nine. Her blessings, albeit manufactured, included a mane of long thick ebony hair (weaves), full, sensuous lips (filler), piercing green eyes (contacts), and a perfect upturned nose that I suspected was the result of plastic surgery along with her D-cup boobs. She could afford to have her features altered. She was rich. Mega rich. "Daddy"—billionaire corporate raider, Victor Holden—was Gloria's Secret's largest shareholder and Chairman of the Board. I could never keep track of how many shares he controlled. All I needed to remember was that he could make or break everything I'd built. And make or break me.

Despite being my assistant, Vivien was never pleased to see me. She narrowed her catty eyes and gave me the once-over. "How did it go today with ZAP!?"

Before I could respond, she huffed, "You know, Gloria, I should have been there. Daddy says advertising is soon going to be under my domain."

Her words irked me. Everything was under *my* domain. I was the CEO and founder of Gloria's Secret. Vivien thought she was entitled because Daddy backed the company. Though she was talented, she wanted to get to the top quickly. It was no secret that she coveted my job. Inhaling deeply, I controlled myself. I couldn't afford to offend her because of her father. Or fire her because Victor's investment in my company was predicated on a life-long job for Vivien. It was a Catch-22 situation that I had to accept.

"No, Vivien, you belonged here. The Gloria's Secret Fashion Show can make or break our year-end earnings. Plus, there's so much you can learn from being on the set."

She scoffed at me. "The only thing I've learned is that I'm surrounded by a bunch of incompetent morons."

God, I wanted to slap her. Or rip off her phony baloney lips. And that was not all.

With a flick of her head, she flung back her mane of hair, one of her annoying habits. "So what was Jaime Zander like? I haven't seen him for years."

My brows lifted. Vivien knew Jaime? Why didn't she tell me? She could have spared me a lot of embarrassment.

"He was very professional," I answered, masking my displeasure. She had no need to know the details of the meeting. The thought of Jaime Zander made my breath hitch in my throat. "I'm looking forward to his pitch, which I want you and Kevin to attend."

Her cat-green eyes lit up. "And I'm looking forward to seeing him again."

She sauntered off before I could I ask her what she meant by that.

CHAPTER 4

Jaime

I managed to clear my afternoon and got to the Lexington Avenue Armory quickly. Located on Lex between 25th and 26th Street, it wasn't far my office. Noting the long line of limos and taxis lined up in front to the venerable Beaux Art style landmark, I had my driver Orson let me out a few blocks before and then jogged over to the entrance, clutching my VIP pass which I'd printed out from my computer. There was a special, much shorter line for VIPs so I got into the building in no time, eschewing the paparazzi that were swarming the area.

The lobby of the Armory was bustling with spectators here to see the Gloria's Secret Fashion Show. I recognized several celebrities in the crowd as well as a few of my past fucks—including a top model, a reality show bachelorette, and a local newscaster. When they made eye contact with me, I shot them back cordial smiles and buried myself in the crowd. According to an announcement, the doors to the auditorium wouldn't be opening for another fifteen minutes. I glanced down at my watch; things were running late.

My mind drifted. I wondered again how Vivien had gotten my email address. And how she had access to an extra ticket to this event. In retrospect, I'm surprised Gloria herself hadn't given me one as seeing the show might inspire my marketing pitch. HA! Maybe I made her so hot and bothered she simply forgot. Or maybe she deliberately wanted to avoid me.

"Surprise!" A familiar raspy voice cut into my mental ramblings as a hand groped my crotch. Forcefully shoving the hand off me, I spun around and met her face to face. She knotted her arms around my neck and moved in closer to me. Her cloying perfume was as toxic as she was. Bristling, I peeled her arms off me in a single sharp move. *Don't fucking touch me.*

"Jesus, Jaime. Is that anyway to treat a lady?" She rubbed her forearm where I'd gripped it. "And someone you haven't seen for over a decade?"

Vivien was the last thing from being a lady. And someone I *never* wanted to see again. I took her in. If I hadn't recognized her sultry voice, I might not have recognized her in the crowd. While not much taller than I'd seen her last, she looked totally different. The former chubby twelve-year old with the mousy brown hair and bucked teeth was now a total vixen—her taut body sculpted with tits the size of melons and a wasp-like waist, her hair now thick and jet-black, and most significant, her facial features sculpted to make her look like a modern-day Elizabeth Taylor. She'd had tons of work done, something her father could well afford.

"Well, Jaime, aren't you even going to say hello?" Her voice dripped with sarcasm. Her new look seemed to have made her even more obnoxious.

"What are you doing here?" I asked, deflecting her question.

With a roll of her wicked green eyes, she flung her head back. "Seriously, doll boy, do you really have to ask?"

The hairs on the back of my neck stood up. What didn't I know? "Enlighten me." My monotone voice was as cold as ice.

Another eye roll. "Didn't Gloria tell you about me?"

She knew about my meeting with Gloria Long? Anger was unfurling inside me. "Tell me what?"

"That I work for her and that one day I'm going to run the entire company."

"What are you talking about?"

"Puh-lease. Don't you know? Daddy's the Chairman of the Board. He controls everything."

The news hit me like a brick. A blunt force to the head. Nowhere online had I read that Victor Holden was involved in Gloria's business. Vivien had stunned me into silence.

"You know what they say. Money buys power." She ran her hand through her witchy mane of hair. "Oh, and by the way, Daddy may come by."

Seeing Vivien was bad enough. But was I ready to confront Victor? Memories of the past rolled through me like nausea. Maybe I should just get the fuck out of here. Pass on the Gloria's Secret account while I still had a chance. Vivien's voice drifted back in my ears as she grabbed my hand.

"C'mon, Jaime, let's take a picture in front of the step and repeat."

Eying the pink and white banner with the Gloria's Secret logo all over it, I jerked myself free of Vivien.

"Let go of me, Vivien, and don't touch me again."

With a shake of her head, she tutted. "Looks like I'm going to have to whip you into shape."

Her words sent a painful chill down my spine. I stiffened.

Then, before I could say a word, the doors to the auditorium opened. As the crowd piled in, I had a split second to make a decision. Walk away. Or walk inside.

My options warred in my head. But not for long. I inhaled a fortifying breath. Fuck Vivien. Fuck Victor. Things were different now. I was a man who got what I wanted. Rich and successful. No longer subject to their torture.

I wanted the Gloria's Secret account.

I wanted *her*.

And the fuckers weren't going to stand in my way.

CHAPTER 5

Gloria

"In five, four, three, two, one ... Showtime!" Hot techno music blasted; my heart hammered. Watching from backstage, I gaped in awe as our gorgeous long-legged supermodel angels, their D-cup bodies clad in the skimpiest lace bras and thongs, descended from the ceiling through a cloud of dry ice onto the runway and began to strut down it, one after another, in their six-inch stilettos. Their outrageous colorful feathered wings, attached to their backs, fluttered like butterflies as they vamped to the beat of the pulsing music. Loud gasps, whistles, and applause emanated from the celebrity-packed audience and press. I let out a deep breath. Yes! They loved it! My beloved Kevin had pulled it off again. It truly was an unforgettable spectacle. Almost surreal, otherworldly. I was totally in the moment but wouldn't be relaxed until it was over. Every muscle in my body clenched.

Twenty minutes into the show, Kevin joined me backstage. While I was still an exposed nerve waiting for the worst to happen, he was like a child in a candy store. His long-lashed eyes lit up like lanterns. "It's f*aaa*bulous!" he crooned, squeezing my hand. In my anxious state, his hand was a welcome comfort.

"Have you seen Vivien?" I asked.

"Not for ages."

I wondered where she was. She was supposed to be with me, updating me on the live webcast. Once things settled down and we were back in Los Angeles, I was going to have a come to Jesus meeting with her, regardless of who her father was. That girl needed to learn what it meant to be a team player.

Without a hitch, the show continued to blow the audience away. Oohs, aahs, whistles, and cheers filled the air. Forty minutes in, Rihanna descended from "the heavens" in a cloud of pink smoke. The crowd went wild. She looked amazing, her dazzling body clad in a diamond-studded black leather bra and thong we had custom-made for her. The cost to make the ensemble was one million dollars, but it was being auctioned off later tonight for charity at the after-party that Victor Holden was hosting at Touch. My hunch was that some billionaire pervert was going to buy the matching set and put them to his nose every night at bedtime. I chortled silently.

With raw sexuality, Rihanna belted out her new song, "Open Your Mind." *"Mind over body; body over mind. Open your legs wide. Baby, let him know you're mine."* Closing my eyes, I found myself thrusting my hips, getting lost in the words and beat of the stunning superstar's sensuous song. Without warning, the image of a stunning man flooded my head. Jaime Zander! We were face-to-face. Heart to heart. Hip to hip.

My heart was vibrating. And then I realized it was actually my cell phone that I'd stuck inside my shirt pocket. I'd put it on mute, having informed all my employees to text me during the show only if it was an emergency. I silently cursed. This must be an emergency. My eyes flew open. I immediately checked my messages.

Ms. Long~

What does this song do for you?

xJ

The air escaped my lungs. *Holy Shit! He's here?*

With grinding dance moves to match, Rihanna continued to exude sex with her sultry song. My core was pulsing, my heart racing. What was wrong with me? Jaime Zander! This man, who I hardly knew, had no right to invade my head. And stalk me, no less! Damn him!

"Gloria, it's almost over!" piped Kevin, snapping me back to reality.

My mind was elsewhere as Rihanna took a bow, and the show moved into the grand finale. In a file, all the sexy, winged models paraded down the runway, their faces aglow with megawatt smiles. The audience leaped up from their seats, applauding and cheering as the last model did her turn.

"Glorious, go! It's your turn to take a bow." A remixed version of the late great Laura Branigan's popular 80's song "Gloria" was always my signal . . . *calling Gloria.* Taking my phone out of my trembling hand, Kevin had to virtually push me onto the runway. I was so distracted with thoughts of Jaime Zander that I'd forgotten about this mandatory ritual.

Wearing our popular black leggings and an oversized button-down white blouse that I'd changed into before the show, I staggered down the runway, my legs like jelly. Thank goodness, I was wearing ballet flats. The models and standing audience applauded and cheered loudly. I inhaled deeply. Once again, I was in the moment, in control. Without a doubt, this show had been our best ever; we had outdone ourselves. Taking my bow, I was both humbled and elated. Fireworks went off, and a flurry of confetti cascaded from the heavens, temporarily blinding me. When the confetti and smoke settled, my eyes grew wide. Sitting in the front row was Vivien. And right next to her, was Jaime Zander, wearing a cocky grin. My gaze met his with a gape, and suddenly I felt as naked as the scantily clad models embracing me.

Then, Vivien locked her eyes with mine as she put her hand on his thigh and shot me a wicked smirk. As her hand crept up his leg, Jaime leaped up from his seat and made a beeline for the exit.

My eyes followed him as a tidal wave of confusion and anger washed over me. What the hell was going on?

CHAPTER 6

Jaime

I wanted to stay.

To surprise Gloria backstage. And congratulate her. With a hug that forced her body to brush against mine. And feel my hard-on. Then find a hidden corner where I could fuck her senseless. And give her angel wings that sent her flying.

But fucking Vivien didn't allow me that opportunity. Sitting in the front row next to me, she was about to make a spectacle of herself. Right in front of Gloria. In front of everyone.

Her unwanted touch made my stomach churn, her cloying scent adding to my malaise. This had to stop. Before she could take her hand any further up my leg, I shoved it away, jumped up from my seat, and split. Without looking back, I made my way up the already crowded aisle to the exit. My gut twisted with every harsh, determined step.

Swinging the auditorium door open, another unwanted encounter awaited me.

"What the hell are *you* doing here?"

The voice steely cold. Too familiar. Chilling. Victor Holden. Vivien's father.

The expression on his face was as sinister as ever. Venom poured from his eyes.

And so did it from mine. An eye for an eye. A tooth for a

tooth. So close to bashing in his perfect implants, I balled my hands by my sides.

"None of your fucking business."

Before he could respond, I pushed myself past him and hurried out of the building. Pulling out my cell phone from my jacket, I speed-dialed Orson to pick me up. Beating the crowd, he got here in no time.

I leaned back against the leather seat, letting my nerves calm down. Once my pulse returned to normal, I asked Orson to take me to The Walden. Clarity and strength surged inside me. And I made a decision. I wasn't going to let Victor or Vivien fuck me figuratively or literally. Fuck them. The game was on. And I wasn't backing away. I wouldn't let them get in the way of the Gloria's Secret account. Or Gloria.

Not now. Not ever.

I was ready for my next move.

CHAPTER 7

Gloria

After the models got back into their own clothes and congratulated me backstage, I searched for Vivien. I was fuming. I needed answers. What the hell was Jaime Zander doing at the fashion show and who had invited him? I had asked Kevin, but he had no clue and was as surprised as I was.

And there was more that fueled my rage. Why the hell were Vivien's hands all over him? Rather than feeling relief that the show was over, anxiety consumed me. Vivien was nowhere to be found backstage, and she wasn't picking up her phone. I was getting madder by the second, but my bladder was begging a trip to the restroom. I hadn't peed for hours.

I ran to the nearest ladies' room and flew inside. There she was. I should have guessed—in front of a mirror. Leaning into the glass, she pursed her plump lips as she applied a fresh coat of pink lip-gloss. My reflection met hers.

"Oh, hi, Gloria," she chirped after smacking her shimmering lips. "The show looked great online. We've had three million hits. I bet it's going to get fabulous ratings."

Great. But that was not on my mind at the moment. "What was Jaime Zander doing in the front row?" I asked, followed by a silent question. *And why the hell were you sitting next to him and feeling him up?*

She slipped the tube of lip-gloss back into her quilted designer purse and did that obnoxious hair fling. "Oh, I hope you don't mind. I sent him an invitation. I thought it would be good for business. Give him a little edge in terms of winning the Gloria's Secret account."

Inside, I was seething. How dare she go behind my back and invite him without telling me? My eyes narrowed with fury. "You should have told me, Vivien."

She shrugged her shoulders. "Ooh, I'm sorry. I totally forgot. I was so busy." Her saccharine voice was oozing with phoniness. *Liar!*

I clenched my hands and zipped my mouth. It wasn't worth challenging her because in my heart I knew I'd get nowhere with her; she would just twist and turn things around. I loosened my fingers and splattered some cold water on my face as she shimmied toward the door.

"By the way, Jaime's as gorgeous as ever."

I swirled around, but she was already gone. Then, I mentally kicked myself. I'd forgotten to ask her how she knew Jaime Zander. I'd also forgotten to pee. Tonight at the after-party, I was going to find out.

CHAPTER 8

Gloria

The Gloria's Secret Fashion Show after-party was one of the most coveted invitations in the city. While many would give the shirts off their backs to be invited to the glamorous *New York Post Page Six*-worthy event, I usually found it boring. Lots of A-list beautiful people, wannabes, booze, drugs, and loud music. After the stress of this afternoon's show, I was exhausted. What I really wanted to do was order in room service and curl up in my luxurious bed with a good book. But I had no choice. As founder and CEO of Gloria's Secret, I was expected to attend and party like there was no tomorrow.

I considered myself pretty low maintenance and prided myself on how fast I could transform from a high-powered executive to a glamorous night owl. Tonight, however, I was taking my time. I needed to unwind. I poured myself a glass of wine from the mini-bar and then drew myself a hot bath, pouring a capful of soothing lavender bath salt from our Bed & Bath Collection into the rapidly rising water. Stripped naked, I dimmed the bathroom lights and lit a fragrant Gloria's Secret candle, something I always traveled with on business trips.

Pinning up my braid with a few loose bobby pins, I stepped into the deep tub and sunk into the steamy water. On contact, I let out a loud sigh and felt my tension melt away. I leaned my head against the marble basin and stretched out my long legs. Reaching for the large sponge, I circled my firm, heavy breasts, brushing over the pronounced scar I wore above my heart. Out of habit, I closed my eyes to block out the memory—the secret—that scar harbored. It never worked. I always relived it. I always shuddered. As I swept my hand over my sensitive nipples, my mind, unannounced, switched channels from the memory of that horrible night to another unsettling reality show—Jaime Zander.

He was back in my head. I had to admit he was gorgeous. Sexy as sin. The way he looked at me with those intense denim blues and cocky smile was unnerving enough, but seeing him today with Vivien had totally unhinged me. What kind of mind-fuck game was he playing with me?

It had to stop. Control was something I clung to and needed to survive. The thought of losing control petrified me. I had spent hours in therapy dealing with my control issue and the roots of it. Dr. Pepperdine, my shrink, believed it stemmed from my mother . . . that I feared to become her, a pathetic addict who craved sex as much as she did crack, relying on men to feed her sick habits. In part, she was right. But what she didn't know was that my need for control was attached far more to the scar. The secret. Boris Borofsky was out there somewhere and could take everything that was precious to me away from me. Including my life.

Enough. It was time to step out of the tub and focus on getting ready for the party. With the towel draped around me, I stood before the mirror and did my makeup. My routine was simple, even for a glam night out—mascara, eyeliner, a little blush, and some lip-gloss from our growing line of cosmetics. Refreshed and polished, I padded back to my bed where I'd carefully laid out what I was going to wear. Shedding the towel, I began with my lingerie—an underwire, front-closing black lace bra, matching bikini, and complementary garter belt—all part of our bestselling "Sexy Nights" collection. After dabbing my inner thighs with some of our perfume, one of my beauty rituals, I lowered myself to the bed and languidly inched the sheer lace-trimmed silk stockings up my smooth, waxed legs. Real silk stockings from Paris were my one non-Gloria's Secret must-have—an indulgence I'd inherited from my mentor, Madame Paulette, who I was visiting tomorrow.

Rising from the bed, I slipped into my dress. Okay, confession. It, too, was not from the Gloria's Secret catalogue. It was a splurgy little black number by Chaz Clearfield, an up and coming designer whose line I admired and was backing. I was thinking of asking him to design a reasonably priced line of dresses for Gloria's Secret the way Target and H&M were approaching top designers. His cutting-edge sexiness was a good fit. There was definitely money to be made.

After pulling up the side zipper of the dress, I stepped into my black-satin, red-soled Louboutins, another designer I wanted to approach for a collaboration. I quickly re-braided my long hair—something I could do with my eyes closed—and glanced at myself in the floor-length mirror opposite the closet. I was pleased. I looked polished and confident. Ready to work the Gloria's Secret after-party.

Grabbing my black pashmina shawl and my vintage beaded clutch, a gift from Madame Paulette, I was about to scoot out of my suite when my cell phone rang. I expected it to be from Kevin, who likely was already manning the after-party. Not. Instead, it was from my driver Nigel.

"Miss Long," he hedged, "my daughter's water has prematurely broken."

It took me no time to put two and two together. His beloved only daughter, who was married to a Brooklynbased writer, was giving birth. I knew what he was going to ask me before he could utter another word.

"Nigel, you must be with her. Get to the hospital right now. I'll just take a cab."

"Are you sure, Miss Long?"

I smiled. We'd been together for a long time. Although he knew nothing about my past, he genuinely cared about me and protected me. I loved him like a godfather.

"Of course. Call me the minute the baby is born."

"Thank you, Miss Long."

"No, thank you, Nigel. Congratulations!"

I sighed as I hung up the phone. At thirty-three years old with no long-term relationship in sight, a baby and a family were likely not going to be mine for the having.

I'd forgotten how hard it was to get a cab during rush hour in Manhattan. Make that impossible. It made me appreciate Nigel even more.

Forget who I was. It didn't matter. I was lined up behind at least twenty other guests at the hotel's entrance where a valet was desperately trying to hail cabs with the help of an ear-piercing whistle. Occupied cabs kept whooshing by, with only one pulling up to the hotel so far. At this rate, I'd probably be in line for the rest of the night. Maybe I should walk. But at the thought of walking close to twenty long city blocks in my heels, that idea flew out of my mind as quickly as it had entered it. A bubble of frustration was about to burst inside me. I needed to be at the Gloria's Secret party. Now!

"Can I give you a ride?"

The familiar male voice, deep and sexy, purred in my ear as I tightened my fingers around my purse. I spun around and gawked. It was him! Jaime Zander. What was he doing at the hotel . . . again? Was he stalking me? Or was it just a coincidence?

My eyes drank him in. He was wearing another sexy black biker jacket, black tight-ass jeans, a V-neck white T-shirt, and alligator loafers with no socks. Damn! I loved the way he was dressed. My skin prickled and my pulse quickened. *Take a deep breath, Gloria. Breathe!*

"Is that a yes or no, Ms. Long?" He shot me a saucy smile that was daring me to take him up on his offer.

I silently debated if I should. The long cab line hadn't budged an inch. I had little choice. "Fine." I stabbed the word at him like a dart just as his shiny black Range Rover pulled up to the curb. He shuffled me toward the car as his driver opened the back passenger door. I tingled at his warm touch.

"After you." Jaime followed behind me as I gracefully slid into the plush SUV. I sat as far away from him as I could, but he sidled up right next to me. I could feel his warm breath on my neck and smell his heavenly cologne— again our spicy made-for-him fragrance. I suddenly felt lightheaded. Maybe it was the way it mixed with the scent of his skin and the leather of his jacket.

"What were you doing at the fashion show?" I spluttered.

"Research."

"How did you get invited?"

"I have connections."

Vivien?

His sparkling eyes gave me a long once-over. "You look hot."

All at once, I felt hot—make that near the melting point. I crossed one leg over the other, trying to calm the sudden pulsing sensation between them.

"You got a big date tonight?" He brushed the tip of my braid under my chin, coaxing a response.

I squirmed. "I'm going to a Gloria's Secret party at Touch."

That cocky grin curled on his lips. "Then we'll arrive together."

Creasing my brows, I flinched. "What do you mean?"

"I'm on the A-List."

I mentally grimaced. I bet Vivien had invited him. The little vixen wants to get into his pants. I was going to have to watch her like a hawk tonight. I took a deep calming breath and shot my companion a challenging look.

"Shouldn't you be home or at your office working on the Gloria's Secret pitch? You know, I expect to see it on Friday with my team. That's less than forty-eight hours away."

His chest vibrated with a deep, sexy laugh. "Don't worry. It'll come to me."

I cocked my head. "Really? So you're that sure?"

"Yeah, you inspire me."

"What else do I do to you?"

"You make me hard."

His words made me jolt. I glanced down at his crotch and my eyes widened. Holy shit! He wasn't kidding. There was a substantial bulge between his legs that was straining against his jeans.

I was still in shock when he grabbed my right hand and placed it on his cock. A hot, rock-hard mound met my palm. Before I could move a finger, he cupped his warm hand over mine, pressing it against his arousal. My pulse was in overdrive, and I was bristling all over.

"Gloria, look at me."

Hesitantly, I turned his way. I met his penetrating gaze.

"I'm not a bullshitter. I want your account. What do I have to do to win it?"

His eyes not wavering, he brushed his upper lip with his tongue.

Kiss me! My breath hitched. What this man could do to me with the simplest gesture! My heartbeat sped up and wet heat gathered between my thighs. Looking down, I squirmed in my seat and spit out the words.

"First, let go of my hand."

He slowly lifted his hand. My fingers flew off his cock.

He shot me a wry smile. "What else?"

"Come up with something I love."

"I've got something you'll love, and it's right here in this car."

For a New York minute, I froze, positive he was going to unzip his fly. I didn't know whether to sigh with relief or cry out in frustration when he swung open the door of a built-in cabinet and pulled out a bottle of champagne in an ice bucket along with two flutes. After uncorking the bubbly, he poured us each a glass and proposed a toast.

"To our relationship." He clinked his glass against mine. Normally, I drank very little, but I was in mighty need of a drink. This man was getting under my skin. And I more than liked it.

CHAPTER 9

Jaime

Tonight was going to be fun.

It was already fun.

She looked hot.

She smelled hot.

And she got hotter as I sidled up next to her in the back seat of my vehicle. So close our knees touched and heat radiated off her flesh.

Outside the car, the city traffic pulsed. Inside, there was another pulse. One thudding against my fly. This feisty powerhouse of a woman had a way of making me hard and I wanted her to know it. I put her hand to the steely bulge between my thighs and I secretly smirked as she jolted. She could have resisted or reprimanded me, but she didn't and kept her hand there longer than needed before asking me to free it. I'm sure because her fingertips were burning with my heat. Obliging, I couldn't hold back a smug smile as her hand fell onto her lap. Her long slender fingers fidgeted and I wondered: What would they feel like around the base of my cock?

Her spine straight, her gaze forward, she looked uptight and I offered her a glass of champagne.

After filling our flutes, I proposed a toast. "To us."

Clinking her glass against mine, she immediately

downed the bubbly.

"It's quite lovely."

So are you.

Um . . . could I please have a bit more?" Her voice was unsteady.

"Of course." I reached into the bucket and refilled her flute.

Slowly sipping mine, I watched as she again gulped the bubbly as if it were going out of style. Her unusual dual colored eyes glinted as if she was getting high. Loosening up.

"Do you always try plastering your potential clients, Mr. Zander?"

"Only the ones I like."

She shot me a glaring look. "Very funny."

Squirming, she uncrossed her long legs, but then quickly refolded them, this time the left over the right like she was defensively squeezing her pussy tight.

My cock twitched. It was going to take a lot of determination to get between them. And an equal dose of creativity, I mused as we reached our destination.

CHAPTER 10

Gloria

There was already a major scene outside when we pulled up to Touch on West Fifty-Second Street. Wannabes were clamoring to get past the bouncers and the red velvet rope, and paparazzi were stepping over each other to get shots of the arriving celebrities and supermodels. Jaime clasped my hand as he elbowed our way through the crowd. His grip was firm, warm, and powerful.

"Gloria!" shouted out several paparazzi, blinding me with their flashes as they snapped my photo. I plastered a big fake smile on my face. God, did I hate this part of the job. Only Kevin knew I was actually rather shy. And that I harbored deep insecurities—leftovers from my past—beneath my powerhouse façade.

As much as he irked me, I was glad to have Jaime Zander by my side. Protectively, he ushered me through the mayhem, wrapping his strong arm around me, shielding me as I bowed my head. I hoped a photo of the two of us together wouldn't appear tomorrow on *Page Six* of the *New York Post*. I took a calming breath. There were way more intriguing people than me to feature. Like Kim Kardashian, who I'm sure would be here with her entourage or Justin Bieber who was also on the VIP list. Not to mention all the Gloria's Secret supermodels.

Inside the vast, three-story nightclub, loud, pulsating music blasted while candy-colored lights bounced off a giant disco ball. On the flat screen TV above the U-shaped bar, the Gloria's Secret Fashion Show was playing; it looked even more dazzling on television. I felt confident the ratings would be sensational.

The place was packed. Beautiful body after body was draped everywhere. Over lounges. Over the bar. Over each other. The smell of marijuana was thick in the air. Kevin found me quickly and ushered me away from Jaime to meet some of the VIPs. From the corner of my eye, I saw Jaime mingling in the crowd. He was turning heads, and before long, a dozen gorgeous supermodel types were fawning all over him. I recognized several of them from our fashion show. Former Jaime Zander fucks?

"Glorious, you look *faa-bu-lous*!" crooned Kevin, diverting my attention and unfounded jealousy away from Jaime.

"You look great too." True to himself, he was back to being outrageous. He was wearing an open white peasant shirt over Gloria's Secret leopard-patterned leggings and combat boots. Kev could one-up the hippest designer any day.

"No one can stop talking about the show. And we're killing it in the ratings!"

"Thanks to you." My eyes lit up though I was feeling a little claustrophobic in this dark, frenetic environment.

He gave me a signature peck on both cheeks. "No, it's all you. Your dream. Your vision. I just make it happen."

Kev and I were a great team. He always made things happen—even the one thing we both wanted to forget. We had been through thick and thin. If we could survive our abusive childhoods and the unthinkable crime we'd committed together, we could survive anything.

While I shied away from events like this, Kevin thrived on them. He was in his element. Taking my hand, he swept me away. "Come on, I want you to meet some of the VIPs. Actually, they want to meet you."

I stole a glance backward and I spotted Vivien heading Jaime's way. My stomach twisted and I had the urge to intercept them. But I didn't have the chance as Kevin led me deeper into the crowd and they disappeared from my line of vision.

Bubbling with energy, Kevin introduced me to numerous VIPs that included top models, recording artists, and big-name stars from Broadway, television, and film. While I was cordially smiley-faced with all of them, my mind was focused on Jaime and Vivien. What was with them? My eyes searched the pulsing crowd, but I could no longer find them. Had Jaime left with her? My mental ramblings came to a halt when Kevin told me he had to split and get the charity auction for Rihanna's diamond-studded bra and thong started. I was not standing alone for long.

"Gloria, lovely to see you." The cold, affected drawl was unmistakable. Victor Holden, Vivien's father. My multi-billionaire biggest shareholder and Chairman of the Board.

He cupped his hands on my shoulders. His fingers, as usual, were as icy as his voice and penetrated my shawl. With a shiver that shimmied down my spine, I spun around to face him.

Victor was in his mid fifties though his fit body and handsome face made him look at least ten years younger. He was a tall, lean, debonair man with slicked back salt and pepper hair, a permanent tan, and elegant features that included piercing steel gray eyes and an aquiline nose. Wearing an expensive tweed jacket, open-collar dress shirt, and well-cut gabardine trousers, he exuded old money. A shrewd businessman, he was known for making vulnerable companies his prey. Many on Wall Street called him "The Vulture."

His eyes roamed down my body, lingering on places they had no right to be. But which he thought he had the right to claim. He was always hitting on me. I was his prey too. I inwardly shuddered as he planted a wet kiss on each cheek.

"Well done today, darling. I'm sure the show will drive up first quarter sales. Our shareholders will be pleased."

"Thank you, Victor." I hated when he called me "darling." The less I said to him the better. I always tried to keep it to dollars and cents.

"Why don't we celebrate with a dance?"

The last thing I wanted to do was dance with him. He moved uncomfortably close to me. The rancid smell of his breath—cigarettes mixed with alcohol—assaulted my senses. He squeezed my jaw.

"Don't disappoint me, Gloria." He squeezed my jaw tighter.

"Please, Victor, you're hurting me." I jerked away. My pashmina shawl fell off my shoulders to the floor. Before I could bend down to pick it up, it was back on me, draped perfectly over my dress. I instantly recognized the scent of my hero. Jaime!

"Sorry, she's with me," he growled, wrenching me away from Victor. Their eyes clashed, the air between them thick with tension and animosity. Unspoken words flew between them. Victor's eyes narrowed into sharp slivers of glass as Jaime led me deeper into the crowd. As we neared the bar, I stole a glance back at Victor. He stood there motionless, his glacial eyes fixed on me. It was not the look of defeat but rather that of a man who wouldn't take "no" for an answer. He frightened me.

"Do you know who that was?" I asked Jaime.

"A fucking asshole." His face hardened.

"Do you know he's the Chairman of—"

"Yeah, I know," he said, cutting me off. "I don't give a flying fuck."

His contempt for Victor shocked and enthralled me. "He could get in the way of you winning the Gloria's Secret account."

His jaw stiffened. "He won't." It softened. "Do you want a drink?"

"I'd love one," a familiar female voice responded. Slinking up to us was Victor's daughter, Vivien, dressed to the nines in a fuchsia strapless bandage dress that hugged her curves and pushed up her D-cup boobs. Matching platform stilettos completed her ensemble. She flung back her loose ebony hair with a shake of her head and gave Jaime a wide toothy predatory smile.

"Hi, Jaime," she purred. "How about a dance?"

"Later," Jaime said coolly.

Vivien's face took on the expression of a miffed spoiled little rich girl who was used to getting anything she wanted. She glowered at me as she sauntered off. My face didn't move a muscle. *Bitch!*

"So where were we?" asked Jaime, his tone now sexy and seductive.

"Um, uh, a drink," I stammered. Drinking at business events was against my rules, but I sure could use one.

"What would you like?"

"A vodka martini with extra olives."

"Don't move." He strode over to the bar and returned quickly with two martinis, one for me, one for him.

"Thanks." As I put the cold smooth liquid to my lips, the pulsating music came to a sudden halt. The auction for Rihanna's diamond-studded bra and thong had begun. All eyes, including Jaime's and mine, were riveted on the wiry auctioneer standing behind a podium at the front of the club. The items were displayed on a curvaceous mannequin to his right.

The bidding opened at $100,000. It quickly escalated to $500,000. My heart was palpitating. While I was seriously amazed that someone would pay so much money for a set of underwear (Okay, they were diamond-studded and Rihanna-strutted), I was thrilled because all the proceeds would go to Girls Like Us, the charitable organization I had started to help under-privileged and troubled teen girls pursue their dreams. Like me.

At $900,000, a new bidder stepped in. I recognized the icy voice immediately. Victor!

"I have $900,000. Do I hear one million dollars for these treasures?" shouted the enthusiastic auctioneer.

Dead silence. Everyone in the room held their breath.

"One million dollars."

I gasped. Jaime Zander had just shouted out that exorbitant figure. I shot him a wide-eyed look. A smug smile sprung on his face. What the hell was he doing?

"One million dollars to the man with the gorgeous blonde."

I cringed. His smile widened.

"Do I hear one million five hundred thousand dollars?"

"Over here," chimed in Victor hastily. I turned my head, and my eyes met his. They burnt with fire and desire.

The auctioneer beamed behind his podium. "One point five million dollars. Do I have any more bids?"

Silence again. I glanced again at Victor. He shot me a smarmy smile. The tension in the air was as thick as cement.

The auctioneer: "Going once . . . Going twice . . . Fair warning . . . Going down at . . ."

"Two million dollars!"

Jaime again! He raised his martini glass high in the air to

confirm the bid. Was he out of his mind? I gasped so loudly I was embarrassed. Fortunately, the din of the crowd's collective gasp drowned it out.

The auctioneer grinned. "It's back to the gentleman with the gorgeous blonde. Do I hear anything further?"

I eyed Victor once more. He was quietly fuming. I'd seen that sinister expression on his face before when he couldn't get what he wanted—especially at the price he was willing to pay.

The auctioneer slowly raised his hammer. "Going once." Silence. "Going twice." Silence. "Going . . . going . . . GONE!" He slammed his hammer down on the podium. "Sold for two million dollars to the gentleman with the gorgeous blonde. Congratulations, sir!"

Raucous applause and cheers broke out. The loud disco music started up again. The crowd began to dance wildly. The party was now just getting started. But I stood motionless in shock.

"Aren't you going to congratulate me, Gloria?" Jaime asked, catapulting me into the moment.

"Why did you buy the Rihanna undergarments? They cost a fortune."

"Because I could afford to. And the money's going to a good cause." He winked at me as he punctuated the words "good cause."

Smartass! "So, you think by impressing me with your money and audacity you'll win the Gloria's Secret account?" I countered, my voice testy.

His lips curled up into that sexy cocksure smile. "No. I'll win your account with my creativity and agility."

Arrogant asshole! But there was no denying that his words made me flush. Before I could utter a sound, he tugged at my braid.

"Dance with me, Gloria!" An order. Setting his half-finished martini onto a nearby cocktail table, he whisked me into his arms, drawing me tight against him. The dance music was pounding, and so was my heart . . . along with the wet bundle of nerves between my inner thighs. Against my silk dress, I could feel the rippled muscles of his chest and the rigid mound between his thighs. He pressed his arousal harder against me as he gyrated his hips against mine. I was as stiff as a board.

"Relax, Gloria," he commanded. "Just trust me."

He splayed his long fingers on my jutting hipbones, rotating my hips to follow his. I chugged my martini, and as the velvety liquid coursed through my bloodstream, I felt myself loosening up. Soon I was rhythmically moving with him as if we'd danced together forever. His undulating movements were fluid, sensual, and controlling. Boy, did Mr. Agility know how to move!

A waiter passed by with a tray full of cocktails. Plunking my depleted martini glass down on it, I grabbed another drink, not knowing what it was. I polished it off in two gulps in time to return the emptied glass back onto the tray. I reached for one more. Jaime gripped my wrist forcefully, holding it back.

"Careful, Gloria." Jaime's voice whirled in my ears as the room started spinning around me. Was this some kind of special effect? One of my favorite songs, "Blurred Lines," began to play. I was totally into it, singing along at the top of my lungs.

"Do you think I'm a good girl?" I asked Jaime, slurring each word.

"Come on, let's get of here." Jaime's voice took on urgency.

"No!" I protested. "I want to dance." I looped my arms around his neck, brushing them along his silky tousled hair, and glued my forehead to his. My hot breath caught his, and

I started to move wildly, bumping every part of me against his rock-hard body. My hips. My butt. My boobs. Without losing physical contact, I pulled off my shoes.

"Don't need these!" I chirped and tossed them deep into the crowd.

"Let's go. Now!" ordered Jaime, his voice gruff.

Before I could protest again, Jaime yanked my arms off his neck, grabbed a hand, and dragged me through the crowd. Dazed and dizzy, I tottered behind him, barely managing to keep up with him.

I passed by Vivien and waved at her. She fired me a scathing look. I was confused. Everything was a whirling blur.

Finally, we were outside. The cool, crisp air enveloped me but did little to bring me to my senses. The world, which revolved around the devastatingly handsome Jaime Zander, was still spinning out of control. I felt myself swaying. Thank goodness, this gorgeous hunk of manliness was holding me up, his muscled arm clamped around my waist. He slipped his spare hand into his jeans pocket and pulled out his phone. He speed dialed a number and I heard him mumble, "Orson, I need the car brought around to the entrance of the club immediately."

"How do you feel?" Jaime asked upon ending the call. His voice was now tender.

"Like shit," I murmured. Nausea had settled in. Bile was rising to my chest. *Oh God, please don't let me throw up in front of him! Please! NO!*

The next thing I knew, Mr. Zander was scooping me up in his arms and loading me into the back seat of his Rover. He cradled me in his lap, his hard length pressing into my backside, and let me lean my head against his chest. Though his chest was pure steel, the softness of his buttery leather jacket was comforting.

"I'm sorry," I rasped, barely able to get out the words as I fought back nausea.

"Don't be." He smoothed my hair along my scalp and then twisted my long platinum braid around his fingers.

"Rihanna's garments!" I mumbled, the events of the night whirling around in my head.

"Don't worry. They're in the back of the car." He pressed his warm lips against my forehead. Even in my drunken stupor, his touch zapped every fiber of my being.

I gazed up at him. Gah! There were two of him! Double the gorgeousness. "Do you have an identical twin?" I slurred.

"Ah, my Gloria." He chuckled. "You'll soon find out that I'm a one and only. Just like you."

The muffled sounds of late night traffic in the city that never sleeps drifted into my ears. Somewhere during the ride back to the hotel, everything faded to black.

CHAPTER 11

Jaime

The doormen at The Walden were used to seeing me escort a lot of beautiful women into the hotel. But I sure as hell didn't want them to see me carrying one inside so I had my driver take me to my private entrance, which was around the corner on Fifty-Sixth Street. With Gloria passed out in my arms, her long braid dangling, I managed to punch in the code with one finger and the door slid open. Holding her limp body, I stepped into the secret elevator that took me directly to my suite.

After all that had transpired tonight, I craved a drink, but my priority had to be getting Gloria back to her room. And preferably before she came to. Setting her gently down on my couch, I hurried to the door of my corner suite and swung it open. Retrieving Gloria, I stepped outside and suddenly remembered her purse was still in the Rover. Shit. I didn't have her key. Just when I thought I was fucked, a familiar voice drifted in my ears. My gaze stretched down the hallway.

"Good evening, Mr. Zander." Dolores, one of our long-time nightshift custodial workers. Heading my way, she was pushing a cart filled with fluffy white towels and assorted bathroom amenities. At this late hour, she was most likely fulfilling a request from a demanding guest. I suspected many used a different towel for every body part or were hoarding our exclusive shampoos and lotions.

"Dolores, can you do me a big favor?" I asked. "Open the door to Room 2018."

"Of course, sir." Though I'm sure she'd seen a lot of my hook-ups coming in and out of my fuck pad located on the floor below, I'd never entered a guest's room. If my trusty employee was surprised or questioning what I was doing carrying this passed-out, gorgeous woman, she didn't show it and silently obliged using her master key.

"Thanks," I said, stepping inside the junior suite and making a mental note to give her a generous anonymous tip in the morning.

"Have a good evening," replied the housekeeper with a wink, closing the door behind us.

Without looking back, I got Gloria onto the couch. Sliding off her shawl, I covered her body with it. Her chest evenly rising and falling, I kept my eyes on her serene, beautiful face, the face of an angel. The sooner I was out of here the better. Temptation gnawed at me, but thank fuck I was a man of honor. Like my father. As I cranked the handle of the door, eager to get back to my suite, a raspy voice called out to me.

"If you want me, just whistle. You know how to whistle, don't you, boys?"

I looked over my shoulder. Still seeing double, Gloria was conscious and on her feet. Teetering, her eyes glazed over, her face a ghastly shade of green. She met my gaze and winked.

"You just put your lips together and blow." Demonstrating, she pursed her lush lips as if she was blowing me a kiss. She was still drunk. And so damn sexy.

Before I could say a word—or whistle for that matter—her lips parted, and with a cry of "Oh God," she bent over, folding in half, and gripped her midriff. One belch and then she puked. And then another round of vomit poured from her mouth. Most of it landing on the hardwood floor, some of it splattering on her dress and long limbs.

"Oh my God," she sobbed out again. Tears were already falling from her eyes, one a cloudy sapphire, the other topaz.

Pivoting, I hurried back to her, wondering if I should get her into the bathroom or tuck her into bed.

"Are you going to be sick again?" I asked, holding her steady.

"I don't know," she stammered. One look at her contorted face, I knew where we had to go. And fast.

Sixty swift seconds later, she was on her knees on the tiled bathroom floor, barfing up everything inside her into the toilet bowl as I held up her braid. Sobs mingled with the belches, which came one after another. Finally, a reprieve.

"I think I'm okay." Her voice was raw and hoarse.

"You sure?"

She nodded, her hands clinging to the sides of the toilet as I flushed it for a third time. She tried to stand up, but wobbled on her feet.

"Here, let me help you." Letting go of her braid, I helped her stand up and led her to the sink as she clung to me. I turned on the cold water and soaking a washcloth, I wiped her sweat-laced face as her color returned. Then, I found her toothbrush and coated it with a squeeze of her toothpaste.

"Open your mouth," I ordered, wondering what it would feel like wrapped around my cock.

Gloria Long was strong but vulnerable. In her moment of weakness, beautifully controllable. Obliging, she let me brush her perfect pearl white teeth as I fought the urge to run my tongue over them. I filled up a glass with water and made her rinse before downing a couple Advils. Then, she glimpsed herself in the mirror, her glazed, bloodshot eyes not recognizing her reflection.

"I-I'm sorry," she stuttered. "I never get drunk."

Meeting her reflection, I smiled. "Hey, there's a first for everything." Then gently, I tugged on her silky braid. "C'mon, let's get you to bed."

"I'm covered in vomit."

She was right. And the stench lingered. She fumbled with the zipper of her dress.

"Let me help you."

Silently, she submitted and let me unzip the tiny black sheath and slide it down her body, each tug revealing another inch of her supple flesh and luscious curves. She clung to me as she stepped out of it, and in the mirror, I admired her lithe, sensuous body, now clad only in her lace push up bra, bikini, garter, and stockings. My cock throbbed. How could it not? She was sexy as sin even in her wasted condition.

Still unsteady on her feet, I lifted her again in my arms and brought her into the bedroom of the suite. Gently, I set her down on the bed and then dashed back to the main room to clean up the mess she'd left behind with a wet towel. Returning, I rummaged through her chest of drawers for some nightwear. Jeez. There was a fuck load to choose from, each piece sexier than the one before, but I quickly settled on a two-piece lavender baby doll. Should I undress her? Put the sexy as fuck garment on her? The temptation was great, but I forced myself to lay the ensemble on her bed.

"Remember, just whistle," she murmured, gazing up at me with a faint smile.

Fuck. I wanted her. Maybe I *should* put my lips together and whistle, but on her next breath, she was out like a light. It was time to make my exit except I couldn't get my feet to move. I just stared at her, mesmerized by her beauty. She was flawless except for a shiny raised mark on her chest, the size of a dime. A scar. Not dwelling on it, I wondered what she looked like with her hair loose as my eyes roamed down her gorgeous body, stopping to admire her exquisite breasts, the contours of her tummy, the pronounced curves of her hips, and those long, taut legs. On a whim, I decided to take off her stockings so she'd be more comfortable. One by one, I unhooked the garters and then slid off the sheer silk hose, my knuckles brushing against her smooth satin skin as I lowered them. Scrunching them in my hands, I put them to my face and inhaled them. They smelled intoxicating like her—a delicious mixture of pure woman and something else—perhaps she dabbed perfume on them or along her long limbs. I yearned to touch and taste her everywhere. Cup her mounds in my hands, pinch her nipples between my fingers, run my tongue up her legs. Then, suck on her clit and lick the slit of her pussy. And that was just for starters.

My dick strained against my fly. I could virtually hear it whistling through my pants. My carnal fantasy was making me lose control. I had to get out of here. Stuffing the stockings into a pocket, I hurried out of the room, forcing myself not to look back.

I longed to fuck Gloria Long.

Knowing I was the one who might get fucked in the end.

By a sick bitch and a bastard.

CHAPTER 12

Jaime

Back in my suite, I poured myself a much-needed nightcap. An expensive cognac. The warm amber liquid coated my throat before heating my veins as the events of this evening whirled through my brain. Though I'd paid a hefty price for my booty, it was worth every cent to beat the fucker who'd once beaten me. Literally and figuratively. Taking another sip of the velvety liquor, my victory—or should I say Victor-y—fed my ego. The look on his face when I outbid him and won the diamond-studded garments was priceless and made me forget about his equally toxic daughter Vivien. Neither of them was going to get in the way of what I wanted. When my thoughts settled and my tumbler was drained, all that remained in my head was one name. One person. One face. Gloria.

I was insanely attracted to her. I'd been with a lot of beautiful women, but none had ever had the effect she had on me. In fact, most I never saw again. I had a simple set of rules. It all boiled down to two words.

Fuck

And forget.

But Gloria was different. Unlike the many others I'd been with.

I had no interest in getting to know the women I fucked.

But with Gloria, I wanted to know everything about her before I sunk my cock into her.

I never saw the same woman twice. I couldn't wait to see more of Gloria.

I only bedded easy to get women who let me be in control. Gloria was almost an equal. Hard to get yet I loved the challenge.

I mostly cared about getting myself off. With Gloria, her pleasure was mine. In fact, it came first.

Despite her effect on me, I hadn't fucked her. And I couldn't forget her.

I poured myself another shot and chugged it in one long gulp. My head fogged up, clouded by doubt. Maybe this was all wrong. Getting involved with her on any level—business or personal. She was dangerous territory. A land mine filled with time bombs. Forces of evil that could potentially blow up in our faces and destroy us both.

Shoving the ominous perils to the back of my mind, I poured myself one more shot and ambled to the desk where I worked from when not at my office. It was a massive Herman Miller creation that had belonged to the original owner of the hotel. Upon his retirement and the sale of the hotel, he'd left it to me, but instead of keeping it on the ground level where he had an office, I'd moved it to this large corner suite, which served as both my residence and home office. Strategically, I'd placed it facing one of the many windows that wrapped around the unit and allowed me great views of the city.

There was nothing like New York City at night. The lit-up skyscrapers licking the navy-blue sky and the bright headlights of the vehicles below swirling around the city streets like strings of Christmas lights. Looking out the window from this height was both empowering and inspiring. I felt invincible, like nothing could get in my way.

Not even those who would do anything to own me or destroy me.

On my next breath, I found myself whistling. Something I did either when I was stressed or totally relaxed. I was neither . . . rather totally aroused as the memory of carrying Gloria in my arms, almost naked save for her sexy black lingerie. Totally mine.

Just whistle if you want me.

Without warning, inspiration hit me as hard as my raging erection.

I suddenly envisioned the new Gloria's Secret ad campaign. Clear as crystal. Hot as lava.

Digging my hand into my pocket, I pulled out Gloria's stockings and took another whiff of them. I could smell sex and success. Setting them down on the desk, my fingertips jumped to my keyboard and began to type frantically. I was forty-eight hours away from winning her account.

And winning her.

CHAPTER 13

Gloria

Jaime Zander was pounding into me. His thick pulsing cock taking me to the hilt. Hitting a magic spot again and again. Driving me insanely wild. I moaned with ecstasy and dug my nails into his flesh. He was on top of me, the weight and strength of him holding me captive.

"Let go, Gloria. Come for me," he ordered, his hot breath in my mouth. He grinded faster and deeper, each stroke bringing me closer to the edge. I clung to his biceps as my muscles began to convulse. Inside my body, a spiraling tornado was taking everything in its wake. My head was ringing, spinning out of control.

The loud ringing wouldn't stop. Reality set in, and I realized it was my room phone. It stopped before I could answer it.

Drenched in sweat, I pried my eyes open, one at a time, and after blinking several times, took in my surroundings. I was back at the hotel . . . in my bed. My head was pounding and my sandpaper-like tongue was stuck to my dry as cardboard palate. It must be morning; a ray of sunshine beamed through a slight gap between the blackout curtains. I must have kicked off the fluffy duvet sometime during the night. Splayed on the bed, I was wearing only my black bra, bikinis, and the matching garter from last night. On the pillow next to me, a lavender baby doll ensemble was neatly laid out. It looked like it hadn't been worn.

Wait! How did I get back here? What happened to my little black dress? My stockings? My shoes? The events of last night spun around in my head. Slowly, the fuzziness gave way to clarity. Fuck! I got drunk last night! I vaguely remembered Jaime Zander escorting me out of the club and lifting me into his SUV. And after that, I couldn't remember a damn thing. Oh, God! I must have passed out.

My breath caught in my parched throat. Had that cocky asshole brought me up to my room and undressed me? My mind raced; my heart raced. Holy, holy shit! Had he taken advantage of me and fucked me? Was that a dream or was that for real? A wave of panic swept over me.

The phone on my nightstand rang again. This time I managed to reach for it with an outstretched arm. It was Nigel, my driver.

"Good morning, Miss Long," he piped, his voice bright and chipper. "I shall be waiting for you at the entrance of the hotel at ten o'clock as you requested."

My brain still in lockdown, it took me a long moment to remember what I was doing today. *Gloria to brain. Come in now.* Yes. I was going to visit my beloved mentor, Madame Paulette. Thank goodness, Nigel had called because I hadn't arranged for my customary wake-up call. Raising myself to a sitting position, I freed my tongue from my palate.

My voice hoarse, I thanked my trusty driver. And then I remembered something else. "A boy or girl?"

"A six pound four ounce baby girl!" beamed Nigel on the other end. "Her name is Annabelle."

"That's wonderful, Nigel!" Despite my sorry state, a smile spread across my face. "Congratulations! I'll see you soon."

After returning the phone to its cradle, I made myself a

mental note: Make sure the gift is sent today. I had already purchased an expensive stroller along with a travel bag full of baby care necessities online. It gave me pleasure knowing that Nigel's daughter would appreciate everything. After my visit to Madame Paulette, I was also going to give him the rest of the day off so he could spend it with his daughter and new grandchild.

The mental diversion was short lived. My mind jumped back to Jaime Zander. A shudder rippled through me. I'd made a total fool of myself and now, I was fucked—in maybe more ways than one. How could I ever face him again?

I picked up the phone once more and dialed room service. I ordered a large pot of coffee—something I desperately needed if I was going to make it through the day. At least, I had some time to figure out how I was going to handle Jaime. His pitch wasn't until late afternoon tomorrow. Getting out of the city might give me some clarity.

My visit to Madame Paulette was something I looked forward to as much as I dreaded. It would probably be the last time I saw her. She was, along with Kevin, the most important person in my life. With a heavy heart and hangover from hell, I dragged myself out of bed and staggered to the bathroom.

I glimpsed myself in the bathroom mirror. My reflection startled me. I looked as bad as I felt. My skin was pasty and my eyes bloodshot. Waves of nausea were still rolling through me. I brushed my teeth to freshen my stale breath and swallowed down a couple of much needed Advil. I desperately needed a shower. As I took off my bra, the alluring scent of Gloria's Secret men's cologne invaded my nostrils. I instantly buried my nose in the lacy fabric. The intoxicating scent of him was embedded in the fibers. My stomach bunched. Oh God, had he? Panicky, I yanked off the matching bottoms. Scrunching them in my hand, I checked my body for more evidence. There were no signs of bruising, and neither my breasts nor my privates were sore or engorged. I took a whiff of the bikinis—oh no, the distinct scent of him again! Yet, there was no trace of any physical telltale sign of him on the crotch. I impulsively rubbed my cleft and put my wet fingers to my nose. The distinct sweet smell was definitely all mine, but I still couldn't be sure. Maybe he washed off all the evidence. Damn him! Damn me for losing control!

The hot, pulsing shower was revitalizing. I tilted my head back with eyes squeezed shut and let the jets of water spray my face while I lathered up my body with the fragrant soap. Nothing felt out of the ordinary except the lingering nauseous feeling. Turning off the faucet, I stepped out of the shower and wrapped a giant bath towel around me. Feeling refreshed, I studied myself in the bathroom mirror. I looked better than expected. The hot shower had done its magic. My porcelain skin was glowing, and there was only a trace of broken capillaries in my duo-colored eyes. I re-braided my long blond wet hair and applied a dollop of lip-gloss. I wanted to look groomed for Madame Paulette. Appearance was important to her.

Returning to the bedroom, I looked again for my missing garments and shoes. And again the question: Who the hell took them off me? I searched the drawers, looked under the bed, and scanned the closet. *Gone. Gone. Gone.* I glanced at the alarm clock on the night table. It was already nine forty-five. Nigel would be here soon to take me to Connecticut. Hastily, I donned a lacy gray bra and bikini set, matching garter, and sheer gray silk hose. A lady-like A-line gray dress and pewter pumps followed. I always matched the color of my underwear to what I was wearing. It was something Madame Paulette had taught me to do. My life lessons from this incredible woman were many and meaningful. Sadly, she would soon be gone.

The coffee still hadn't arrived. As much as I craved a major dose of caffeine, I couldn't wait for it. Grabbing my coat, purse, and a canvas bag full of goodies that I knew Madame Paulette would adore, I skirted out of the room and headed to the elevators.

"Hey, wait up!"

That deep, sexy voice. Fuck! It was him! Jaime Zander. What the hell was he doing here?

Bristling, I kept marching without a single turn of my head. I could hear him jogging down the corridor. He caught up to me, and we stood side by side waiting for the lift. Staring straight ahead, I refused to look at him. Not even a little glimpse.

Unlike yesterday, the elevator took its time arriving. In fact, it felt like an eternity. Maybe it was stuck somewhere—explaining why my coffee had never arrived. My stomach tightened and I was losing patience. And then he started whistling—"Gloria" of all songs. *Bastard!* He was trying to distract me and get my attention.

"Stop that!"

"You don't like my whistling?"

"I don't like you." And then it just came flying out. "Did you fuck me last night?"

"Gloria, I would never take advantage of you in that state. In case you don't remember, I carried you up to your room and then you threw up all over yourself."

Holy crap! Mortification raced through me. I kept facing the elevator, too embarrassed to look him in the face.

"There's nothing to be embarrassed about. You're just

not used to losing control."

I never lost control! *Never!* What had this man done to me?

"By the way, I gave your dress to the valet for cleaning. It should be back in your room by five. Unfortunately, someone else may be wearing your shoes. You may not recall this, but you took them off and tossed them while you were dancing with me."

I couldn't care less now about my eight hundred dollar designer shoes. Every muscle in my body clenched. The reality of him undressing me and seeing me almost bared consumed me.

"Don't be ashamed. You have a beautiful body. While taking off your vomit-coated dress was not exactly something I enjoyed, peeling off your silky stockings from those long legs was quite a treat."

I felt my cheeks flare. In fact, my whole body was heating up. *Come on, elevator. Get here already.* His words got in the way.

"Your body should be among the wonders of the world. I wouldn't mind getting a taste of it some time. When was the last time you got laid?"

"None of your damn business!"

"That's what I thought."

He was infuriating me. What's more, he was setting every fiber of my being on fire, especially the area between my thighs. Where the hell was the elevator? I had to get away from him. Finally, a car arrived. As soon as the doors open, I stomped into it. I slammed my palm against the "L" button, but the doors wouldn't close. That's because the asshole was leaning against one, his arms and legs seductively crossed.

For the first time this morning, he was in full view. All six foot three of his manly gorgeousness. Today, he was wearing a fringed tan suede jacket with faded blue jeans that hung low on his narrow hips, a plaid flannel shirt that exposed his chiseled pecs . . . and cowboy boots. Mr. Urban Cowboy! God, he looked sexy. Right out of *GQ*. And on top of all that, his hair had that perfectly tousled, just-fucked look going on.

An unnerving thought shot into my head. Did he fuck someone else after he left me? A beautiful supermodel? Vivien? Maybe he kept a room at this hotel as a fuck pad. Lots of successful men did that kind of thing.

My eyes narrowed. "Can you please either leave or get in?"

That cocky half-smile curled on his lips. "I just want to get a good look at you." His sexy denim blues gave me the once-over. "You look lovely, Gloria."

I grimaced. "It's Ms. Long."

"You're not very polite, *Ms.* Long."

"Thank you," I grumbled. *Screw you!*

"That's better." With a thrust of his hips, he strode into the elevator and stood right next to me. The doors closed instantly, and we began our high-speed descent. I inhaled his intoxicating scent but kept my eyes focused straight ahead.

He broke the silence. "Oh, by the way, did you like the negligee I picked out for you?"

My face flushed crimson and my stomach muscles scrunched. In my mind's eye, I could see the wicked grin on his face.

"To be precise, it was a baby doll and it sufficed," I murmured through gritted teeth, my muscles tightening again at the thought of him rifling through my lingerie. There was no need to tell him that the lacy lavender peek-a-boo set from our "Sweet Temptations" collection was one of my favorites. Or that I never woke up from my drunken stupor to put it on.

"I hope you'll be a little more enthusiastic about my pitch." His voice dripped with sarcasm. "I think I've nailed it."

I pressed my lips together and said nothing. To my relief, he remained silent for the rest of the ride. We reached the lobby in no time, and the elevator doors re-opened. As I moved to dash out, he fisted my braid, holding me back. The nerve of him! Fuming, I turned on my heels to face him. My eyes met his equally intense gaze.

"Are you visiting another ad agency today?" he asked, his brow cocked. "There's really no need to."

His presumptuousness was getting under my skin. Should I tell him that I was visiting a dozen more, just to make him think he had a lot of competition?

"No," I finally said.

"Good." With a satisfied smile, he let go of my hair and accompanied me to the hotel entrance, keeping up with my slower than normal pace. There was no physical contact between us. Whatsoever.

A refreshing blast of cool air hit me as I stepped outside. It was another beautiful New York City winter day. Sunny and not too cold. The usual array of cabs and limos crowded the driveway. Jaime Zander stood next to me.

"Do you want to grab breakfast with me?" he asked.

God, a coffee would be so good. Even if I had to put up with the pompous asshole. I glanced down at my watch. Nine fifty-five. "I can't. My driver will be here momentarily."

"What about lunch?"

"I'm visiting someone out of town."

"Oh, a boyfriend?"

"Yes!" I shouted the word and didn't know why I lied.

"Happy Valentine's Day!" He winked.

My jaw clenched. "Same to you."

Thankfully, before Mr. Nosy and Infuriating could probe further, Nigel pulled up to the curb.

Wearing a warm smile, my driver jumped out of the Town Car and opened the back passenger door. As I slid into the car, Jaime Zander never took his contemplative eyes off me. His lips twisted again into that maddening grin as the car rolled away. Fuck. I bet he saw right through my white lie . . . the tinted windows . . . and my coat.

CHAPTER 14

Jaime

I watched as her car drove off. A smirk curled my lips as she turned her head to see if I'd skirted off. When our eyes met, she made a face and jerked around as her car turned east on Fifty-Seventh Street. She was out of sight, but not out of mind. I couldn't stop whistling the song "Gloria" as Orson pulled up.

After my morning workout at the gym, which I alternated with an hour-swim in the rooftop pool, I was invigorated and eager to get to my office. The Gloria's Secret pitch had come together in my head and I couldn't wait to share it with my team.

Looking out the tinted window, I took in the morning rush hour traffic. I loved going to my office. ZAP! was my baby and my family. Though they were young, I had the best creative team in the business. Their loyalty to me was equaled by my loyalty to them, and together we had made ZAP! one of the top agencies in the cutthroat advertising industry. No one could surpass our cutting-edge creativity.

Several of my clients had suggested I move my office uptown to be closer to my residence. And to the other Madison Avenue ad agencies. I, however, loved the vibe of downtown, and the drive from The Walden to Soho was now a part of my routine. For me, it was both productive and relaxing. I used the time stuck in traffic to respond to clients around the world and often, some of my best ideas came to me.

Like now. Tonight she would be mine. I immediately pulled out my cell phone and speed-dialed Maurice, my trusted head of guest relations. Without questioning me, he agreed to do what I asked. Valentine's Day. Today would be productive. Tonight would be divine.

Orson dropped me in front of my office, which was housed in a 19th century brownstone on Spring Street. I told him there was no need to hang around as I knew I would be sequestered in my office all day working on the Gloria's Secret pitch. Sending my driver off enabled him to make a few extra bucks via fare-rides to and from Kennedy airport and throughout the city. He would be back at six to pick me up and take me back to The Walden.

"Good morning, Izzy," I called out to my receptionist as I whizzed by her. "Please have everyone meet me in the conference room in fifteen minutes."

"I'm on it," she replied already composing an email as I thanked her.

Taking long strides, I headed to my corner office, stopping only at the coffee station to grab a cup of the aromatic steamy brew. Sipping it, I threw my suede jacket over the back of my chair, and with my laptop bag flung over my shoulder, I hurried to the conference room. My creative juices were flowing. Adrenaline was pumping.

I reached the conference room in no time. My small creative team—affectionately known as the ZAPPERS—was already gathered around the conference room table in their favorite spots. My chair in the middle was vacant; I preferred to sit here because it gave me an egalitarian connection to my team and eliminated the feeling of superiority that came with sitting at the head. Regardless of where I sat, my crew knew I was their creative leader—the force that inspired them. Some people like Victor Holden led through intimidation, but I preferred inspiration. And passion. That's how I made people tick and do their best.

Without wasting time, I filled my eclectic team in on yesterday's meeting with Gloria Long, the head of Gloria's Secret . . . how she was looking for a new agency to help her market her upcoming BDSM-inspired line of lingerie. The team sat wide-eyed, their brains churning.

"This could be so hot," beamed my assistant, up and coming art director, Ray Wallace. "Sex sells."

"Exactly," I replied. "Every agency in town is courting her, but I want us to be the one to blow them away." *And blow her away.*

"How much time do we have?" inquired my chief copywriter Chloe.

"Forty-eight hours."

In unison, my team groaned. Eyes rolled. Panic.

"That's impossible!"

"We're on deadline to complete the SIN-TV spot!"

"We need to do research!"

I calmed the group down. Impossible was *not* possible in my book and we had time to finesse the SIN-TV commercial. It was right on track. Plus, I wasn't going out to LA until the end of the month to meet with Blake Burns, the head of the popular erotic cable network. We'd be fine.

"Listen, guys, calm down. We've been in this boat before. Let's start off with some word association." Their eyes didn't waver from me as I leapt up from my chair and ambled to the white board. "What comes to mind when you hear the term 'BDSM'?"

"Don't hold back," I added as I grabbed a marker.

"Bondage," shouted out Ray.

"Control," shouted another Zapper.

I scribbled both words on the board as they fired more at me.

"Possessive . . . pain . . . domination . . . sex . . . alpha male . . . submissive . . . blindfold . . . handcuffs . . ."

Before long, the board was covered with words. I smiled at my team. They had just reconfirmed my creative direction. And more or less, described me.

"Great job. You're all on target. And now I'm going to save you all a lot of time and effort."

Eyebrows shot up; eyes widened.

"I had an 'ah-ha' moment last night. This is what I'm thinking."

In a few words, I explained my vision of the campaign. The group listened intently, throwing out suggestions, which I loved. They were the best. The campaign was crystallizing in my head. I could see it in my mind so clearly it was if I was watching it on a big screen TV. The only thing that was still not quite right was the tagline. It was close, but no cigar. So we went around the table, trying to refine it.

" . . . let Gloria's Secret possess you."

" . . . let Gloria's Secret seduce you."

" . . . let Gloria's Secret capture you."

And then badda bing. I had it.

The team broke into raucous cheers and applause. The meeting breaking, everyone scurried back to their work-stations to make my vision a reality. The excitement in the air zapped every nerve ending of my body.

And as if things couldn't be more promising, I got a text from Maurice when I returned to my office that things were underway for tonight.

I pulled out Gloria's silk stockings from my jacket pock-et. Scrunching them, I put them to my nose, knowing I'd be doing that all day.

My cock flexed beneath my desk.

I didn't know what I was more jazzed about—tomorrow's pitch or tonight's dinner. Both were equally creative and hot as shit. One or the other was going to melt her.

Maybe both. I was back to whistling "Gloria."

CHAPTER 15

Gloria

The drive along the scenic Merritt Parkway to Connecticut was relaxing. I alternated between catching up on emails and gazing out the window. A fine layer of snow dusted the lawns of residences we passed by. Snow was something I rarely saw living in Los Angeles.

I would be lying if I said I didn't think about Jaime Zander. I couldn't get him out of my head. He was having an effect on me like no other man had before. I'd never met a man who could reduce me to a nervous wreck with just the wink of an eye. Make me feel so totally out of control. It scared me. Big-decision-maker-me didn't know how to handle it. Why the hell didn't I just tell him to fuck off? And forget about the pitch for my business? Walk away from him while I had the chance? The truth: He had gotten under my skin. I was undeniably drawn to him—both to his sexy good looks and his challenging personality. He was as tempting as he was toxic. Even now, just thinking about him, I was a wet bundle of nerves. Conscious of the stickiness between my legs, I sat back against the soft leather seat, glad to be away from him.

To get my mind off him, I went back to checking my emails. I opened Kevin's first; there were several. The first one brought a big smile to my face.

Happy Valentine's Day, Glorious! Xoxo~Kev

I emailed him right back.

MWAH! Same to you!

Kevin had been my one and only Valentine forever. Neither of us had ever had much luck in the love department. But we had each other. Hopefully, tonight we could celebrate together although we hadn't made any firm plans. Our traditional pity party for two could be on the agenda.

Waiting for his reply, I read the rest of his emails. All great news. The televised broadcast of the Gloria's Secret Fashion Show had rocked in the ratings, and sales were at record high levels at our stores worldwide. Yes, women were flocking to Gloria's Secret last minute to buy seductive lingerie and sleepwear for the romantic Valentine's night ahead. And they were standing in line with men, who were purchasing them as gifts to be worn after a candlelit dinner. I found it bitterly ironic that I sold love and sex but was never on the receiving end. Always on this day, my elation over sales was met with a pang of sadness. My mind jumped again to Jaime Zander. I bet he had a hot date tonight; women were all over him; I saw it with my own eyes. With a heavy heart, I eagerly awaited an email from Kevin to cheer me up.

An hour and a half into the drive, we exited the parkway and followed a rural, wooded road to the retirement home where Madame Paulette was residing. A magnificent gated estate soon came into view. Once the Normandy-styled mansion of one of America's great oil barons, it was now the Cadbury

House for Assisted Living. What I'd read about it had put my mind at ease. The pedigreed staff was attentive, the surroundings luxurious, and the cuisine delicious—prepared by a French chef. I was thrilled that I was able to afford to place my beloved Paulette here for her final years. Even though I had made her a wealthy woman with Gloria's Secret stock, there was no way I could let her pay for her care. I owed her everything.

The call I had received from the head caretaker just before I'd left for New York had been unsettling. In fact, it had brought tears to my eyes. Madame Paulette's health was failing rapidly, and it was unlikely she'd make it to the summer. Even if I didn't have business in New York, I would have hopped the corporate jet and come East to visit her. She meant the world to me. She was my mentor, my role model, and the mother I never had. Upon learning about her numbered days, I vowed I would confess the secret I had harbored my entire adult life. She needed to know. I needed to tell.

Standing in the elegantly appointed entrance with her bag of goodies in hand, I anxiously awaited for someone to show me to her room. Nurse Perez, a jovial, curly-haired buxom woman, appeared in no time and escorted me up a magnificent winding marble staircase to the second floor. "We all love Paulette," she said as I trailed close behind her. What was there not to love? She was a magnificent human being who would be sorely missed.

Madame's suite was located at the end of the corridor. Her door was wide open. She gasped when she saw me. I hadn't told her I was coming. It was a surprise.

"*Ma chérie!*" she exclaimed. Her voice was deeper and raspier than ever. Over the course of her long life, she had smoked way too many French cigarettes and drunk way too many glasses of wine.

Clad in an elegant lace-trimmed white nightgown, she was propped up in a luxurious down-covered bed against half-a-dozen plump pillows. Despite her age—she must have been close to ninety though she'd never admit to it—she was as beautiful to me as ever. Her strong-featured face seemed to be wrinkle-resistant, and her hair, now a shimmering silver, was tied back as usual in a regal chignon. Even in her old age, she epitomized elegance and style.

Fighting back tears, I sprinted over to her. We exchanged lots of cheek-to-cheek kisses.

"It *eez* so good to see you," she said as I plunked down in an armchair next to her bed.

"I'm in New York on a business trip." There was no way I was going to divulge the real reason behind my visit. "I've brought you all your favorite magazines."

I handed her the bagful of fashion magazines. Her face lit up as she removed the contents, one by one. *"Mes favorites!"* Her expression turning dour, she examined the cover of a recent *Vogue* featuring Jennifer Lopez. "But why do *les américains* always put those Hollywood *célébrités* on the cover?"

She made me laugh when I wanted to cry. Even our Gloria's Secret catalogue now featured celebrities like J-Lo on the cover. The bottom line: celebrities moved merchandise.

As she flipped through some of the magazines, we spent time chitchatting, catching up. She complained about the food—way too *nouveau* for her taste. And why couldn't she have more than one glass of wine? I, in turn, told her about how well Gloria's Secret was doing. *"Beezness shmeezness,"* she muttered. "Are you in love, *ma chérie?"*

I flushed. Jaime Zander's gorgeous face unexpectedly flashed into my head. I tried my damnedest to make it go away. No luck.

"No," I replied.

Madame Paulette studied my face with her intense cappuccino eyes. *"Ma chérie,* you cannot fool me. Your glow gives *eet* away." Signaling with her index finger for me to move in closer to her, she said, "You must tell me everything about *zee* new boyfriend."

"He's not my boyfriend," I protested as I slid my chair up to her bed railing.

"What *eez* his name?"

"Jaime."

"How do you spell that?"

"J-A-I-M-E."

"Ah, like *'J'aime.'* In French, that means, 'I love.'"

Of course. I suddenly remembered Madame Paulette telling me *"Je t'aime beaucoup."* *I love you very much* . . . when I thought love had abandoned me.

"So, *ma chérie,* are you in love with him?"

In love? I blushed. "I just met him."

"AH! *Zee* best! Love at first sight."

I still couldn't get Jaime Zander's beautiful face out my head. My heart pattered. No, it was not possible.

A melancholic smile flickered on Madame Paulette's face. "Always remember, *ma chérie,* it *eez* better to have loved and lost than never to have loved at all."

I wondered—had Madame Paulette ever been in love? While she always referred to herself as Madame, she had never mentioned a spouse, and I'd never been comfortable asking about her love life or her past. I'd always had a hunch, however, that she had once been married and had tragically lost the great love of her life. Once a year, on the eve of the Jewish holiday, Yom Kippur, the Day of Remembrance, she lit a candle that burned for twenty-four hours. I had asked her about the significance of the candle, and she had told me it was to commemorate someone special. While she always had dashing suitors who brought her flowers or French bonbons, she dismissed them all with a roll of her eyes. Whoever she had once loved couldn't be replaced.

A cheery Nurse Perez entered the room, carrying a tray. "Your lunch, Madame."

"Merci," growled Madame Paulette.

Smiling, Nurse Perez placed the bed tray over her lap, setting out the cutlery and linens. "Bon appétit," she said before parting.

"Bon appétit," Madame Paulette mock-mimicked. She was as feisty and as brutally honest as ever. "This *eez* French TV dinner," she grumbled, reluctantly digging a fork into the mishmash of food. *"Gar-bahge!"*

Stifling a laugh, I reached into my large designer bag. "I've brought you something else." I handed her a medium-sized, gold-foiled box that was sealed with a red velvet ribbon. She opened it with her still long and elegant fingers. The fingers that had adjusted thousands upon thousands of bra straps to bring out the best in women.

Her face lit up. "Ah! Bonbons. *Je les adore!"*

I pecked her cheek. "Happy Valentine's Day!"

"Ah, *zee* day of love. So silly! Every day should be a day of love."

A bittersweet smile tickled my lips. I was going to miss Madame's words of wisdom.

She popped one of the rich chocolate treats into her mouth and savored it. *"Merci beaucoup, ma chérie.* You must have one."

I helped myself to one of the chocolates and let it melt in my mouth. It was pure deliciousness. After swallowing the last morsel, the sweet taste of the dark chocolate dissolved into the bitter taste of dark memories. It was time.

"Madame," I said hesitantly. "I must tell you something."

"What *eez eet, ma chérie?* There *eez* sadness in your eyes."

My mind flashed back fifteen years. Kevin and I were both teenagers—sixteen-year-olds who had run away from our small rural upstate New York town. Him to escape the brutal beatings of his father, a macho local sheriff, who had no tolerance for his son's homosexuality, and me to escape the wrath I endured as the daughter of the neighborhood crack whore. "Who's your daddy?" the kids at school would taunt when I was a skinny pigtailed youngster. For all I knew, it could be any one of their fathers. My narcissistic, never-there-for-me mother (I was an unwanted accident discovered too late to be aborted) slept with them all to indulge her sick addictions. Then, at fifteen, late-bloomer me sprouted five inches, and my flat-as-a-board breasts morphed into spheres. Boys would grab at me, try to pull down my pants, and call me names like slut, whore, and skank. They equated me with my mother, who I was not.

Kevin was always there to protect me. He'd learned Taekwondo to protect himself from his own share of bullies and could send one of my molesters to his knees with a roundhouse kick. But this was not the life we wanted, so we decided to run away together. To find a new life in a big city like New York where we could fit in or disappear.

Kevin stole a gun from his father along with a few hundred dollars, which he kept locked in a safe. The gun and the money were all we had to start off on our new life together. We managed to hitch our way to New York City where we ended up in Brooklyn in the heart of Brighton Beach. Kevin charmed his way into securing a small one-bedroom rental apartment and used the money to buy some flea-market furnishings. We both needed to find work fast. Kevin, who had a flair for words, found a position teaching English to the children of neighborhood Russian immigrants, and I landed a sales job at a local lingerie store. Madame Paulette's.

I'd been combing the busy streets for work for hours when I came upon the big "Sales Help Wanted" sign in the storefront window. I'll never forget walking into her shop. With Edith Piaf's "La Vie en Rose" playing in the background, I took in all the luxurious silk and lace lingerie that Madame Paulette imported from Paris. Tables of delicate, perfectly folded brassieres, panties, and garters mingled with carefully organized racks of beautiful slips, negligees, and robes. There was also a carousel filled with package after package of fine silk stockings. Standing erect behind the cash register, the petite but chic Madame Paulette was dressed in her signature gray A-line skirt and perfectly pressed white blouse and drinking a glass of red wine. I introduced myself and told her I was interested in the sales position. She gave me the once-over and nodded approvingly. In her deep raspy voice, she said, "*Ma chérie, zee* shape of a women's breasts lies in *zee* straps. Let me see if you know how to adjust one."

Leaving her wine behind, she led me to a small dressing room in the rear of the store where a well-heeled buxom woman was trying on numerous bras. Madame Paulette beheld the half-naked woman in her ill-fitting lacy bra and shook her head. "Ah, *non, non, non. Eet eez* all wrong for you." Sorting through the pile of bras strewn on a petite gold-leafed chair, she found another and handed it to her. "Please put on *theese* one, and *mademoiselle* will adjust *eet.*" With a tilt of her chin, she looked my way.

The stocky woman nervously slipped on the big-cupped bra, front to back, and I hastily hooked it for her. Madame Paulette shot me a pleased smile. I surveyed the customer in the bra; the bra had potential but was not fitting her quite right. With nimble fingers, I tightened both straps, lifting up her boobs. I had learned how to put on a bra from watching my mother prepare for her "dates." At least the crack whore had been good for something. And being a difficult fit myself with my full C-cup breasts, which I'd inherited from her, I was quite an expert on making bras fit, though mine were the cheap cotton K-Mart variety.

"Now bend over and wiggle your breasts into the cups," I said after I finished adjusting the straps.

The woman did as I asked and then stood up. She looked at herself in the floor length mirror, and her face lit up. The lacy, underwire bra fit her perfectly and did wonders for her saggy boobs. "I'll take it and two more just like it!"

"*Superbe!*" Madame Paulette beamed. "I will have my *new* assistant wrap *zeem* up."

My heart broke into a happy dance. I had landed the job as Madame Paulette's sales assistant. Always good with my hands, I wrapped up the bras in beautiful layers of delicate, scented tissue paper. The ecstatic customer couldn't wait to hand over a crisp hundred-dollar bill for the three bras.

From that day on, I worked from ten to six every day except Saturdays when Madame Paulette, who I learned was Jewish and from Paris, took a day off to observe Shabbat. Despite her diminutive size, she was an incredible, bigger-than-life woman who understood people, understood life, and understood the basic need that women had to look and feel beautiful under their clothes. She taught me how to examine the quality of lace, how to tell the difference between nylon and silk stockings, how to take a woman's measurements, how to make alluring window displays, how to charm customers, and even how to handle gentlemen who were shopping for something sexy for their secret mistresses. "Life *eez* no fun without sex or wine," she often preached. Twice a year, she went to Paris and handpicked items for the boutique. In between these buying trips, she gave me daily French lessons so that one day I would be prepared to go to Paris. "*Zee* French are so *difficiles*," she'd always complain in her charming accent.

The one thing I'd noticed while working at her store was the number of young women who stopped in on their lunch breaks or way home from work, allured by the beautiful display windows. Inside the shop, they lusted for the exquisite but exorbitant French lingerie that they, like me, couldn't afford. I was convinced there was a market for gorgeous, sexy underwear at a reasonable price. When I shared this thought with Madame Paulette, she shooed me away with a dismissive wave of her hand. "*Mon dieu!* I cannot sell anything but *zee* best!"

I'd been working for her for a little over two years and had just turned eighteen when over a bottle of Bordeaux, which we shared every Friday evening to welcome Shabbat, Madame Paulette broke the news that she wanted to retire and was going to sell the business. My heart sank. There was no guarantee the store would remain a lingerie shop or if I was promised a job. "Would you like to buy *eet, ma chérie?*" she asked. After the shock died down, I told her I would love to, but there was no way I could come up with the twenty-five thousand dollar down payment. Madame Paulette was as disappointed as I was but needed the money for her retirement.

A potential buyer was in the picture—Boris Borofsky. He was a tough Russian gangster—a freakish pink-eyed albino—who wanted to buy the business for his idle, bottle-blond trophy wife, Ina. The latter took a strong disliking to me, and I knew if the deal went through, I'd be out of a job. I wanted the business so badly. I had visions for it and dreams! But with my meager wages and the cost of living in Brooklyn, I hadn't managed to save a penny.

Kevin knew how much I wanted to own the shop. With his boyish good looks and winning personality, he had gotten a job as the host of an underground "men's club" that happened to be owned by the obnoxious Russian pursuing Madame Paulette's business. He'd been able to save five thousand dollars and offered the cash to me.

"Kev, I can't take your money," I sobbed, touched by his offer. "Plus, I would need to come up with twenty thousand dollars more."

"I have an idea," he said.

I listened without interruption as he explained his plan . . . to rob the club. He hated the abusive Russian more than I did. He was a cheap, foul-mouthed womanizer without an ounce of humanity. Moreover, he was a gay-basher, who had threatened Kevin with both his job and life. Because many of his business deals involved drugs and human trafficking, he kept hoards of loose cash in a safe in the basement. A single security guard made regular deposits after hours.

A deep shudder ran through me as I flashed back to that terrible night. A night I wish I could forget but couldn't. The night of terror that had scarred me forever, emotionally and physically. The vault . . . the alarm . . . the assault . . . the gun shots . . . the screaming . . . the pain . . . the blackness . . . the blood. My eyes grew watery.

"Madame, I did something terrible." A tear trickled down my cheek. "I hope you can forgive me." I recounted my crime with no detail spared. By the time I was done telling her the secret I'd hidden all these years, I was a blubbering mess.

She took my icy cold hands in her warm ones. "*Ma pauvre petite*, you are lucky to be alive."

Her reaction stunned me. I thought for sure she would condemn me. She tenderly brushed away my tears and continued.

"Do you know, *ma chérie*, the Russian came to my store looking for you?"

My tear-soaked eyes widened. "He did?"

"*Oui*. I knew there was something terribly wrong because you did not come to work or call in for several days. *En plus*, he was missing teeth, and there was a thick bandage on each cheek."

Kevin's bullet! It must have gone through one cheek and out the other. I faintly remembered hearing Boris curse as I lost consciousness in Kevin's arms.

Madame continued. "He was very angry but could barely move his mouth. He wanted to know your name. I made up a different name and told him you no longer worked for me. Since I paid you in cash, there was no way for him to find out your real identity."

I was speechless. Unbeknownst to me all these years, Madame Paulette had protected me and helped save my life.

"I immediately called your apartment. That handsome young gentleman friend of yours luckily answered *zee* phone. I told him that I believed your life was in terrible danger and that you should get as far away from Brooklyn as possible. I offered him money, but he told me there was no need."

The hazy memory of a panicked Kevin telling me that Boris was after me flitted into my head. I was weak, still in bed, barely recovered from my gunshot wound. Kevin threw together a duffel bag full of basics, and two hours later, he was pushing me in a wheelchair through Kennedy Airport with the sack of money on my lap. I vaguely remembered him telling the suspicious security guard that the cash was for a much needed surgical procedure. Glib Kevin could talk his way through anything. Soon after, we were on a plane to Los Angeles on our way to safety.

A harsh cough from Madame Paulette brought me back to the moment. My heart was melting. She was both my mentor and savior. Blinking back tears, I wrapped my arms around her frail body and hugged her. "Madame, how can I ever thank you enough?"

"You must stop crying, *ma chérie.*" Her expression grew wistful. "We've all done terrible things we've regretted to survive."

My sobbing came to a halt. "What do you mean?"

She looked away with sudden remorse in her eyes, then turned to face me. "When I was a young woman, I slept with a Nazi officer to save my family."

I gasped. Had she lived with this horrible secret her whole life?

"Had I not, we would have all been sent to a concentration camp."

I was speechless.

"Alors, ma chérie, you must forgive yourself. You have redeemed yourself and done many noble things with what came of it. I am proud of you."

I hugged her again. It was probably the last time we'd embrace.

She sighed against me. "I still wish you could have bought my *beezness.*"

Boris Borofsky had purchased it, but sadly, his incompetent wife ran it into the ground. It was now a Starbucks. The fate of Madame Paulette's boutique tugged at my heartstrings. If only things had worked out . . . but "what ifs" didn't matter anymore. I gently squeezed her hand.

Another caregiver stepped into the room. This time a handsome silver-haired doctor. "I'm afraid, Ms. Long, that Madame must take her nap now."

"Bah! Sleep *eez* for *zee* dead!" grumbled Madame Paulette after he left.

Her words at once amused and saddened me. The reality that she was going to die soon hit me hard. I held back more tears.

I gave her a final double-cheeked kiss, and then we just held each other. Her frail bones warmed mine. When we finally broke away, she wearily said, "*Ma chérie,* there *eez* something else I want to tell you." She paused while her eyes grew watery. "I had a husband. His name was Henri Lévy. He died fighting for the Résistance. I want to be buried next to him." She ripped out a sheet of paper from the note pad on her night table and scribbled something on it. "This *eez* where he *eez*," she said handing it to me. I folded the paper in half and placed it in my bag.

"*Oui,* Madame. I will take care of it." A fresh round of tears was verging.

She smiled contently and closed her eyes. Softly, she repeated what she'd said earlier. "Remember, *ma chérie*, that it *eez* better to have loved and lost than never to have loved at all."

I tiptoed out of the room with a less guilty conscience and the newfound knowledge that Madame Paulette had indeed known true love.

CHAPTER 16

Jaime

My creative team was doing an outstanding job readying the Gloria's Secret pitch. Like me, they worked well under pressure. In fact, better. The office was buzzing with creative energy and electricity. Several times during the day, I strolled by their offices to see how things were coming together. I couldn't be happier. Thai food was ordered in for lunch as no one wanted to go out or take a break when they were on a roll. Devouring skewers of chicken satay at my desk, I spent more time thinking about my dinner with Gloria than my pitch to her tomorrow. I was the king of winging it and had learned over the years that over-rehearsing my pitches got in the way of my passion and salesmanship. My style was the antithesis of those Madison Avenue suits with their buttoned-up presentations. I preferred to shoot from the hip and keep things loose.

Finishing my Thai ice tea while catching up with emails, my attention was diverted from my computer screen when my door creaked open. I swallowed hard. Standing at the doorway was the last person I wanted to see.

From behind him, our receptionist dashed into my office, panic on her face. "I'm sorry, Jaime. I tried to stop him."

"It's okay, Izzy," I gritted. "Just close the door behind you," I added as my unexpected visitor stepped into my office. As she skirted past him, my eyes took him in. He was dressed in an impeccable three-piece charcoal suit with a black wool overcoat draped over his shoulders. His sinister gaze met mine.

"What do you want, Victor?" Was he angry I'd won the auction last night?

"My daughter tells me you are pursuing the Gloria's Secret account."

"So, what if I am?"

His steel-gray eyes narrowed at me. "Drop it. And stay away from her."

My blood simmered. Bitter disgust for this man filled my mouth. It tasted repulsive on my tongue.

"You can't tell me what to do, Victor."

He snarled. "That's always been a problem. I should have disciplined you harder. To show some respect for me."

For a moment, my mind flashed back to thirteen-year-old me. I relived the radiating pain. The sting of humiliation. The dark memories faded as a Molotov cocktail of rage and hate pounded through my bloodstream.

"Get the fuck out of my office, Victor."

"Watch your language."

"Fuck you, bastard."

He just stood there, motionless and unfazed. "You're going to be sorry, Zander. Don't get involved with things that belong to me."

"Is that a threat?"

"No, it's a statement. I will take you both down if I have to."

"Get. Out."

With a smug smirk still pasted on his face, he wordlessly pivoted and swung open the door before slamming it shut behind him.

My nerves crackled like lightning. My chest tightened.

To calm myself, I took several deep breaths, inhaling and exhaling from my nose. Fuck him. He couldn't control my life anymore. And I wasn't thirteen-years-old anymore. The scrawny, insecure adolescent was now a grown man. I could fight fire with fire.

The ping of an incoming email cut into my raging thoughts. It was from Ray. The creative team was ready to show me the mock up.

With a final gulp of my ice tea, I scurried out my office to the conference room. When I saw the board, my excitement knocked my anger out of the ballpark. It was fucking brilliant.

There was no doubt in my mind that I was going to win the Gloria's Secret account. And when I saw the email from Maurice upon returning to my office that all was set for tonight, I was positive I was going to win her too. Unwavering confidence sailed through my blood vessels, heading straight to my cock.

Fuck Victor. If anything, his threats only propelled me to win what I wanted. And who I wanted.

My cock high fived me. Yeah, fuck him.

CHAPTER 17

Gloria

The journey back to the city was uneventful. We were in counter-traffic and made excellent time. I thought about what Madame Paulette had told me . . . and Jaime Zander. I wondered if I would bump into him at the hotel or have to wait until tomorrow's pitch at his office. Either way, flutters clustered between my thighs for the duration of the ride. Confession: I hoped sooner than later.

We got back to the hotel by four p.m. I headed straight to my room, caught up on some emails, took a short nap, and showered. As I towel dried myself, the room phone rang. My heart galloped. Could it be Jaime? Wrapping the towel around me, I sprinted to the phone. With a shaky hand, I picked up the receiver.

"Glorious."

It was Kevin.

"I'm sorry I haven't been in touch. I've been crazed all day with the press. I have to go to dinner with some of the models and a network executive. Do you want to come along?"

After such an emotional afternoon, the last thing I wanted to do was have dinner at some pretentious restaurant with a bunch of bubblehead models and some fawning network guy.

"If it's okay, I'm going to pass, Kev. I'm beat." At some point, I needed to tell him about my encounter with Madame Paulette, but this wasn't the time. Nor did my talky best friend let me.

"It's Valentine's Day. Are you sure you're going to be okay?"

Kevin knew how downtrodden I got on this holiday. "Yeah. I'm going to order room service and curl up with a book boyfriend."

Kevin mock-sniffed. "But I'm your one and only Valentine."

I laughed. "Don't worry. You are. Have fun tonight!"

"Mwah! Happy Valentine's Day, Glorious. I love you."

"Love you back."

As I hung up the phone, a pang of sadness stabbed me. Book boyfriends were as close as I'd ever gotten to the real thing.

Though it was now only 5:30, I was ravenous. Other than the chocolate, I hadn't eaten a thing all day. My body was crying out for food. Maybe a good steak, a baked potato, and an iced tea. Definitely no alcohol after last night's binge, the effects of which still lingered a little.

As I was about to reach for the phone, it rang again. I picked it up on the second ring.

"Have you had dinner yet?"

Jaime! I sucked in a gulp of air. "Don't you have a hot Valentine's date?"

"No. I don't do love."

"Neither do I."

"Then, come eat with me."

Silence.

"My suite is three doors down to the right."

Silence.

"We can talk business."

Silence.

"Just get your lovely ass over here."

Jaime's corner suite was triple the size of mine—a mini palace in the sky. Floor-to-ceiling windows wrapped around it and overlooked the sparkling city. The views were breathtaking.

The lights were dimmed, and scattered candles scented the air. He ushered me to a black leather couch and strode over to a built-in veneer cabinet in the corner. Putting on some soft jazz, he said, "Room service should be here any minute. I hope you don't mind that I've already ordered for both of us."

"Perfectly fine." I couldn't take my eyes off him. Casually dressed in charcoal sweats that hung low on his hips and a soft white tee—and barefoot—he looked freshly showered and sexy as hell. How could he always look this way? Having slipped back into the gray ensemble that I'd worn earlier in the day to keep things businesslike, I felt overdressed and uptight.

I surveyed his suite. While mine was decorated with mid-century reproductions, I got the sense that the furnishings in his were authentic and included pieces from Bauhaus, Charles Eames, and others. He had moreover personalized the spacious interior with a bold geometric patterned rug and colorful pillows that picked up the hues of the many intriguing abstract paintings scattered on the walls. They were similar in style to the ones in his office and all signed PAZ.

He crossed the room with his long-legged confident gait and sunk into a creamy leather armchair opposite me. He casually folded one leg over the other and I tried not to look down at intersection between his thighs.

"Do you live here full time?" I asked, fumbling for conversation.

"Yeah."

Okay, so it wasn't a fuck pad, but it was still an odd living arrangement. Was it because he could fuck transient women and never have to see them again? I mentally slapped myself and asked, "Why do you live in a hotel?"

"It's convenient. I work long hours and travel a lot, so having all these amenities makes things easier."

I could understand that because I lived in a full maintenance high-rise building in Los Angeles that catered to my every whim—except room service.

He paused. "And because I own it."

My eyes popped. He owned this hotel?

Before I could inquire further, there was a loud knock at the door. Jaime jumped up to open it. A handsome, college-aged waiter wheeled in a white linen-covered cart with two silver dome-covered platters on warmers. I was surprised there was also a bottle of Cristal in a bucket of ice— especially after my embarrassing episode last night.

"Mr. Zander, would you like me to set up a table here or would you prefer to eat in the dining room?" asked the eager-to-please waiter.

"Right here is fine," replied Jaime, pointing to the area between his chair and the couch.

The waiter magically transformed the cart into a small dining table, complete with linens, utensils, and a votive candle.

"I'll take it from here," said Jaime, slipping the waiter a hundred-dollar bill. The thankful young man scurried out of the suite.

I watched as Jaime expertly uncorked the champagne and poured the bubbly into a pair of flutes.

"Just a little for me," I said hastily as he filled my glass. *Careful, Gloria. Control yourself.* The last thing I wanted was a repeat of last night.

With an amused look, he respected my wishes and filled my flute only halfway. "To a fine meal and fine company." He clinked his glass against mine, brushing his fingers along my flesh. I nervously took a sip of the champagne. The bubbly did little to calm the butterflies swarming my stomach.

His eyes stayed on me as he drank his champagne. "I hope you like filet mignon. I asked for it rare—like you."

The breathy way he said "rare" led me to take another gulp of my champagne. The truth was I did like my steaks that way.

He lifted the silver dome. A plate with a small, succulent steak, buttered peas, and potatoes au gratin grazed my senses. It all looked and smelled divine.

He slid back into his chair and scooted it up to the table. His clean, fresh scent mixed with the mouthwatering aroma of the food.

"Eat!" he ordered.

"What about you?" I asked after placing my napkin on my lap.

"My dish has to simmer. Besides, I want to watch you eat. I'll enjoy it."

Anxiously, I cut into the tender steak and put a forkful of the juicy pink meat to my mouth.

His eyes never left me. "Ah, you cut your meat and eat the European way," he mused. "I find that very sexy."

I choked. Madame Paulette had taught me this way of eating. It was one of her many life lessons. "Eating like a European will give you class and mystery," she had told me.

"Swallow!" he ordered.

Nervously, as he watched, I gulped down the first morsel

of the meat. Getting it past the big lump in my throat wasn't easy.

I continued to eat my dinner under his intense, watchful gaze. As delicious as the meal was, I was losing my appetite with each bite. In fact, my gut was cramping, and a tingling between my legs was distracting me. Why did he affect me this way?

"Aren't you going to eat?" I asked.

A saucy smile curled on his lips. "I'm getting rather hungry and think my meal might be nicely heated up now." Slowly, he lifted the silver dome covering his entrée.

My eyes practically popped out of their sockets. Artfully displayed on the platter were Rihanna's diamond-studded brassiere and thong.

"Gloria, are you done with your dinner?"

Speechless, I just nodded. I couldn't eat a bite more even if I tried.

"Good. Then stand up."

As if under a hypnotic spell, I did as he asked.

He rose to his feet and came around the dining cart. In one swift, smooth move, he swept down the back zipper of my dress, swooped it over my head, and tossed it to the floor.

Quivering, I stood semi-naked in front of him, clad only in my lacy gray lingerie and silk stockings. And my heels.

His lustful eyes roved up and down my body. I suddenly became very conscious of the scar above my heart that peeked out from my bra, but to my relief, he ignored it.

"I like the way you match your undergarments to what you're wearing."

Madame Paulette had ingrained that in me. In a state of semi-shock, I mumbled a throwaway thanks.

He continued to study me. "You have such a sexy body. Custom-made for your lingerie line. But it's such a shame you don't enjoy what you sell. Let me show you how."

My body, indeed curvaceous, was a trembling mess. Words stayed trapped in my throat while I tried to steady myself on my feet.

"Relax, Gloria. Trust me." He shoved the dining cart out of the way. There was nothing standing between the two of us except a blazing storm of electricity.

He squatted halfway to the floor and clutched my thighs with his warm, manly hands. With his teeth, he snapped open each garter. I stood motionless as he slid my silk stockings down my long legs. His hands brushed against my skin, sending goosebumps all over me. I anchored my palms on his broad shoulders as he removed my shoes and stockings. The garter and my skimpy lace bikinis were the next to hit the floor. He slipped the shoes back on my feet and then stood up and removed my bra. My scar in full view, my body didn't move a muscle. A contemplative smile spread across his face as he gazed at me.

"Ah, Gloria, you are so, so, beautiful." He reached for the diamond-studded undergarments and handed them to me. Please put these on."

What?

"Don' t worry. I had them thoroughly cleaned. They're like brand new."

It wasn't Rihanna's crotch I was worried about. It was mine. I was on fire.

"Put the thong on first. I want to stare at those exquisite tits for as long as I can."

My nerves on edge, I bent over and slipped each high-heeled foot into the leg openings of the thong and then pulled it up until the patch of diamonds covered my patch of gold. The diamonds formed a heart—the iconic signature of Gloria's Secret. All our merchandise bore the insignia heart somewhere. There was even a heart instead of a dot over the "i" in the Gloria's Secret logo.

He examined me. His eyes seared my flesh.

I felt light-headed. The heat of his gaze mixed with the warmth of the buttery leather. He was making me melt. Hot juices gathered between my thighs.

He smiled. "Perfection. Now, the bra."

With jittery fingers, I put the back-closing bra on backward and fumbled with the clasp. After hooking it, I twisted the bra around, slipped my arms into the straps, and plumped my milky-white globes into the push-up cups. Hearts of diamonds surrounded my erect nipples.

Jaime gazed at me reverently. "You look more beautiful in these works of art than I ever imagined."

My brows rose to my forehead. "You bought them for me?" I asked, finding my voice.

He let out a light, sexy laugh. "No, I bought them *for me* to look at on you."

Semantics. A chill ran down my spine in anticipation of what was next.

"Turn around."

I pivoted on my heels and could feel his eyes on my very exposed ass.

"Beautiful. Now come over here. I think my dinner is ready."

Hesitantly, I stepped into him. In my stilettos, we were eye to eye. Chest to chest. Organ to organ.

His eyes bored into mine. "You're so fucking edible. I bet you're going to taste so good."

Edible . . . Taste?

In one smooth move, he yanked down the thong to my ankles and dropped to his knees. He gazed up at me with his ravenous eyes.

"Spread your legs," he ordered.

They shifted apart as though I was contractually obliged.

In a breath, my butt cheeks were cupped in his hands, and his mouth was buried between my thighs, sucking and nibbling at my tender flesh.

Why the hell am I letting him do this? What's the matter with me?

"You're so fucking delicious," he moaned. "And so wet."

His hot, velvety tongue swept across the folds of my cleft. "Mmmm. And so sweet." Stroking and licking, he was clearly enjoying his dinner.

I had the answer to my questions. I was enjoying it too. Okay. That was an understatement. I was in a state of rapture. The movements of his aerobic tongue were sending a heat wave through my body. I squeezed my eyes and stifled the moans that were begging to be released. It took all the willpower I could muster not to squirm. *Control yourself, Gloria!*

And then his tongue stayed in one place—my clit. He alternately flicked it with the tip and sucked it hard with his mouth. My body quivered as overwhelming pleasure flooded my senses. I bit down on my lip to quell the sounds clogging my throat.

Still working my nub furiously, he shoved his fingers up my hole. I jolted. There must have been more than one inside, judging by the fullness. They felt divine! He slid them up and down, bringing a new level of erotic pleasure to my being. All the while, his tongue stayed focused on my clit, working it vigorously.

Control was no longer an option. I was totally losing it. Wetness pooled between my thighs. Whimpers escaped my throat; sweat escaped my pores. My legs turned to jelly and my heart beat into a frenzy. Writhing against him in my stilettos, I clung to his shoulders for support as the insufferable throbbing between my useless legs threatened to undo me. Truthfully, I wasn't sure if I could hold on any longer. He was driving me to the point of no return. *Oh my God. Oh my God. Oh my God.*

"Fall apart for me now, Gloria." As he breathed my name, I shattered on command with a ragged scream. Waves of ecstasy crashed through me like a tsunami taking everything in their wake. Shattering all of me. Beautifully broken into a million pieces, I thought I might pass out.

He gripped my hips to steady me and then flicked my clit one last time, gifting me with yet another dizzying orgasm. Oh, what this man could do to me!

He finally pulled away and gazed up at me. With sexy half-moon eyes, he lifted the three, yes three, deft fingers that had been inside me, now glistening with my juices, to his lush mouth and sucked them. Then, he lowered them and licked his lips.

"Ah Gloria, you are like fine caviar. I hope you enjoyed your dinner as much as I enjoyed mine. Would you like dessert?" he asked before pulling up the diamond-studded thong and rising to his feet.

Still breathless, I didn't think I could handle dessert, whatever that was. When I glimpsed the bulge, now bigger, beneath his sweats, I had an idea. "I'll pass," I managed.

"Oh, do you feel sated?" I could tell his eyes were hungering for more.

"Yes," I stammered. *Very.* "I need to go to sleep." Shaking, I collected my clothes that were strewn on the floor.

He smirked at me. "*My* brassiere and thong, please."

"Right." Before I could make a move, he one-handedly unhooked the bra and slipped it off. Scrunching it in his hand, he pulled down the diamond-studded thong with the other. I held on to his broad shoulders for balance as I stepped out of it. Embarrassment crept through me. The silk crotch was now drenched.

He bent over, retrieved his prize and, to my shock, put the soaking wet undergarment to his nose. He inhaled deeply. "I don't think I'm going to wash these."

At a loss for words, I donned my dress, not bothering to put my underwear back on. I swept up the lacy pieces in my hands; he didn't need more souvenirs.

"Thanks for dinner." I rushed the words and pivoted toward the door. My body was still trembling from my head to my toes.

He tugged my braid hard, holding me back. "Thanks for letting me feast on you."

I spun around to face him. "Let go of me."

Coiling my braid around his hand, he roped me in closer to him. So close, his breath heated my cheeks. "What are you doing tomorrow?"

"I have a busy day. Store visits. Our Fifth Avenue store is our largest. I'll be there all afternoon."

"Ah, Gloria. All work, no play. I'm going to change that." He did the hair thing again—coiling my braid tighter. "The hotel has a splendid pool on the top floor. Meet me there at six a.m. when it opens. No one will be there except us. We'll have it all to ourselves . . . have a little fun and get in some exercise . . . maybe burn off this meal."

He let me go. As my weak legs carried me to the door, he breathily said, "Don't be late."

"I never am." I didn't turn my head to look at him but knew his glimmering eyes were lingering on me, his smile cocky from his little victory.

As I limped down the hall to my suite, he called out to me. "Hey, Gloria. Happy Valentine's Day."

A smile that he couldn't see curled on my lips. Confession: It was the best Valentine's Day I'd ever had.

CHAPTER 18

Jaime

D inner was smeared all over my face and I loved it. The taste of her lingered on my tongue, the scent of her still on my fingers. She tasted as delicious as she smelled, so sweet and intoxicating her juices should be bottled. Like an elixir or fine perfume. Something rare and sensual to savor.

I leaned back against my couch, still in my sweats, too wound up to go to sleep. The room was dark, lit only by the myriad lights of the towering city outside. I stared out a window, replaying tonight's events.

My dinner had gone perfectly as planned. In fact, better than planned. I didn't realize how submissive she'd be. How responsive. How fucking sexy she'd looked in those diamond-studded garments. It was if they were made for *her* body. That gorgeous body that had come all around my tongue and my digits. I could still feel those vibrations flooding her core with each successive orgasm and see the look of tortured ecstasy on her exquisite face. Feel her trembling thighs, envision her quivering tits.

Did she have any fucking idea what she did to me? My cock was already semi-hard before she showed up. Just from anticipation. And it got harder as I watched her eat, hungering for her. Straining against my sweats as I undressed her. And ready to burst through the fabric the minute she slipped on those leather undergarments. Jesus. I devoured her like Valentine candy, licking and sucking her succulent pussy, and as I made her come, I thought I was going to combust in my pants. It was not my M.O. to solely pleasure a woman. Or even care about that. My physical needs always came first. The pleasure I derived from pleasuring Gloria could only be measured by the size of my dick. It took all I had—every atom of control—not to slide out my cock and thrust it into her spectacular hot, wet, pussy. Coiling her braid around my hand as she departed my suite was a metaphor. In my head, I imagined what it would be like to have her tight as fuck cunt coiled around my cock, setting it on fire as I thrust in and out of her.

The problem was my cock had not recovered. I was still so hard it hurt. As the city lights shimmered in my eyes, my unyielding erection throbbed from need and lust. I was restless, desperate for relief. Grabbing the diamond-studded thong from the coffee table, I put it to my nose. It was still damp and smelled of her. Sex and sweetness. Yanking down my sweats with my free hand, I clutched the base of my pulsing cock and began to rub it up and down, each stroke harder and faster, each intake of her wetness and scent bringing me closer to the edge. Searing heat surged between my legs and spiraled through my body as an orgasm of epic proportions built in my groin. Then, with a groan of her name, I exploded, hot cum spilling between my fingers.

Wasted, I closed my eyes and she was all I could see.

In my mind, I was seducing her.

In reality, she was seducing me.

CHAPTER 19

Gloria

I thought for sure that I would meet Jaime at the elevator, but he wasn't there. I was wearing the plush white terry-cloth robe that came with the room over a bright red bandeau bathing suit. One of our popular catalogue items, it was cut in a way that made my long legs look even longer. I had also packed a bikini but decided on the one-piece because it was more comfortable and enabled me to swim fast without any worry of it falling off. Besides, no bikini could compete with the diamond-studded underwear I'd worn last night. Unable to force that memory away, I pressed the elevator button and, when the doors slid open, headed up to the pool. I stared down at the sparkly flip-flops on my feet—last summer's unexpected bestseller—trying impossibly hard not to concentrate on the throbbing that lingered between my thighs.

To my surprise, he was already doing laps up and down the Olympic-size pool when I showed up. His form was beautiful . . . long elegant strokes with his brawny arms and long tapered fingers, and powerful kicks that spliced the water with little splashes. Upon catching sight of me on a breath, he finished his lap and hauled himself out of the pool. Dripping wet, his soaked hair slicked back, he lifted his goggles on top of his head and broke into that dazzling smile. "Good morning, Gloria. I'm looking forward to our swim together and to seeing you all wet."

My heart skipped a beat. This was the first time I'd seen him without his clothes on—well, almost. He was wearing one of those latex Speedos made for racing that exposed a body that could belong to an Olympic champion. His shoulders were broad; his chest chiseled, his arms sculpted, and his legs long and muscular. For sure, a body of steel. A fine layer of dark hair coated his limbs and descended from his amazing washboard abs to the most fabulous V-section I'd ever seen on a man. Then, I almost gagged. The sizable package between his taut thighs was like nothing I'd ever seen before—actually, make that, monstrous—and sent a shockwave reeling through me. The throbbing between my legs intensified; I could actually hear the thrumming like a heartbeat.

Once again, he knew the effect he was having on me and shot me a cocky smile. "C'mon, I'll race you for dinner. The winner of two out of three laps gets to pick a restaurant; the loser gets to pay."

Defensively, I crossed my arms. "What makes you think I want to have dinner with you, Mr. Zander?"

"Ms. Long, after last night, there's no doubt in my mind."

I bit my lower lip. Tongue-tied, I managed one word: "Fine."

I shrugged off my robe. Jaime's sparkling denim blues traveled down my body. "You are simply magnificent. A feast for the eyes. Maybe the winner's prize should be ripping off the other's bathing suit."

At his unexpected words, I suddenly felt more naked than I was and the thought of seeing him in the raw stole my breath. I almost choked. *Control yourself, Gloria!* Pulling myself together, I wrinkled my nose at him; I couldn't let him unhinge me. "Forget it. A deal is a deal. Come on, let's race."

I was looking forward to the challenge. He had no idea whom he was dealing with. Having lived in Brighton Beach, I had become a masterful swimmer thanks to the nearby ocean and large community pool. My long lean muscles and broad square shoulders reflected my passion. I still swam regularly in the heated pool at my condo complex. Little did he know, I was extremely competitive.

Lowering our goggles over our eyes, we lined up side by side at the edge of the pool's deep end. His slick wet body deliberately brushed against mine, sending a chill up my spine. We wished each other good luck. Snark and smirks. Neither of us meant it.

"Okay, on your mark, get set, go!" I called out and with that, we both dove into the water.

To my relief, the pool was heated. I wasted no time propelling myself ahead, stroking and kicking furiously. Damn it! Mr. Challenging was keeping up with me, even at the halfway mark. When I got to the other end a mere second before him, I quickly did a flip turn and headed back to where we'd begun. On a breath, I stole a glance backward. Yes! My competitor was losing steam and was now several lengths behind me. Picking up speed, I raced ahead and reached the starting point way before he did. Breathing hard, I popped up from the water and, with a triumphant smile, watched him struggle to meet me. "Fuck!" he cursed under his labored breath.

"I'm thinking of a very expensive restaurant," I taunted and flipped back my heavy wet braid.

"I am too," he said, catching his breath and flipping up his goggles.

I dwelled on his glistening face. God, he was beautiful, his lips lickable and his eyes, two glimmering blue gems with crowns of thick dark lashes. My heart thudded, an unstoppable reaction to the sight of the god-like man beside me and the challenge that faced me. Ha! He was no match for me. One more race and it would be over for sure. This time he said "on your mark," and we took off. I reached the other end way before he did and turned around quickly. I could taste victory. About a third of the way back, I noticed he was picking up speed. My limbs and lungs burning, I surged ahead. Three breaths later, he passed me; I gaped when I glimpsed his cocky smile. He was beating me to the finish line by several yards. An amused glint flickered in his eyes when I finally reached our starting point. I was panting. He wasn't even breathless. Huh? Had he possibly let me win the first race? Faked all that heavy breathing? I was fuming.

"Are you still thinking about a very expensive restaurant?" he asked with playful sarcasm.

I scowled. "Yes!"

He tugged at my thick wet braid. "You're cute when do that little frown thing with your brows."

I was seething. Simply seething. "Cute" was the last thing I was.

The third and final race. The race that would determine who was taking whom to dinner. I mentally psyched myself up for it. *Come on, Gloria, show him!*

"Good luck, Gloria. May the best man win."

"Or woman," I scoffed.

He winked at me as we took off.

I was off to a strong start. *Just focus on the race*. I forced myself not to take any breaths—a means of keeping him out of my field of vision and not letting him distract me. Kicking and stroking at torpedo speed, I flipped around at the other end and finally came up for a much-needed gulp of air. To my horror, there he was . . . several lengths ahead of me. Calling upon every muscle in my body, I caught up to him only for him to swim ahead of me again. He shot me a cocky smile on a breath as he passed by me. Rage surged inside me as I silently cursed. No way could I let him win! Furiously, I propelled myself forward, stroking and kicking harder than I'd ever had. We were neck to neck. Breath to breath. Splash to splash. Every muscle in my body stung as I took my last stroke. My head shot out of the water. Clinging to the edge of the pool, I was panting like a dog. I couldn't catch my breath. Beneath my fogged up goggles, my eyes fluttered. He was in my face. At the finish before me.

"Get over here, you," he rasped. Breathing heavily, he took me in his powerful arms and drew me against him. I was too exhausted to resist. My heart pounded against his; I hadn't been this close to someone else's heartbeat in years. Before I could say a word, he lifted up my goggles, tilted back my head by the tail of my braid, and crushed his mouth upon mine. The warmth of his breath permeated my body. His kiss was passionate and fierce. I was panting into his mouth. Once again, I was losing control to this outrageous man. I don't know why, but I just let him do it. Even deepen the kiss as his tongue parted my lips. Inside my mouth, his tongue did a synchronized swim with mine. Swirling and twirling. It was as if we had practiced these moves for years. I couldn't get enough, and if kisses were part of the Olympics, this one would have been the gold standard. Close to losing consciousness, my body grew slack as the electricity between us zapped every fiber of my being. If tendons held muscles to bones, I had none. I was boneless. Finally, he broke away, leaving me breathless, incapacitated, and begging for more.

"Wrap your legs and arms around me and just relax."

Without questioning myself or him, I complied, folding my limp limbs around his broad shoulders and buns of steel. I was glad to be off my feet. The buoyancy of the water helped hold me up.

His glistening wet skin brushed against mine. I longed for his mouth. His tongue. His breath.

With a devilish grin, he read my mind. "Ms. Long, you obviously need to be kissed. And kissed often by a man who knows how."

On my next heated breath, he moved his hand from my braid to my lower back, pulling me closer to him. His lush mouth consumed mine once again, gnawing, sucking, tongues colliding, reawakening my senses, infusing me with strength, and sending carnal waves of desire to my core. Closing my eyes, I could feel his erection digging into me through the thin material of his Speedo as I squeezed my legs around him and pressed my breasts against his steely chest, needing to feel him with every part of my body. My hand fisted his slick wet hair. He moaned into my mouth and I moaned back, the erotic sounds kindling my desire.

I don't know how long we stayed in this position, when a crotchety voice brought us abruptly to our senses.

"I wish I could do that."

Our eyes snapped open. We had company. A slight, elderly, balding man, who was wearing swim trunks two sizes too big for him, was hunched over above us. My face flushed with embarrassment.

"Don't let age stop you," chuckled my companion, not the least bit embarrassed.

"Can you find me one as pretty as her?" cackled the octogenarian and then plowed into the pool with a loud splash-worthy belly flop. He swam away in quite good form for a man his age.

"Guess I won't be able to fuck you here," murmured Jaime.

The F-bomb resounded in my head. Goosebumps erupted along my arms. Now what was I getting myself into? And why wasn't I running away?

Jaime hauled himself out of the pool and then helped me out. He wrapped me up in my fluffy white robe and then slipped on his. He held me against him and again I was unable to resist. It felt so good to rest my head on his strong chest against the soft terry cloth.

"Come on, let's take a hot shower together," he said softly in my ear.

"In your suite?" I gasped.

"No, here. There's a great handicapped steam shower in the men's room." He pressed his heavy erection against me. "And right now, I'd say I'm handicapped."

Oh was he! I swallowed hard and let him lead the way, his hand clasping mine. The thought of showering in the men's room made me feel like a very naughty schoolgirl.

There was no one in the men's room. The spacious handicapped shower, complete with support railings and a bench, occupied a corner at the end of a row of shower stalls. We shrugged off our robes and hung them on the hooks bracketing the shower door.

Jaime's hands gripped the top edge of my bathing suit.

"What are you doing?"

"What does it look like? I'm taking off your bathing suit."

"Wait! Remember? This was not part of the prize package!" Too late. The wet suit was already a crumpled heap at my feet.

"Not fair."

"Don't worry." He immediately slid his off too. "Now we're equal."

For the first time, I got an eyeful of his cock. Holy cow! It was huge. And the veined, pink pillar of flesh was pointed my way. *Run, Gloria!* Forget it! My legs had turned to jelly, and the air had left my lungs.

Taking my clammy hand, Jaime led me into the shower stall. Trailing him, I noticed a series of faint white lines streaking his back. Stretch marks? This was the only imperfection on his otherwise perfect body. They didn't distract from his beauty.

With his free hand, he slammed the glass door shut. He jiggled the shower knob, and a forceful spray shot out from the showerhead. He wrapped his muscled arms around me from behind, spooning my body into his. His powerful arousal brushed against my backside.

The hot water pounded on the two of us. He tightened his grip around me and nuzzled the nape of my neck, then the sides. I'd never realized how sensitive my neck was. The erotic sensation made me buzz all over.

"Gloria, you are so fucking beautiful," he whispered into my ear. He nibbled the lobe, then rolled his tongue inside the shell of my ear. The strangely erotic swooshing sound was turning me on even more.

Slipping off the simple black elastic at the end, he started to undo my braid. Slowly, section by section. I closed my eyes, and when I reopened them, my thick platinum hair hung loose to the base of my spine. He raked his fingers through the long soaked strands.

"I want to see you with your hair down tonight."

Not wanting to think about how long it would take me to blow dry my mane, I asked, "Where do you want to eat with me tonight?

"I'll eat with you anywhere you breathe."

His words sent a shiver up my spine. A restaurant was not what I was thinking about.

I felt him kiss the top of my head; he buried his nose into my scalp and inhaled.

"Mmmm. I can't get enough of your hair. It's like wet silk." He squirted a dollop of shampoo onto his palm from the canister and then rubbed it gently all over my head. He began to lather the creamy soap into my hair, digging the tips of his deft fingers deep into my scalp. I tilted my head back and closed my eyes, allowing myself to savor the sensual physical sensation and erotic squishy sound. God, it felt good. So good. Like a scalp fuck. As he worked conditioner into my hair, I moaned with pleasure. What these beautiful, nimble fingers could do!

Still standing close behind me, he moved his hands to my full breasts and began to knead them, squeezing and caressing. One of his thumbs passed over the raised scar above my left breast, but once again he seemed oblivious to it.

"So, so, beautiful," he hummed, nuzzling my neck, the sensuous touch of his lips and fingertips shooting a stream of hot tingles to my core.

With a breathy sigh, I undulated my hips, brushing my backside against his erection. His hips moved with mine as he cupped my breasts.

"They're for real," he murmured, plumping them up in the palms of his hands. "So fucking soft and supple."

For a brief moment, I wanted to punch him. Obviously, he'd fondled the surgically enhanced type way too many times. Maybe even Vivien's? I stiffened then relaxed. I had to remember: he was a player, the gorgeous millionaire kind, who'd probably fucked a gazillion beautiful women. And felt up twice as many breasts. The sensuality of the massage and the debilitating effect it was having on me didn't allow me to dwell long on his extracurricular activities.

I always knew I had sensitive breasts, but not this sensitive. Each time his thumbs trailed across my nipples, a jolt of pleasure zapped me. I moaned and moaned again. The peaks swelled, and the more he rubbed them, the more my body pulsed with desire.

Jaime breathed into my ear. "Ah, those perfectly puckered rosebuds of yours are so tender."

Leaving a knowing hand on one tit, he slid the other down my torso until it made its way to the fiery triangle between my thighs. Beelining for my clit, he fingered it with single-minded fury. My own wetness mingled with the shower. My nub hardened beneath his touch as he continued to circle it fast and hard. My breathing grew ragged. He was driving me wild and I wanted, no needed, to come badly.

"Please make me come," I cried out.

He abruptly withdrew his fingers—almost like a punishment for asking. "Not yet, Gloria. I want you do to something for *me* first."

Anything.

He flipped me around and swung my arm up to the liquid soap canister. He squirted a clump onto my palm. "Get down on your knees and wash my cock. I want to see your eyes. So look up at me as you do it."

Without the slightest hesitation, I dropped to my knees and wrapped the soaped-up hand around the crown of his huge erection. It shot straight out of him and was practically in my face. The heat of it singed my fingertips. My soapy hand skated down the rigid shaft to the base and then glided back up to the tip. How velvety smooth it was! And how big! Its extraordinary girth fit tightly into the curl of my fingers.

"Good, Gloria. Now squeeze harder and hold my balls with your other hand."

My left hand cupped his heavy sacs as I slid my right hand back down his thick length, applying more pressure. Then back up. I repeated the movements, picking up my pace. My eyes never left his enraptured face. I watched with awe as he threw his head back and parted his luscious lips. A loud groan escaped between them. His balls felt heavier. Was he going to come?

He gazed back down at me with his hooded blue eyes. "Ahh, you're doing it just right. Now, I want you to rinse me off with your mouth."

So, he wanted me to give him a blowjob—like I owed him one for last night. Okay. I could handle this. Confession: The thought of giving this beautiful man head excited me. I opened my mouth wide, but before I could take him, he yanked me up by my hair.

"Go down on me standing." He placed his hand on top of my head and pushed it down toward his erection. I had to bend my knees for my mouth to make contact with it.

I flicked my tongue across the glistening crown, glad to discover that the soap had washed off, and then wrapped my lips around its impressive perimeter. As he let out a moan, I went down on his slick, hard length until I could go no further. My mouth came back up, and I repeated the movements. Again and again. Up and down. Faster and faster. His magnificent cock became my mouth's obsession.

Without breaking contact, I placed one hand on his muscular thigh and the other around the side handicapped railing to give me the support I needed in this semi-squatting position. My thighs were burning. I felt like I was doing one of those loathed "chair positions" with my yoga instructor.

"Oh, baby, you suck me so good. So hard."

I gazed up at him. The expression on his face was one of pure tortured ecstasy. I was amazed by how much pleasure I got from pleasuring him. Despite my discomfort, I wanted to please him.

I came up for a quick breath of air. Arching his back, he hissed.

"Don't. Stop."

Before I could tell him not to worry, he pressed down on the crown of my head, urging me to descend on him once again. This time, my tongue lapped the shaft as I headed back up toward the tip.

He groaned. "I'm going to come in your mouth."

One spurt. Two. Three. He let out a deep guttural grunt and cursed under his breath as his release spilled into my mouth. The taste of it was sweet and salty and oh so good. I swallowed every drop.

"We're not done. Suck me dry."

My eyes gazed up at his impassioned face as I feverishly went back down on his cock, taking in only the upper one third into my mouth. Removing my hand from his thigh, I squeezed the base as my mouth bopped up and down. The silky, soaked hair along his groin brushed against the back of my hand.

"Oh, Gloria!" he roared as he coated my tongue one more time. His eyelids lifted. "This time, I want to watch you swallow."

I eagerly gulped it down. Smiling with satisfaction, he withdrew his thick, slick dick. Smiling back, I straightened up, glad not to be in that painful crouching position. My legs felt like Jell-O.

The shower washed away the last traces of his cum. To my shock, his cock was still semi-erect.

"Christ, that was fucking amazing. You never stop surprising me. Now, I'm going to finish what I started."

Smacking a kiss on my lips, he stepped out of the shower. In a split second, he was back. The belt of his terry cloth robe was dangling around his neck. *What the . . .*

Stopping me in my thoughts, he scooped me up in his arms and then set me down on the teak wood planks of the built-in handicapped shower bench. "Trust me, Ms. Long, you're going to be handicapped once I'm done with you."

I eyed the belt. A shudder ran through me. "What are you going to do to me?"

"I'm going to make you fall apart and then attempt to

put you back together again."

I snickered. "You think I'm some kind of Humpty Dumpty?"

He smirked. "You're much more fragile. At least on the inside."

My breath hitched. He knew me. "What if someone has to use the shower?"

"They'll knock." He knitted his brows. "Are you on birth control?"

I nodded helplessly. My pills helped me with my cramp-ridden periods.

A smile danced in his eyes. "Good. Now, lie down."

Wait! What about him? Given his promiscuous past, could I trust him?

"Don't worry. I'm clean. I've been tested. Now, lie down."

Hesitantly, I lowered myself to a reclining position. My torso spread across the length of the bench while my limbs hung over the edge.

"Now, Gloria, I want you to open your mind and open your legs. For. Me."

In one swift move, he spread my dangling legs and threw my ankles over his broad shoulders. Looming above me, he gazed at my sex. His glorious cock, now almost fully erect again, pointed my way. The shower began to fog up. There was something otherworldly about seeing his god-like body in a cloud of steam.

"You're such a pretty shade of pink. You may, however, be a shade of red when I'm through with you."

I cringed. Was he going to pussy-whip me with the belt?

"Relax. I'm not going to hurt you." *The mind reader.* "But I am going to tie you up. You'll enjoy it. Now lift your arms high."

Relieved, I did as he requested. With whip-like speed, he

wrapped the long belt around my wrists, binding them together, and then attached them to the handicapped railing directly above me. I writhed my arms to see if I could free myself. Forget it. He had me tied up too tightly.

"I need to get harder, and you need to get horny." He kneeled on the edge of the bench and reached across me to fondle my mountainous breasts. Crawling closer to me, he planted his enormous cock between them and then squeezed the mounds against it. He moaned with pleasure while I, too, got off on the sensuous massage I was getting. Erotic pleasure rushed to my core. Oh God! I was ready! My body was crying out for him while my mind screamed no. *Gloria, let go. Open your mind!*

"Your breasts are such sweet pillows of flesh," he murmured as he continued to rub them against his cock. "Now let's see if I've aroused you."

He shoved a finger into my opening. I moaned but wanted something more.

"Ah. You're so hot and wet. But not quite ready."

He pulled his finger out and began to play with my tender clit. Vigorously circling it like a finger-painting child. I groaned.

"How does that feel?"

My clit was a lit up firework ready to explode. I didn't know how much more I could take. I desperately wiggled my bound arms attempting to free myself; it was futile.

"Answer me, Gloria." His tone was demanding.

"Oh, yes!" I moaned.

"Good enough."

Still fingering my clit, he used his other hand to rub the crown of his thick length up and down the folds of my cleft. He was teasing me when I was aching for him to be inside me.

Then, he leaned into me, placing his hands on the bench

for support. "I'm going to come inside you now and give you an orgasm that's going to blow that uptight mind of yours to pieces."

"Please," I begged.

He grinned wickedly. "I'm going to fuck you until you can't walk. I'll be carrying you back to your room."

Oh, yes! Handicap me!

Balancing on one hand, he used the other to position his pulsing arousal. I felt his hot cock at my doorway to pleasure. A thrust away from penetrating me, there was a loud pounding on the fogged-up shower door.

"What's going on in there?"

I recognized the voice immediately. It was the old man who had gone for a swim.

"Fuck!" muttered Jaime. "I'm not going to rush this." He leaped up from the bench and stormed out of the shower, leaving me tied up and throbbing. I assumed he was going to return right away with our robes. *Hurry!*

The door re-opened. The little old man's skin was prune-like from his long swim, and a towel was wrapped around his waist. He took it off before shuffling inside. His waterlogged eyes widened as they stared at me, naked and bound to the handicapped railing.

He grinned wickedly and then his shriveled cock twitched. "I want whatever he had."

I gasped with horror. He wasn't just an old man. He was a dirty old man! Oh God! Had Jaime abandoned me? Left me helplessly stranded with this horny geezer? My panic button sounded. But just as my mind skipped to the worst possible scenario, the shower door burst open.

CHAPTER 20

Jaime

Damn it! Why did that frickin' altacocker have to show up when I was so close to taking Gloria? One millimeter away from penetrating her. One second away from giving her a fucking she'd never forget. So close I could practically hear her screaming my name and feel her shuddering around my cock as I came inside her.

I had learned in business that timing was everything. It was part of my secret to success. Plus, one always had to be prepared for the unexpected. And here lay the problem. I wasn't prepared for our rude interruption. My pent-up lust mixed with my frustration. Standing at the urinal, I quickly jerked off and then slipped on my robe.

What was I to do? Yeah, I could have told him to use another shower. Or taught the old fart a thing or two, but I didn't want to share Gloria with anyone. At that thought, my gut twisted with concern. What if he'd decided to use the occupied shower? Tied-up Gloria was prey. Was he touching her? Worse, fucking her? Jesus, with her hands bound so tightly to the handicapped railing, she had no way of escaping. And seriously, who could resist Gloria? She was a goddess. All wet and naked, she was a temptation to any man whatever his age.

My heart racing, I adjusted my robe and hurried back to

the shower, praying that Gloria was okay. The fact that I didn't hear any signs of a struggle was somewhat reassuring, but she could still be in harm's way.

Unsure what I'd do if I found this man touching Gloria in any shape or form, I yanked open the fogged up glass door and burst inside the stall. The octogenarian, stripped of his swim trunks, was scrubbing himself, the steamy rivulets of water pouring down his shriveled body like varicose veins. His voice croaked in my ears.

"Sweetheart, when I was your boyfriend's age . . ."

I cut him off.

"Excuse me, sir," I said calmly, relieved that he seemed harmless. "My girlfriend needs to take her meds."

"What?" shrieked Gloria, still flat on her back and tied up.

Knowing that Gloria was safe and there was no chance of the geezer fucking her in the shower, it was time to have a little fun. I actually had to suppress my laughter at the hilarity of the whole situation. I untied Gloria, looping the belt to my robe around my neck. The old man's eyes stayed on us.

"I haven't gotten this close to such a beautiful woman in thirty years. This hotel deserves a five-star review on Trip Advisor. I'd give it a ten if I could."

Gloria seemed mortified. Before she could say a word, I swept her up into my arms. The old man looked at us, baffled.

"Sorry," I said as I kicked-open the door and carried Gloria out. "She swoons in showers."

Once outside the shower, I could no longer contain my laughter. "Jesus, that was priceless. I can't wait to read that review."

My companion, on the other hand, found none of this funny. Her face scrunched, she was simmering mad.

"Your girlfriend? Meds?" She flung the words at me like slaps to my face.

Still holding her, I shrugged. "C'mon, Gloria. You have to admit that was creative."

My response only made her madder. Damn, she was cute when she got mad.

"Where the hell did you go? Why did you leave me for so long?"

"Sorry. I had to take a leak." I left out the jerked-myself-off part as I set her down on her feet. I hastily belted my robe to hide the evidence as she narrowed her eyes at me. The truth: beneath the terry cloth, I was growing hard again.

"Don't be mad at me. It wasn't my fault. I'll make up for it at dinner."

She pouted her kissable lips, her brows knitting together. "There's not going to be any dinner." Angrily, she yanked her robe off the hook and shrugged it on, knotting the belt tightly around her waist. As if she was shutting me out.

"Hey, remember what you said." I tugged at the belt ends. "A deal is a deal."

Admitting defeat, she scoffed at me. "Do you have a place in mind?"

"Rafael's. It's *very* expensive."

She scrunched her face again. "Fine. Meet me down-stairs at the entrance of the hotel at eight."

"Perfect."

She shot me a dirty look and, without another word, stomped out of the spa area. When she was out of sight, I fisted my hand and punched the air. Score another one for me. When it came to competitiveness, I had met my match. She liked to win as much as I did. I could have let her win our little race, but that would have fed her ego and put her in the driver's seat. There was no way I was going to relinquish control.

I was breaking her bit by bit.

Beneath my robe, my cock thickened, then jumped like it was meeting my air punch.

Touché.

CHAPTER 21

Gloria

I spent the rest of the day running around the city doing store checks. We had retail outlets in every borough—except Brooklyn. *Borofskyland.* It irritated Victor that I refused to open a Brooklyn store; it was a missed opportunity, especially since Brooklyn, now a chic place to live, catered to affluent Gen X'ers. The money-hungry opportunist didn't understand I could never go back there. It held a terrible memory for me and it was too risky. Boris was still living there according to Intelius.com, and I was sure that he'd recognize me immediately.

Thank goodness, I had Nigel to get me around because the city traffic was impossible. As he expertly navigated it, transporting me from one store to the next, I couldn't stop thinking about Jaime Zander. He was unraveling me, bringing me to sensual places I'd never been before. And I was letting him. I hardly knew this man. It had to stop, especially if we ended up working together. The last thing I needed in either my personal or professional life was a fucked up relationship. I made an executive decision. Over dinner, I was going to bring this all to an end. Just keep everything to business.

The store visits were a welcome distraction. For the most part, the city retail outlets were all in good order. I enjoyed spending time with the general managers as well as sales personnel. It was also good to observe first-hand the shopping patterns of customers. I even chatted with some and got some valuable consumer insights. All were very excited about the possibility of Gloria's Secret sex toys.

I caught up with Kevin and Vivien at the Fifth Avenue flagship store in the mid afternoon. We were having a special in-store event there—a fashion show. A scaled-down version of our big extravaganza. There was going to be coverage by one of the local cable channels as well as by numerous bloggers. Gift cards and coupons were being offered to shoppers in attendance. Kevin, as always, was handling everything beautifully. Vivien, however, wore a resentful expression. She had actually texted me that she wanted to go shopping while she was in Manhattan. I had to remind her this was a business trip, not a vacation.

The show went off without a hitch and customers loved it. Sales went through the roof another day in a row. Shortly afterward, Kevin strolled up to me. "Glorious, want to go out for dinner tonight?"

I twitched a regretful smile. "Can't. I'm having dinner with Jaime Zander."

"Oh," chimed in nearby Vivien. "Business or pleasure?" The sarcasm in her voice was hard to miss.

"Strictly business." Though my tone was nonchalant, Vivien eyed me suspiciously.

"Do you know Jaime Zander is one of Manhattan's most eligible billionaires?"

I digested this new piece of information. While I'd never seen his name on the Forbes 400 List, I guess if he owned The Walden Hotel and could afford to spend two million dollars on Rihanna's leather undergarments, he must be mega-rich. Though ZAP! was quite a successful ad agency, it didn't seem enough to make Jaime so wealthy. I wondered—how did he make his fortune? Maybe I'd find out at dinner.

I checked my watch; it was almost six. "I'm going to split. I need to get ready for my dinner."

The thought of having dinner with Jaime Zander made my whole body quiver with anticipation and apprehension. I was anxious about seeing him. Would I be able to keep my emotions—and hormones—in check and keep things purely professional? What concerned me as much was that I was looking forward to seeing him.

The twinkle in Kevin's hazel eyes clued me in that he knew there was something going on between Jaime and me. After all these years together through thick and thin, he could read me like a book. Vivien's eyes, however, were shooting daggers my way.

"Where are you going for dinner?" she asked, her tone snarky.

"Rafael's." I immediately regretted telling her.

Back at the hotel, I showered and rewashed my hair. I remembered that Jaime had asked me to wear it long and loose. I debated whether to give in to him, but ultimately decided in his favor. It took me almost an hour to blow dry my waist-length locks. There was a reason why I wore it in an easy braid, but had to admit it looked gorgeous cascading down my back and over my shoulders like a whimsical cape. My mane of hair was my treasured asset. After my wicked, narcissistic mother chopped it off with meat scissors in a drugged-out fit of rage, I vowed never to cut it short again. My long hair, in some way, was my security blanket. And it covered my scar.

After the blow dry, I did my makeup, keeping it light

and simple. I studied my heart-shaped face in the bathroom mirror and was pleased. I looked soft but sexy.

I put on some light jazz and went through my ritual of matching my outfit to my undergarments. The dress I chose was a flowy powder blue chiffon V-neck number that accented my narrow waist and my full breasts without giving too much away. Beneath it, I wore delicate lacy blue lingerie from our popular "Hot Nights" collection—an underwire bra, G-string panty, and matching garter that held up my sheer silk hose. While slithering the stockings up my legs, I once again thought about my beloved mentor, Madame Paulette. Sadness swept over me. I was relieved that I had told her my secret. The one that had haunted me my entire adult life. Yet, I still bore the weight of my misdoing on my heart. And the nightmares had never stopped.

Forcing negative thoughts to the back of my head, I stepped into a pair of strappy, silver stilettos that went well with the demure dress. Grabbing a soft blue pashmina shawl and a clutch, I headed toward the elevator. I was purposely fifteen minutes early. I wanted to be at the entrance to the hotel before Mr. Zander. And have the time to rehearse what I was going to say to him about mixing business with pleasure. Okay. Sex. The very thought of his cock sent a rush of wetness to my panties. *Stop it, Gloria. Get a grip! You can't let this man do this to you!*

As I stood anxiously at the hotel's entrance, Vivien came flying in with a bunch of shopping bags in her hand. All of them were from high-end Madison Avenue designer boutiques. A little shocked to see me, she gave me the once-over.

"Enjoy your business dinner." With an emphasis on the word "business," she shot me smirk.

I quirked back a semi-smile. "I'll see you down here at 8:30 tomorrow morning. We've got a full day of agency meetings."

Without another word, she skirted past me. Vivien was just too damn impetuous for her own good. Lucky for her, Daddy was Gloria's Secret largest shareholder and Chairman of the Board and protected her surgically enhanced ass. If I could, I would fire the entitled little bitch in a New York minute.

A warm, firm pair of hands on my bare shoulders stopped me in my thoughts. And then through parted hair, I felt soft warm lips nuzzle the nape of my neck. Tingles raced down my spine. I jerked and spun around. Jaime!

I swear my eyes were drooling. Tonight, he was Mr. Preppy—clad in a crisp blue and white striped collarless shirt that was unbuttoned enough to flaunt his taut chest. The shirttail hung loose over perfectly fitting jeans. Navy suede loafers covered his sockless feet, and a rich cashmere sweater, almost the same blue as my shawl, wrapped around his broad shoulders. Draped over his arm was a stunning black wool overcoat. Bottom line . . . he looked sexy as hell. And smelled intoxicating.

I sucked in a breath. "Your car or mine."

"Mine." He studied me. "My sex goddess, you look like an angel. Blue is definitely your color, and you should always wear your hair that way."

"Thanks," I mumbled, trying to hold it together while he called his driver. Why did he have to say the word "sex"? Though I had mastered my "all good things must come to an end speech," my hormones were already raging. I bit down on my lip.

His car pulled around outside, and as his driver held open the rear passenger door, he slid in after me. I moved away from him. A bemused smile flitted onto his face. "So, Gloria. Are you playing a game tonight? Hard to get?"

I wrinkled my nose. He chuckled. "That nose thing is

one of the things I love about you."

I cringed. Why did he say the L-word? He wasn't making it easy for me to stay in control.

He told his driver Orson to take us to Rafael's on Prince Street.

"Have you ever eaten there?" he asked.

I'd heard of the restaurant, one of the city's original French bistros, but had never eaten there. I shook my head and muttered a "no."

"Then, you're in for a treat. The food is delicious. And the atmosphere's great. There's even a fortuneteller who holds court in the loft. Maybe you can ask her about our future."

I cringed. I knew the answer to that already. There was none.

The restaurant was located downtown not far from Jaime's office. The jam-packed front room resembled a classic bohemian bistro, with leather banquet tables and funky paintings, including nudes, hung all over the walls. The attractive brunette hostess welcomed Jaime with a warm embrace; he was obviously a regular. Flirtatiously glancing back at him from time to time, she led us through the crowded, noisy restaurant and then through the busy kitchen to a back room. I couldn't help but wonder if he had fucked her and all the other beautiful women who stopped him along the way.

Unlike the frenetic front room, the back room was low-key and romantic, filled with candlelit tables draped with fine white linens. A vaulted glass ceiling added to the atmosphere. We were escorted to a table for two, closest to the blazing fireplace. I could feel the warmth of the fire against my back.

A heavy-set, jovial waiter came to our table. "Good evening, Mr. Zander. What will it be tonight?" As Jaime pondered the menu, the waiter looked me over and smiled. I wondered—was this where Jaime brought all his fucks? And how many had sat in this chair before me? I mentally kicked myself. Why should I care? This wasn't even a date; it was a business dinner. And I was about to set the womanizer straight.

Jaime gazed up at me. The flickering candlelight and blaze in the hearth bathed his face in a soft glow, making him even more breathtakingly gorgeous than he already was. Despite myself, tingling desire was spiraling inside me. *Stay in control, Gloria*, I silently chided before he broke into my damning thoughts.

"Gloria, I hope you don't mind if I order for the two of us. The steak tartare is divine and so is the grilled artichoke. And we'll share a bottle of Bordeaux."

"We'll have the Latour 2009 Controllé right away," he told the waiter. Trusting his choices, I let him place the rest of the order. The attentive waiter smiled and sauntered off.

The wine arrived quickly. I'm sure it was mega expensive. The waiter poured a little into Jaime's glass. Jaime sampled it and then nodded with approval. The waiter continued to pour wine for both of us. After he parted, Jaime clinked his goblet against mine.

"To winning," he said with a seductive smile.

I quirked a smile back at him, wondering if he was referring to our swimming competition, the Gloria's Secret account, or me. Or all of the above.

My eyes still on him, I took a swallow of the wine. It was delicious. Rich and velvety. It reminded me of the French wine Madame Paulette would treat me to on Friday evenings.

After a few sips, Jaime eased into conversation. His tone was inquisitive as his long-lashed eyes held me captive.

"So, Gloria, tell me something about yourself that I haven't already read on the Internet."

"What exactly do you know about me?" I countered.

"Not much . . . Self-made business woman extraordinaire. Built Gloria's Secret into a billion-dollar company from the ground up."

This was true. After Kevin and I touched down in LA, we stayed at a rundown Hollywood motel until we found a tiny but charming two-bedroom apartment to share in Beachwood Canyon. We were able to secure it with a first and last month rent deposit from the money we had stolen from Boris. Kevin quickly found work as the manager of a hot Hollywood night club, frequented by celebrities, and I, once recovered from my gunshot wound, used the money to rent some studio space downtown and to purchase bolts of lace and silk as well as a dozen used sewing machines and necessary supplies. Once settled in, I hired a handful of talented, eager-to-work laborers to stitch up my lingerie designs. I shortly found a small, affordable storefront on Hollywood Boulevard to sell my wares. Gorgeous French-inspired lingerie at a reasonable price.

With the help of Kevin, who sent the "beautiful people" who frequented his club to my no-name boutique, my business boomed. Women and men alike fell in love with the innovative, sexy, and reasonably priced undergarments; it became the word-of-mouth, in-the-know place to shop for lingerie . . . leading me to call my boutique, Gloria's Secret. With my success, I was able to secure a small business loan and six months later, I opened the flagship store, Gloria's Secret, in the Beverly Center, a popular LA mall. The store was an overnight success; a catalogue followed along with a robust website. Kevin quit his job to become my partner and head of Public Relations and Marketing. One year later, enter billionaire businessman Victor Holden, who smelled a winner, invested millions, and took the company public. The rest is history. One store grew to thousands worldwide and a billionaire dollar a year business.

I took another sip of my wine. Meeting Jaime's gaze, I didn't go into details. Very little of this backstory was online—Kev had carefully guarded it—and I surely wasn't going to reveal it now. "What you see is what you get."

"So far, I like what I've seen." He paused. "And I like what I've gotten."

The double entendres weren't lost on me. I shifted in my seat and crossed my legs under the table to quell the tingly sensation between them. His eyes traveled down my body.

"By the way, what's that scar on your chest?"

My breath caught in my throat. I almost spit up the wine. While my dress covered most of it up, he must have noticed it in the shower or the other night when he undressed me. The scar I despised. The reminder of everything I wanted to forget.

"None of your business," I snapped at him.

"Ah, so Gloria has a secret."

Impulsively, I fixed my shawl so it was hiding the scar. This man was unnerving me. There was no way I was going to open up to him about my past. That one regrettable moment in time. I didn't want to go there. It was bad enough to live it every waking hour and in my dreams. I quickly changed the subject, focusing on him.

CHAPTER 22

Jaime

"So, Mr. Zander, tell me, how did you get into advertising?"

Gloria was definitely hiding something. It had something to do with that scar. The fact that she adjusted her shawl over her dress to cover it and abruptly changed the subject attested to it.

She took a sip of her wine waiting for me to respond. "Well?"

Just like her, I needed to be guarded about my past. There were things she didn't need to know. *Couldn't* know at least not yet. I had to be careful about saying anything that might get in the way of winning her account. Things that might cause her to leave me alone with the check. And walk away. Taking a long sip of the velvety wine, I contemplated what to share with her.

"I had a talent. An artistic one. Rather than going to college, I came East and set up meetings with one ad agency after another to show them my portfolio."

Her two-toned eyes locked on me, my dinner mate looked intrigued as I continued.

"I got hired by one of the big Madison Avenue agencies—which I'm sure you've met with—to be an art director. The business of advertising suited me. I discovered I had a way with words as well as graphics. The art of manipulation."

"I'd say you're a master of the art of manipulation."

I smiled, taking her comment as a compliment.

"I was touted as a wunderkind, but the corporate world wasn't for me. Too many rules; too much bullshit. I stuck it out for five years, then finally called it quits. A few key clients left with me. Long story short . . . they rounded up some investor money, and I started ZAP! Zander *And* *P*eople."

"So, how did you become a billionaire?"

My brow shot up. I wasn't expecting that question. "Ah, so you've done your research too, Ms. Long. I'm impressed."

She flashed a half-smile, holding back how she'd found out. My fortune was not a well-publicized fact and I preferred to keep it that way. I proceeded slowly, my voice growing guarded.

"I inherited several million dollars from my mother, and during the recession a few years ago, I made some lucky investments."

"So you were born with a silver spoon in your mouth."

"Hardly." My body tensed, my facial muscles tightened. "My mother married someone very wealthy when I was thirteen."

"It must have been fun being a rich kid."

"Money comes with benefits. It also comes with baggage."

"Oh, is that your tagline for your poor little rich boy poster?"

Her words felt like knives to my chest. I suppose I deserved that jab given her apparent rags to riches past. But the one thing I wasn't was entitled. In fact, I despised entitlement. It stunk of Victor and Vivien. Just the thought of them brought a rush of bile to my chest. Before I could swallow it down and defend myself, our waiter returned with our dinner. Just in time. I'd had enough of talking about the past. I didn't want to go back to that dark, toxic place.

I lifted my wine glass, proposing a toast.

"Bon appétit, Ms. Long."

CHAPTER 23

Gloria

Jaime's face tensed, making me immediately regret what I'd just said. His somber expression suggested that his childhood memories, like mine, might not be happy ones. Perhaps, he was harboring some dark secret too. I flashed back to the faint white marks on his back I'd noticed in the shower. Scars? Before I could say a word, the steak tartare and artichoke arrived. Jaime's face brightened. The attentive waiter refilled our wine goblets and then scurried off.

I imbibed more wine. The smooth, red liquid poured down my throat and coursed through my bloodstream. I was loosening up. *Slow down, Gloria. You don't want to get drunk.*

Jaime cut into the voice of my inner conscious. "Spread your lips," I heard him say.

I found myself spreading my legs.

My companion let out a sexy little laugh. "I was referring to your mouth. I want to give you your first taste of the steak tartare."

Gah! How did he know what was happening under the table? I felt flushed with embarrassment. He was affecting me again. The area between my inner thighs was getting hot and wet. This was not supposed to be happening. I was losing control!

"Excuse me, I have to use the restroom," I said, leaping to my feet. I needed to get away from him. Compose myself. Focus on business.

"It's in the front of the restaurant, up the stairs," he said, eyeing my body. "I'll be here waiting for you."

I felt his eyes on me the entire time as I made my way to the packed front room and up a rickety spiral staircase. There was a long waiting line for the ladies' room.

A portly, dark-haired woman who resembled a gypsy was stationed at a table outside it. "Let me tell you your fortune, my dear," she called out to me.

Usually, I never did these kinds of things, thinking they were shams, but tonight my unease tempted me, and I really didn't want to wait in line.

I lowered myself into the worn velvet chair facing her.

"You are very beautiful."

"Thank you," I said as she studied my face with her dark eyes.

"Your eyes, one brown, one blue, tell me a lot about you. You are two very different people who share the same face. A woman of contradictions. One side of you is light and seductive, the other dark and secretive."

I inwardly gasped. How did she know?

"Let me see your palm." She grasped my right hand and flipped it so that my palm was in full view.

Her eyes grew wide.

"What is it?" My voice was shaky.

"You are losing control of your life. There is a man."

I heard myself gasp. Jaime Zander was written all over my hand.

She shook her head and bit down on her lip. Her fore-boding gaze slowly met mine. "I usually tell people good things they want to hear, but I must tell you the truth."

My heart hammered. I could hear it thudding in my

chest.

"You are in grave danger. Someone is out to get you."

I shuddered. Boris Borofosky! I'd heard enough. I jumped up from the chair and hurried to the restroom. Thankfully, it was now free.

With my dress raised to my thighs and my panties and garter lowered to my knees, I sat on the toilet longer than I needed. I was shaking. Was Boris on my trail? Was he seeking revenge? Was my life in danger? Wait! That wasn't possible. I knew from Madame Paulette that he didn't even know my name. So, he couldn't possibly know where I lived or what I did. Or where I was this very minute. I took a deep calming breath. Besides, that woman was probably a charlatan though she did seem to know the effect Jaime Zander was having on me. Yes, he was making me lose control, but by hell or high water, I was going to put an end to that tonight. Yet, at the very thought of him, the pulsing between my thighs intensified, and I could feel myself heating. I dragged my hand over my cleft. The folds were even hotter and wetter than I imagined. My fingertips could actually feel the throbbing. For a minute, I thought about masturbating, to put myself out of my glorious misery. Instead, I peed and washed up. My hormones were back to raging. Damn that man!

Jaime's eyes contemplated me as I headed back to the table.

"Are you okay?" he asked as he rose to his feet and pulled out my chair.

"Yes." In truth, I was all hot and bothered.

"Good." Returning to his seat, he refilled our wine glasses. There was a wicked glint in his eyes.

"So let's pick up where we left off." He scooped up a forkful of the steak tartare. "Now, part your lips, Gloria."

Again, the sexy command. This time I did as he asked.

My lips spread apart.

"I love fine raw meat," he purred as he shoveled a taste of the rare delicacy into my mouth. The velvety, moist meat laced with a hint of Worcestershire sauce was beyond delicious. It totally obliterated any trace of Boris in my head. I immediately wanted more. The gorgeous mind reader fed me another heaping forkful. I swallowed. Tingles rose from my core.

He helped himself to a taste. He savored it before swallowing. "Did you know that steak tartare is an aphrodisiac?"

"I read that somewhere." Being in the sexy lingerie business, I was actually quite knowledgeable about what turned women on. And right now, I was totally turned on. I wanted this gorgeous man to ravage me.

I jolted. Under the table, I felt something slide under my dress and snake up my thigh-high silk stocking past my garters to my middle. Gulp! It was his bare foot, and it was running circles over my mound.

"Ah, Gloria, your pussy feels so hot and wet beneath those lace panties of yours." He paused. "They are powder blue, right?" he asked with a fiendish grin.

"Yes," I gasped. His foot was now rubbing hard against my clit. I was getting more feverish by the second as he pushed me toward the edge. My fingers clutched the corners of the white-linen covered table.

"I think you should stop," I gritted.

"There's a difference between I think and I want. Do you *want* me to stop?"

"Yes," I said breathily.

"Your mouth says 'yes,' but your pussy screams 'no.'"

Oh, God! This man had me. He continued working my soaking wet cleft. The pleasure and pressure were so intense I thought I would yelp. I dug my fingernails into the table and chewed my lip, trying hard not to scream. Jesus, how would I look if I broke loose?

Jaime shot me a cocky, confident smile. I wanted to rip it off his face with my teeth.

"Gloria, you want to lose control. Do it!" he commanded as he jabbed his big toe into my sex.

I exploded. Ripples of ecstasy swept through me. It took all my willpower not to scream out. "Oh, God!" I moaned under my breath.

His satisfied eyes seared into me. "Now, it's time to move on to the steamy artichoke, another natural aphrodisiac."

Barely recovered from my mind-blowing orgasm, I eyed the thistle-leafed delicacy sitting in the middle of the table and jolted again. Beneath the table, a hand clutched my calf. Another gulp. My turn to play footsy? My already rapid heartbeat accelerated as he maneuvered off my silver sandal and placed my foot on the mound between his legs. His steamy delicacy. The warmth of his erection beneath my sole intensified the throbbing between my inner thighs.

He began rubbing my foot up and down his length. I could feel it grow harder, thickening beneath my arch. He hissed. There was nothing I could do with him holding my foot prisoner but wait anxiously for him to come.

And then the movements below ceased. My foot rested on his erection. The sole of my foot was burning.

His glimmering eyes burned a hole in mine. "I'm not going to force you to make me come. That would be too much for me here. Too embarrassing. I just wanted to remind you what you do to me, my beautiful angel."

My breath hitched. He called me "angel." His beautiful angel. My heart was melting like the candle on the table. How could one man, one word, do this to me?

Still holding my foot on his length, he peeled off an outer leaf of the large artichoke with his spare hand and dipped the tender edge into the side of melted butter. He raised the leaf, dripping with butter, to my lips. My breath hitched.

"Suck!" he ordered.

I clamped my teeth around the soft buttery artichoke meat and sucked it off the leaf. He discarded the remains onto his plate. With his index finger, he gently wiped off the little bit of butter that had fallen onto my lower lip. He inserted his butter-coated finger into his mouth and moaned.

"Now, you feed me a buttery leaf."

So erotically charged, I peeled off a large outer leaf and repeated his actions.

"Mmm. Perfection," purred Jaime, rolling his tongue over his lush upper lip.

We continued this back and forth consumption of the artichoke until we were down to the heart.

"The heart is the very best part," he proclaimed, his eyes now lustful.

I simply nodded, my foot still resting upon his hard, hot cock. I was in a trance. My head was spinning, and my blood was looping through my body like a rollercoaster. *Hold on, Gloria.*

"A friend of mine once told me that a woman's heart is her real G-spot. You hit that and everything comes apart."

Trembling with arousal, I watched as he stabbed his fork into the fuzzy artichoke center.

"Gloria, I want to win your account. Your cunt. And your heart."

My breath caught in my throat. I couldn't say a word even if I knew what to say.

"And I'm going to win each. One by one, starting with your account."

I impulsively withdrew my foot from his erection. *Business.* It was time to talk business. That's what this dinner was all about. I reinforced myself with a deep breath.

"Mr. Zander, if you are planning on doing business with me—that is, if you indeed have the good fortune of winning the Gloria's Secret account—then I suggest we keep our relationship purely professional."

He burst into laughter, totally unnerving me once again.

"Come on, Gloria. Can you can seriously sit here and say you don't want me?"

I was speechless. Flushed and flustered.

"Doesn't the thought of your pussy submitting to me anywhere make you wet with want?"

Steeling myself, I said, "Go to hell, you arrogant, egotistical asshole."

He laughed even harder and then looked straight into my eyes.

"Gloria, I've wanted you from the moment I set eyes on you."

Our first elevator encounter flashed into my head. Face-to-face. Breath to breath. His organ a fist away from mine.

"Even before the elevator. The moment I saw your photo online, I wanted you."

Wait! Was I hearing that right? He was playing me on the elevator? He'd always wanted me? I was in a bit of a fog from all the wine. And stimulation. Was I dealing with some kind of Christian Grey except fifty shades sexier? At least, in my eyes.

"I don't think I'm your type," I stammered.

He chortled. "You're right. I usually prefer brunettes and like my women to be petite and totally submissive. But that's why you intrigue me, Ms. Long. I never have to pursue woman; they pursue me. You're a challenge. On the outside, you wear armor; underneath you wear lace. Your outerwear says don't touch; your underwear says touch me everywhere. You may be a powerful woman, but the challenge is to unleash the power inside you."

His words whipped around my head. He barely knew me, yet he knew me inside and out. As I sat there wordless and numb, he leaned across the table and ran his fingertips through my long, flowing tresses.

"And by the way, thank you for wearing your hair loose."

I forced a small smile.

"You wouldn't have worn it that way if you didn't want to please me."

Every fiber of my being buzzed. He was right!

A crazy-wicked grin spread across his face. "Come here, you." Rising from his chair, he leaned across the table, fisted a handful of my loose platinum locks, and pulled me toward him. His lips were coming my way. As they brushed against mine, I closed my eyes.

"Well, hello, Gloria."

An all-too-familiar aloof voice startled me. My eyes snapped open, and I jerked away from Jaime. My eyes widened with surprise. It was Victor, dressed in a gray pinstriped three-piece suit, with his daughter, Vivien, draped on his arm. Sandwiched in a tight violet mini dress, that revealed everything, and matching stilettos, she could have easily been mistaken as his high-priced hooker.

Jaime's face darkened. Silent daggers went back and forth between the two men. Was Victor still simmering because Jaime had outbid him on the Rihanna undergarments?

Vivien's pillowy lips parted. "Hi, Jaime." Her voice was a deep sexy rasp. "Fancy meeting you here."

Fancy meeting you here? Give me a fucking break. She knew exactly where we were having dinner. I studied her. She was petite and brunette. Jaime's "type." Reflecting on her behavior at the Gloria's Secret Fashion Show and after-party, I wondered—had she and Jaime fucked? Was she one of Jaime's submissives? There was something more than met the eye going on here. I sucked in a breath.

Jaime responded. His voice was as cold as dry ice. "Nice to see you."

Victor's turn. "So, Zander, I understand from my daughter, you're still courting the Gloria's Secret account." A smug smile slithered across Vivien's face.

Before Jaime could respond, I hastily chimed in. "Actually, Victor, it's the other way around. I'm courting him. I'm impressed by his creativity."

Victor was stunned into silence.

Jaime shot me a surprised look and then broke into a sexy, grateful smile.

"Why, thank you, Ms. Long. I hope tomorrow we can seal the deal." He came around the table and pulled back my chair, signaling me to stand up. As I got to my feet, Victor's steely eyes ran down my body. I could feel him mentally undressing me. "Gloria, you exhibit poor judgment when it comes to men."

I scowled. "That's not for you to judge."

Jaime's eyes narrowed and his lips pressed thin. He clenched his hands so tightly his knuckles turned white. One fist rose. My heart raced. Was he going to punch Victor?

To my relief, he relaxed his hand. "Come, Gloria. We should talk business," he gritted.

Vivien sneered while her father remained steely faced. As Jaime ushered me to the entrance of the restaurant, I could feel Victor's leering eyes on me the whole time.

"Wasn't I supposed to pay for dinner?" I asked while Jaime called his driver Orson on his cell.

"No need. As of yesterday, I own the restaurant."

The drive back to the hotel was fraught with uncomfortable, tense silence. Brooding, Jaime kept his distance. Maybe, he heeded my words. That it was best to keep our relationship purely professional. Still buzzed from the wine, mixed emotions and questions swirled around in my head. So much had gone down tonight. I was dealing with a potential Christian Grey in my life who definitely had some fucked up issues of his own. And I had my own share of fuckedupness that I was not sharing with him. Finally, as we neared the hotel, I broke the thick silence, deciding to get some answers to questions that could affect our potential business relationship.

"What the hell is going on between you and Victor? You know, he's the Chairman of Gloria's Secret and wields a lot of power."

"He's nothing to me," Jaime hissed.

I didn't believe him, but the tone of his voice set up a don't-go-there wall.

"What about Vivien?"

"What about her?" he snapped back.

"Have you ever fucked her? She seems your type."

He took a long second to answer. "No."

Again, I didn't believe him, but let it be. "You know, if you do win the Gloria's Secret account, she may be your point person. She's my assistant, and she's being groomed, under her father's orders, to take over marketing."

"I'll deal with it," he said curtly.

The elevator ride up to our floor was no less tense. He accompanied me down the long corridor to our rooms. When I reached mine, I broke away from him and ransacked my bag for my key card. Shit. I couldn't find it. I must have left it in my other purse.

"Looking for this?" Jaime was in my face, holding up a key card. His mood had lightened.

"That's my key card?" *He had easy entry to my suite?*

He grinned sheepishly. "I had it made the night you were passed out drunk."

He flipped me around and pressed me against the door, pinning me against it with his hips. I could feel the heat of his arousal against my belly through my thin chiffon dress. My breath hitched in my throat as he grabbed my arms and raised them over my head. Like shackles, his fingers locked around my wrists, holding my fisted hands tight against the slab of wood. Once again, I was his prisoner. His to control. Moving in close to me, his intense eyes seared into mine.

"Let's finish what we started, Gloria, before that prick interfered."

My eyes stayed wide open as he crushed his warm lips onto mine. Every part of my body lit up, the sparks flying from my head to my toes. As the kissed deepened with the entry of his tongue, I was aching with desire. Wanting so much more than his tongue inside me. Desperate moans escaped my lips.

His mouth never leaving mine, he slid the key card into my door and kept me pinned against it as he pushed it open. Finally, he withdrew from my mouth. My breathing was shallow, his loud and heated.

"Gloria . . ."

Oh, the breathy way he said my name!

" . . . I meant what I said. I want to own all of you. Every breath, every heartbeat, every surface of your body, and every cell that's inside you."

His words sucked the air out of my lungs. I couldn't breathe. Couldn't speak. Couldn't swallow. He was having that effect on me all over again.

"Do you want to come in?" I finally managed, aware of

the possible double entendre of my words as an afterthought. Confession: I wanted him to say yes in the worst possible way.

Still pinning my arms above my head to the door with one strong hand, he raked the fingers of the other through my tumbled hair. He smirked. "No. I want you to lust for me during my pitch tomorrow."

His eyes burned a hole into mine, setting me afire with desire. He curled a clump of my hair around his long fingers.

"Oh, angel, you have no idea how much my cock wants to be buried inside that soaking wet pussy of yours, but from here on in, we're going to take it one step at time. First your account . . . then your cunt."

He smacked a kiss onto my lips. "Good night, Ms. Long. I want to prepare for my first pitch. The second one will be a piece of cake."

With that and a diabolical wink, he left me plastered on the door, my knees so weak I thought I would sag down it. The manipulator had a new tactic. He was now controlling me with torture.

I masturbated my way to sleep, wishing I had one of those new Gloria's Secret sex toys to expedite my climax. As I came, Jaime Zander's beautiful face filled my head. Drifting off, I looked forward to his pitch and wondered if he would ever win my heart—something no man had ever done except my beloved Kevin. One thing was for sure . . . he was already under my skin.

CHAPTER 24

Jaime

B ack in my suite, I changed into sweats and a T-shirt. While Gloria and I had been out to dinner, my team had been working around the clock to finesse the Gloria's Secret presentation. At my desk, I reviewed the mock-up that Ray sent me via a shared dropbox. It looked fucking hot. Even more sizzling than I anticipated. My team had pulled it off. I gave a few minor notes and told my people to go home. There was no need to pull an all-nighter. Whatever little fixes needed to be made could wait until tomorrow morning. Our meeting with Gloria was in the late afternoon so we had time.

Shutting down my computer, I sat back in my desk chair. While I had high hopes about our pitch, winning Gloria's account came with a Pandora's box. And it had already been opened. My mind flashed back to our dinner. Fucking Victor. His loathing for me burned like a curse. He was out to destroy me. And there was no doubt in my mind that he was out to get Gloria. Where he wanted her—under him, and not just on just on the annual company earnings report. I'd been a breath away from knocking the bastard's teeth out when he made that snide comment about Gloria's choice in men. Vivien couldn't be trusted either. In ways, she was more dangerous than Victor. A loose cannon who had no boundaries. At some point, I was going to have to tell Gloria about them. Reveal my past. I took a sip of my brandy when a knock at my door sounded.

"Room service," a voice called out.

My brows furrowed. That was odd. I'd canceled my usual nightly chocolate dipped strawberries—because the only sweet taste I wanted on my tongue was Gloria's. Perhaps, it was an oversight on the kitchen's part.

Setting my tumbler down, I ambled to the door and swung it open.

My jaw dropped to the floor. My blood bubbled.

"What are you doing here?"

Standing before me in an oversized fur coat and spiky heels was none other than Vivien Holden. A seductive smile slithered across her face as a wicked glint flickered in her feline green eyes. She flashed open her coat and then let it slide off her.

"Jesus, Vivien."

She was scantily dressed. In a provocative one-piece black leather corset that pushed up her fake tits and cinched her wasp-like waist. Garters hung from it and held up black fishnet stockings.

Batting her eyes, she plumped up her melon-size breasts to show them off. "I wanted to surprise you, doll boy." She rolled her tongue over her plump upper lip. "Aren't you going to invite me in?"

My blood was now sizzling. My rage rising in me like mercury. How the hell did she find out where my suite was? No one on my staff was allowed to divulge the location. Knowing Vivien, she'd probably bribed someone. She'd learn all her manipulative tactics from her father. The lies, the bribes, the threats.

Her sinewy arms wrapped around my neck, clinging to me like tentacles. Her snake-like tongue flicked my neck.

Her cloying scent sickened me. And her breath reeked of alcohol.

"Mmm, Jaime, you taste yummy. Can't I come in and play with you?" She scraped her tongue under her teeth, poking it at me. "Just like the old days. I even have some fun toys in my coat pocket."

I glanced down at her coat and then lifted my eyes to meet her lecherous ones as she toyed with the drawstring of my sweats.

Sucking in a deep breath, I stiffened and then in a single moment of rage, I shoved her off me. Teetering on her heels, she gasped.

"How dare you treat me this way? Maybe I should file a harassment suit with your HR person."

Harassment my ass. She was an ugly, sick, delusional chick. "Get the fuck out of here, Vivien, before I call security. And before I do something I regret."

She narrowed her eyes at me, then bent down to pick up her fur coat. Draping it over her arm, she glowered at me. Poisonous darts were shooting from her eyes.

"You don't know what you're missing out on. That cold bitch has nothing on me. I bet she's as frigid as a glacier. Tell me, isn't that the truth?"

"Shut. Up." *You skank.*

She smirked. "You're making a big mistake. Just wait and see."

And with that, before I could slam the door in her face, she stalked off.

I closed the behind me, making sure to slide the security bolt, and thudded back to my bar where I drained my brandy in a single chug.

Fucking, fucking Vivien. She was the worst kind of a parasite—a bloodsucker who could suck the life out of every fiber of my being. As the warm liquor poured through my veins, clarity filled my head. My mind flashed back to this evening's events. Specifically, to the look on Gloria's face when she returned from the ladies' room. She looked frazzled. Upset. Shit. Had Vivien gotten to her? Told her about our past? Fabricated lies about me that weren't true? Is that why she'd asked me if there was something between Vivien and me in the car?

I was about to pour myself another shot when rationality seeped into me. Even if Vivien had smeared lies about us, Gloria wasn't buying into them. The way she held her cool and snapped back at Victor was proof. So was the way she submitted to me at the door to her suite and invited me in.

Suddenly, white-hot desire for her filled every cell of my body. My cock flexed beneath my sweats. My balls tightened with need. The thought of ordering those chocolate covered strawberries resurfaced. In my mind's eyes, I imagined circling them around her nipples, sucking on their sweetness, and then trailing them down her beautiful body to her pussy where I'd drench them with her juices. Give her a bite and then plunk one of them into my mouth before I fucked her madly.

Bottom line. I wanted her so bad I could taste her. In a moment of weakness, I reached for my room phone and asked the hotel operator to connect me to her room.

"Hold on please, Mr. Zander," said the operator.

A few seconds later, her voice—Gloria's—sounded in my ear. It was so soft, so breathy, so angelic. The word hello was like a prayer. I'd awakened her.

I quickly hung up the phone. I didn't need more.

I needed to stick to the plan.

First her account.

Then her cunt.

And then . . . .

And then what?

CHAPTER 25
Gloria

My wake-up call sounded at the crack of dawn. Two minutes later, there was a knock at the door—my wake-up coffee, something I couldn't live without. Groggily, I threw off the delicious duvet and staggered to the door. After the waiter set the coffee and cream down on a small table, I signed the check and handed him a generous cash tip.

Sipping the steamy rich brew, I checked my schedule on my cell phone calendar. It was a crazy busy day. All day long, I had meetings with one advertising agency after another to hear their pitches. The ZAP! pitch was the last one at five p.m. At the end of the day, my team and I would decide on which agency was going to get the Gloria's Secret account. And then I would be on the corporate jet heading back to Los Angeles.

As the caffeine set my brain in action, I couldn't stop thinking of Jaime Zander. I was as excited as I was anxious about seeing him again. Part of me wished that the ZAP! meeting was the first one—just to get it over with. I had no idea how I was going to get through the other meetings without being distracted by the anticipation of seeing him. I wasn't use to a powerful man rendering me powerless.

I showered and got ready. There was only one solution to the Jaime problem. I needed to look and feel extra powerful today. In control. Fierce. I added a thick layer of mascara to my long eyelashes and a hint of blue eye shadow to bring out the intimidating color of my one blue vs. brown eye. I whipped my long hair into a tight French braid. Lastly, instead of the Gloria's Secret lip-gloss I usually wore, I applied a brilliant shade of red lipstick to my full lips. "Red lips can rule *zee* world," preached my mentor, Madame Paulette.

The outfit I chose was all about power and control—a winter white fitted Chanel suit—perfect for an Ice Queen— and a pair of killer Louboutin black patent stilettos that made me over six feet tall. Beneath my suit, I boosted my confidence with an ivory lace push-up bra from our Sexy Angels collection that matched my bikinis and garter. The sheer black silk stockings I selected made a dramatic contrast with the suit and went well with my jet bead necklace and earrings. Grabbing my purse and briefcase, I headed out the door. I was powered up, ready to take on the various pitches. And Jaime Zander.

The elevator once again took its time coming. So much for the saying, "clothes make the person." My short-lived self-confidence morphed into anxiety. I feared the elevator might be broken, never get here . . . and that at any moment, Jaime might show up. My eyes darted back and forth between the elevator and his suite down the hallway. I sighed with relief when the elevator arrived first. I hurried into it and blew out another huff of air when the doors closed sans Mr. Zander.

Kevin, dressed in skinny black leather jeans and a tight knit pullover, was waiting for me in the lobby. He gave me a hug. "Morning Glory, you look sensational!"

"Thanks. Where's Vivien?"

Kevin rolled his eyes. "Late as usual."

I bristled. She had no respect for anyone's time except

her own. Ten minutes later, she showed up acting like the queen had arrived. Carrying an unnecessary fur coat over her arm, she was dressed in a tight, low-cut purple mini dress and thigh-high suede boots with mile-high heels. Her outfit was totally inappropriate for our round of meetings. It screamed: Fuck me! Because she was so late, I couldn't ask her to change into something more businesslike. The truth, knowing the vixen's taste in clothes, she likely had nothing more conservative to change into.

She shot me an obsequious smile. "So, how was your dinner with Jaime Zander?"

None of your damn business. "Very productive." I kept my voice very businesslike. "I'm looking forward to his pitch."

"So am I," chirped Vivien with a smirk. "I'm sure he'll enjoy seeing me again."

Inside, I sizzled. There was definitely something going on between the two of them.

Each meeting was more disappointing than the one before. While the agency heads and their teams pitched us with enthusiasm, everything was SOS. Same Old Shit. A gorgeous big-boobed beauty posing in scanty lingerie. It didn't matter if she was sprawled on a bed or straddling a chair. I was looking for something more. Something beyond the obvious that Gloria's Secret equaled sexiness. I was looking for a story. A story of seduction.

My stomach bunched up with nerves as Nigel drove us downtown to our last meeting with ZAP! While I'd managed to keep Jaime Zander on the back burner for most of the day, I now faced the reality of seeing him again. I reapplied a coat of red lipstick. I needed to stay in control, not let him get to me.

We got there a little before five. Jaime's attractive assistant Ray promptly greeted us in the reception area and offered us waters. I immediately caught sight of the sparks flying back and forth between him and Kevin. Ha! I knew Ray was his type. I shot a knowing glance over to Kev. He mouthed the word "hot." Vivien rolled her eyes. A beaming Ray led us back to the conference room. Already seated at the large conference room table was a geeky twenty-something girl next to whom Ray sat down. I took in my surroundings. Like the rest of the office, the windowless conference room was warm and creative. There was a large flat screen TV on one of the walls and posters of successful ZAP! ad campaigns on the others. Facing me was a large canvas-covered easel. I wondered—was this the pitch?

"Jaime will be here shortly," announced Ray. My heartbeat sped up at the mention of his name.

On cue, Jaime came flying into the room. I inwardly gasped. He was dressed in a tapered, perfectly tailored black suit, crisp white dress shirt, and a sharp blue tie that accentuated his broad shoulders and brought out the blue in his eyes. I'd never seen him in a suit before and was dazzled. As I caught my breath, he took a seat at the head of the table next to me.

His eyes instantly connected with mine, and I could already feel the electricity in the air. I nervously played with my strands of beads.

"Hi, Jaime," purred Vivien. "Great suit."

"Thank you," he replied stiffly.

My blood curdled. What was with them? I was growing more and more convinced they had some kind of thing going on.

Jaime turned his attention to me and I introduced him to Kevin. He, in turn, introduced Ray, his assistant and protégé, and the funky young woman, Chloe, who was his chief copywriter.

"So, Ms. Long, should we get straight into the pitch?"

"That would be good." My tone was very businesslike despite the fact I was buzzing all over. Inwardly, I seethed. The smartass knew his suit would affect me. Knowing that a well-tailored suit is to a woman what beautiful lingerie is to a man.

He flashed a saucy smile that was intended only for me. "Excellent." He rose to his feet and strode over to the easel. My eyes followed him.

"Ladies and gentlemen . . ." He swept off the canvas. "Gloria's Secret. Let yourself be carried away."

I gasped out loud. Facing me on a board, in fifty shades of gray, was the black-and-white image of a gorgeous blindfolded woman with long platinum hair, who was being carried down a sweeping staircase by a breathtaking, bare-chested Adonis. Lying limp in his brawny arms, she wore leather and lace—a skimpy bra, bikini bottom, and garter that held up sheer black stockings on her long dangling legs. Her ankles were bound together by satin shackles as were her wrists. I totally got it. She was submitting to her sex god. Letting him take her. To his bed. Or perhaps to his dungeon! Every atom of my body was buzzing with excitement. This was exactly the story I was looking for. This was the new Gloria's Secret advertising campaign—all in one line. *"Gloria's Secret. Let yourself be carried away."* I could immediately imagine in my head the print ad and television commercial. And the zillion hits on YouTube and our website. I loved the idea of shooting the campaign in black-and-white sepia tones. Fifty shades of gray! So fresh! So forward! So sexy! It gave me the chills.

Breathless, I asked Vivien what she thought.

She scowled. "I like it, but I think the woman should be

a brunette. Our research shows that men prefer women with dark hair."

True, but our research also showed that most women fantasized being a blonde. I turned to my second-in-command. My dear, lifelong friend who made everything happen.

"Kev, what do you think?"

"I think it's fan-fucking-tastic!"

That's exactly what I thought. *Fan-fucking-tastic!* I could count on Kevin for his brutal honestly and to tell it like it is. I so loved him!

Jaime's lush lips curled into a smug smile. He was a total genius and he knew it.

"Do you have any questions?" he asked.

Only one jumped to mind. "Mr. Zander, whom do you see doing the voiceover—a man or woman?

His lustful eyes lingered on me. "Definitely a male voice. It's a story of seduction."

My breath hitched before smiling my approval. "Mr. Zander, please have your business affairs people call mine. I'd like to put this campaign on the fast track."

"Excellent," said Jaime, his velvety voice still very businesslike. He thanked his team and dismissed them. The last bit of eye contact between Ray and Kevin did not go unnoticed.

Jaime gazed at me. "Before you leave, Ms. Long, I'd like to have a word with you alone."

I signaled with a jerk of my chin for my team to leave.

Vivien pitched a snit fit. "Excuse me, but don't you think I should stay? I mean, this would be such a good learning experience for me. I could even be the point person on this campaign."

"Vivien, please just go." My voice was authoritative. "I'll catch up with you back at the hotel."

"Fine." She stabbed the word at me. With an arrogant fling of her hair, she reluctantly stood up and followed Kevin out of the conference room. Her hips swayed with sexy defiance. At the doorway, she turned her head and shot Jaime an arresting smile. "I'm looking forward to working with you," she purred and then disappeared.

Her words got under my skin. I didn't trust her. Not one bit.

Jaime pushed a button on a wall panel and the conference room door slammed shut. Nervous edgy anticipation swept over me. My eyes stayed fixed on his tall lean frame as he loped around the table in my direction. Stopping behind me, he played with my braid, feathering the ends of it against the nape of my neck. The ticklish sensation sent goosebumps crawling all over me.

"So, Gloria, I've won your account."

"Yes. Congratulations."

He let go of my braid and began to knead my shoulders. His touch sent a rush of tingles to my core.

"Now, I want to win your cunt."

My shoulders heaved as my body heated. "I think you should stop."

"Come on, Gloria. After yesterday, you know you want me as much as I want you."

A shiver skated down my spine. It was true! On my next shaky breath, a carnal wave of desire rolled through me.

He kneaded deeper. "Relax, angel. You need to let go. Trust me. Trust my every decision and move. Especially if we're going to be working together."

I chewed my lip and nodded.

"Good."

He released my shoulders. Before I could blink, something whipped around my eyes.

"What are you doing?" I shrieked.

"What does it look like? I'm blindfolding you." I felt him tie a strip of fabric tightly behind my head. A band of darkness shrouded my eyes.

I nervously touched my fingertips to the blindfold. The textured fabric was silky—for sure his tie.

"Why are you doing this?"

"I'm teaching you to trust me. Can I trust you not to take it off?"

Speechless, I nodded.

He lightly kissed the back of my neck. "You just got your first 'A.' Are you feeling more relaxed?"

"Yes," I said breathily. Trust *me*, relaxed was the last word I'd use to describe how I felt. Every nerve ending in my body was buzzing with anticipation.

"Stand up. I'm going to undress you."

"What if someone comes in?" I stammered.

"Don't worry, the door's locked. Now please stand up."

I rose to my feet, my legs unsteady. The first thing to go was my suit jacket. So much for power dressing. He was rendering me powerless.

"Ah! Chanel! Size 6. With those tits of yours, I had you pegged for an 8. Very impressive."

I didn't flinch or say a word as he tore off my blouse and yanked down my skirt. In a few short heated breaths, I was stripped down to my ivory lace lingerie and my jet-black beads. And the lace-trimmed silk stockings and Louboutin heels. A chill swept over me.

"Ah, Gloria. So apropos, you would wear white lace to celebrate our union. Like a bride." He nuzzled the sensitive area between my shoulder blade and neck and played with my bra strap, his fingers grazing my scar. My pounding heart struggled to stay calm.

"You know, the type of lingerie a woman wears provides an outer expression of her inner sexuality."

Madame Paulette had once told me more or less the same thing.

He continued. "And I'd say, Ms. Long, judging by the underwear you have on, you're bottling up a lot of sexual energy. I'm going to unleash that."

Bottling? I was overflowing with lust. I could actually hear bottle caps popping as he bit open the clasp at the back of my bra, his teeth grazing my sensitive flesh. He slid it off me and let it fall to my feet. Exposed, my breasts quivered. With a concomitant moan, his soft hands cupped my full mounds and warmed them. He squeezed them together and massaged them. Heat and wetness gathered between my inner thighs as my nipples peaked beneath his palms.

He breathed into my ear. "It'll be hard to find someone as beautiful and sensuous as you to cast in the new Gloria's Secret campaign."

"I thought you love a challenge," I said, squeezing out the words.

"I do," he said, flutter kissing every part of me.

He flipped me around and lifted me onto the conference room table. I could feel the hardness of the wood beneath my buttocks.

"Lie down, Gloria."

I did as I was told, stretching myself across the length of the table. My chest rose and fell, my breasts still quivering. I felt him tug at my red-soled stilettos.

"Do you know what these shoes are?"

"They're Louboutins," I stammered. *And they cost a bloody fortune.*

"They're Louboutins to you. But I call them 'fuck me' shoes. That's why women wear them."

He was right again. The scantily clad models in our Gloria's Secret catalogue only wore the highest of high heels. I shivered as he slipped them off, one by one, and heard them tumble to the floor.

He clasped my feet in his large, warm hands. His thumbs dug into my silk-sheathed arches, sending a jolt straight to my sex.

"You have beautiful feet. Surprisingly small and dainty despite your stature," he purred as he rubbed his thumbs up and down my inner soles.

"Thank you," I murmured, too caught up with the erotic foot massage to say more. Shoe salesmen were always surprised I wore a size 6.5AA despite my five foot nine height and hearty bone structure.

His thumbs continued making deep circles, sending yet another rush of toe-curling tingles to my core. A moan escaped my throat.

"You like having your feet massaged, don't you?"

I was too enraptured to say a word. I merely nodded.

"Do you know why?"

"Why?" I spluttered.

"Because it releases you. Did you know that the nerves of the feet are connected to various parts of the body? Reflexologists believe you can turn a woman on with just a foot massage. Even make her come."

He definitely knew what turned on women. At least me. From aphrodisiacs to erogenous zones.

He applied pressure again to that particularly sensitive part of my soles. "Tell me. Where do you feel that?" He pressed deeper.

I was throbbing. Growing hotter and wetter by the second. I swear if he continued with this erotic foot massage, I *was* going to come.

"Answer me, Gloria."

"Between my legs," I moaned.

"Your pussy?"

I nodded.

"Say it, Gloria. *My pussy*."

"My pussy," I muttered.

"Good, Gloria. Another 'A' for you." Ending the foot massage with a sensuous kiss on each sole, he unhooked my garters, one by one. My flesh prickled as I felt him peel off my stockings, sensually sliding them down my legs. With a whoosh, the lace garter came off next and then my bikinis.

A dose of reality hit me like a brick. Holy shit! I was lying butt naked on Jaime Zander's conference room table. Me, one of the most powerful women in the world, completely at the mercy of a man I hardly knew. Totally exposed and vulnerable. Something was wrong with this picture. What was the hell was I doing? *I need to stop this! Collect myself and get the hell out of here!* But I couldn't will myself to sit up. It was like I was super glued to the table. And when his hand slid under my ankles, it was too late.

"What are you doing?" I shrieked.

"What does it feel like?"

I didn't have to think hard. He was tying me up. With one stocking, he bound my ankles together, so tight it almost hurt. And then with the other, he bound my wrists. I attempted to wriggle myself free; it was an exercise in futility. Blindfolded and bound, I was now his prisoner. My heart thudded in my ears, and I was breathing heavily. Now what was he going to do? God, I wished I could see.

"Gloria, now you're mine," he said, his deep voice crawling into me. "I want you to relax. To not be afraid and trust me."

Relax? He wanted me to relax? I was totally bared, tied up, and blinded, and he was about to plunder me. My mind flashed back to what he said in the steam shower the other day. *I'm going to fuck you until you can't walk.* A shudder ran through me. I inhaled and exhaled deeply, remembering a breathing lesson from my yoga instructor. I inhaled again, blowing out the air. It wasn't helping.

I shivered again as his warm, velvety tongue glided up my right leg, from my ankles to the apex. He repeated the action with my other leg, this time leaving it where my inner thigh met the triangle between my legs. Spreading my legs a little, he seamlessly moved his tongue to my cleft, lapping the wet folds like a child lapping a melting Popsicle. I moaned with the pleasure he was giving me. Then, I felt his luscious mouth come down on me, sucking and nibbling. While his mouth worked me, he rubbed my clit with his fingers. Two? Three? Writhing, I moaned louder, desperate for a release.

"Oh, angel, you're so hot and wet. And you taste so good," he said breathily, taking a short respite from his sucking and licking. "I think you're ready."

In two quick moves, he unbound my feet and freed my wrists. I wiggled my limbs while his hand clenched my pussy. *What was he doing?* I wanted to scream.

"Ms. Long," he said, his voice again businesslike, "you're free to leave. Sit up, and I'll take off your blindfold though I suppose you could do that all by yourself."

I didn't budge. He squeezed my pussy tighter. I groaned.

"Don't you want to leave?"

Go, Gloria, a voice inside my head whispered. My body shouted something else: *I want more!* I shook my head feverishly, from side to side. I was aching for him.

Jaime let out a deep sexy chortle. "I didn't think so. Now, we're going to finish what we started the other day. Spread your legs wide and then bend your knees."

I did as he asked.

"Good girl."

I heard him unzip his slacks—*Whoosh!*—and climb onto the table—my senses telling me, kneeling between my steepled legs. He grabbed one of my liberated hands and put it to his cock. Its heat penetrated my palm and it was already hard. I curled my fingers around the thick, slab of hot velvet, and despite the blindfold, I could envision it in its full glory.

"Gloria, I want you to put my cock inside you." He squeezed my pussy again. "If that's what you want. You're the client. The client always comes first."

"Yes!" I gasped.

"Do it!" he ordered.

Blinded and frenzied, I grappled until his erection was perfectly positioned at my hungry opening. Inch by thick inch, I inserted it. To my surprise, I took my time to savor the delicious sensation of my pussy stretching to accommodate his thickening magnificence. When it was almost buried to the hilt, he gave his cock a forceful thrust, causing me to yelp, and then held it there. His fullness felt divine. So, so, divine! I clenched my inner muscles around his girth and wondered: did it feel as good for him as it did for me?

"Fucking perfection!" he moaned.

I got my answer. It was perfection . . . my pussy hugging his cock the way a good-fitting bra hugs a boob. His glorious fullness filled every atom of my being, every cell in my brain.

"Now, Gloria, I'm going to fuck you."

Yes, fuck me. Fuck me hard. I'm ready!

Gripping my hips, he slid his shaft back down and then drove it again deep inside me. My drenched walls enabled him to glide smoothly. He repeated the movements, first slowly and then gradually picking up his pace. Harder and faster. With each powerful thrust, hitting an unknown sweet spot deep inside me that made me want to weep with carnal pleasure.

"Gloria's spot . . . the G-spot." He laughed at his own cleverness and then hit it again and again, rubbing against my clit with each masterful stroke.

All I could focus on was the exquisite swelling inside me. Oh, God! What this man was doing to me! He *was* a fucking genius. Pun intended.

I wanted to scream with joy, but bit my lip hard to stifle a shriek.

"Don't worry. The room is soundproof. I always safe-guard my interactions with clients. They're highly confidential."

An unnerving thought ran through my head—how many other clients had he banged on this table? Vivien?

"Besides, I want to hear you. Don't hold back."

His intense pounding hurled me back to the moment. We got into a rhythm, my hips rocking to meet his thrusts, our breaths in concert. Deprived of my vision, my ears took in his ragged breathing and the sound of my beads jiggling against my heaving chest. The deliciously unbearable pressure was building, the blindfold heightening the erotic sensations I was feeling. "Oh, God," I heard myself cry out. My nails dug so deeply into the surface of the table I was sure they'd leave marks. I didn't know how much more I could take. I was falling apart.

"Come for me!" ordered Jaime. "Now!" he grunted with a fervent thrust that was followed by a pinch of my clit.

With a moan that was almost a sob, I let go. Waves of ecstasy began to roll through my body. I was coming. Endlessly coming. The waves traveled from my head to my toes. It was like every cell in my body was being taken out to sea. With yet another deep thrust and a loud feral grunt, Jaime spasmed inside me, blasting his hot release as I blissfully rode out my orgasm.

Folding the weight of his body onto me, he crushed my breasts and yanked off his tie from my eyes. I blinked only once, taking in his expression. It was the face of a man who had just won my cunt—skin glazed, eyes hooded, mouth sated.

His breathing stabilizing, he nuzzled my neck, in the very sensitive crook beneath my chin. "Next time, you're going to watch me come. I want you to see what you do to me."

I wasn't sure about a "next time." I was dazed, confused, wasted; I'd never had such an intense, mind-blowing orgasm. I sucked in a deep breath to oxygenate my brain.

"I've got to go."

"What do you mean? I thought we'd celebrate with dinner. And besides you still owe me one." He shot me that sexy smirk.

"I can't. I'm flying back to LA tonight."

"Change your plans." He played with my mussed up braid, brushing the wispy ends across my sweat-beaded skin. His voice softened. "I don't want you to go."

I tried to deflect the sweet sincerity in his voice as his eyes held me captive. Confession: I wasn't doing a good job. I felt empty. Literally and figuratively without him.

"I'm sorry," I sighed, forcing myself to be strong. "But I've got to. Would you kindly let me get dressed?"

"Fuck. I was ready to bang you again against a wall." He reluctantly rolled off me and dismounted the table.

Sitting at the edge, I watched as he tucked his still semi-hard erection into his slacks. I was still in shock that I'd let this man fuck me on this table and that I'd loved every minute. Still throbbing, I reached for my undergarments that were strewn on one of the conference table chairs.

His hands got there first. The forlorn expression on his face disappeared, replaced by the cocky one so familiar to me. "Let me have the honors. I always cater to my clients."

A shiver tickled my spine as he pulled up my panties and garter. He smiled as the garments made their ascent up my long legs.

"Lift up your gorgeous ass."

Anchoring my hands on the table, I raised myself a few inches so he could get the lacy confections over my butt.

Next the silk stockings.

"Your skin is like satin," he purred as he slinked them up my legs.

My flesh tingled. He expertly rehooked them mid thigh to the garters. I didn't think I'd ever be able to put on another pair of silk stockings without thinking back to this encounter.

He collected my bra. "Slip your hands in," he said with a slight jerk of his chin, holding it up by the straps. I did as bid, and he slid the bra up my bare arms. My tender breasts fell into the cups, my swollen nipples peeking through the lace. His index fingers circled them before moving to hook the back clasp. I stifled a moan as a soft smile played on his face. Next my blouse. His dexterous hands skimmed my chest as he buttoned it up. This time the moan escaped.

Lifting me off the table to my feet, he instructed me to step into my skirt and then shimmied it up to my waist where he zipped and buttoned it. Lastly, he helped me into my suit jacket and adjusted my beads so that they lay perfectly over my collarbone. There was something adoring in the way he dressed me. He made me feel taken care of, though not helpless. It made me want to run my hands along the contours of his face, but I refrained.

"Hold on to my shoulders," he said sweetly as he slipped my Louboutins back onto my feet, where it had all started. The six-inch fuck-me shoes made us once again face-to-face.

I was back to being me . . . albeit a just fucked one. Wobbling, I collected my purse and briefcase. It was back to business . . . so I thought.

"Mr. Zander, don't forget to have your business affairs

people call mine next week. We're going to have to figure out a budget and timeline. I want to move quickly."

His eyes connected with mine. His normally confident, fiendish glint was missing, replaced by something else. A *je ne sais quoi* as Madame Paulette would say. Perhaps loss and longing? The very sentiments I was feeling. Then with a steeling breath, his expression hardened.

"Please tell your business affairs people there's only one deal breaker."

I shot him a puzzled look. "Which would be . . ."

"I want you to be the point person. Only you. No one else."

Well, at least, that solved the problem of Vivien. I agreed.

With a satisfied smile, he coiled my braid around his hand. "Ms. Long, I'm looking forward to working with you. We'll make a great team."

His lips smashed into mine. I melted.

"One other deal point. You must always wear red lip-stick. It becomes you."

Yeah, he was a genius. A total fucking genius.

CHAPTER 26

Gloria

By the time I was back in my hotel room, I regretted what had transpired between Jaime and me. I threw myself into packing my belongings, trying to forget, but the throbbing between my legs and the thudding of my heart made it impossible.

What had I gotten myself into? I made it a point never to mix business with pleasure and now I had crossed the line big time. I had let this gorgeous man fuck me. Right on his conference room table! How the hell were we going to work together? I had no clue.

As I folded up my red bandeau bathing suit, other memories of this week whirled around in my head. Our first encounter on the elevator . . . our first business meeting . . . the Gloria's Secret Fashion Show . . . the after-party . . . our dinners . . . our swim . . . the pitch. A wistful smile—and a tingle—accompanied the flashbacks, and then I mentally kicked myself. Why the hell did I let him do the things he did? How could I—this supposedly powerful, in control, respected woman—be so submissive? So taken? No man had ever done this to me before. And it wasn't just his breathtaking looks and his sexual prowess, though that counted for a lot. I was irresistibly drawn to his cocky, confident personality and his outrageous creativity. His brilliance. I'd never met a man like him. He challenged me. Broke me down. Made me fall apart and then put me back together—making me feel more complete, more alive than I'd ever felt.

Confession: I hadn't taken a shower. Yes, a little gross, but I wanted to wear the essence of him for as long as I could. Feel him on my skin. Smell him on my clothes. Given the three thousand or so miles that separated us and the Internet that connected us, it was unlikely that we'd see other again soon. As I latched the last of my travel trunks, I longed for him to knock down the door and fuck me senseless on it. He had me bad.

With a disconcerted heart, I called the front desk to have someone collect my mountain of luggage. The one thing I was not was a light packer.

The valet came promptly. I followed him to the elevators, my bags piled high on his dolly. I was so hoping, when the elevator doors parted, Jaime would be there, his cocky smile and those sexy denim blues in my face. Ready to take me in his arms and consume my lips with his. Wishful thinking. As the express car descended to the lobby, our first awkward encounter in this elevator replayed in my head. The moment his eyes held mine had been the beginning. And then our fingers touched—a spark of electricity. I shuddered; I could still feel it. Was Madame Paulette right? Was it love at first sight? With a heavy sigh, I wondered: had it been the same for him?

CHAPTER 27

Jaime

Happy Hour.

The bar at The Walden was packed. Three people deep. I couldn't be happier.

Yeah, I was happy that business was so good—the bar was one of the hotel's cash cows—but there was more to my happiness than met the eye.

I'd won the Gloria's Secret account.

My team had worked hard.

And I'd won her sweet cunt.

I had fucked her hard.

Hap-penis.

Internally, I chuckled at my little pun. And my cock got a rise out of it too.

I couldn't get her out of my head. She was a combination of assertive and submissive. Powerful and powerless. Sexy as all fuck.

I knew sex with her would be incredible. But truthfully, I never imagined it to be *that* fucking good. She was a perfect fit—like my cock was made for her pussy—we had the perfect rhythm, and she liked it rough and hard the way I liked to fuck best. She was desperate for me. And most importantly, she trusted me with her body and her mind. We were made for each other in every way.

She'd come apart for me like a beautiful vase, splintering into a million pieces when I thrust into her without mercy and brought us both to orgasm.

Beautiful and fragile. The truth is I loved putting her back together as much as I loved making her fall apart. I'd undressed countless women, but never had I had the pleasure of dressing one. Helping her put back on her sexy power suit was one of the most sensual and intimate experiences I'd ever had. While I could still feel the warmth of her wet pussy cradling my cock and coming all around me, I could also feel the touch of her silky skin on my fingertips and the taste of her on my tongue. And picture her beautiful face, her expression at once so needy and grateful. So vulnerable. There was something about taking care of her that got deep under my skin. Warmed me from the inside out. Made me feel things I'd never felt before. Stirred in me a desire just to hold her in my arms and feel her heart beating against mine. I meant it when I said I didn't want her to go and as I uttered the words, I felt a heavy longing in my chest. That morphed into emptiness as soon as she left.

When would I see her again? She was heading back to LA tonight. I suppose I could go up to her room and fuck her into tomorrow, but the way we'd ended things at my office trumped my desire. I was a firm believer of quitting while you're ahead. And I was ahead. Winning by a landslide.

Fighting my desire, I headed to the bar to quell my thirst for her. A seat opened up and I wormed my way into it. Traveling so much for work, I hadn't been here for a while so the bartender was surprised to see me. His name was George and he was nearing retirement age. I'd snagged him from another hotel that was on the verge of closing. His credentials were impeccable, and as an equal opportunity employer, age made no difference to me. My hunch proved correct, and I learned from Yelp reviews that many patrons returned to the hotel because they loved George. As far as I was concerned, George could work here until the day he died.

His twinkly eyes lit up at the sight of me.

"Boss, what can I get you?"

"How 'bout a vodka on the rocks?"

"Sounds good. Coming right up."

While I waited for my drink, I took in the scene. It was lively mix of attractive men and women—people here at the hotel for business as well as local city professionals. The Walden bar was a popular after-work hangout for singles looking to hook-up. I was amused by the pick up lines I heard around me as well as by the seductive body language that accompanied them. Eye winks. Shoulder rolls. Lip pouts, tongue flicks, and more. I'd done my own fair share of picking up beautiful women at the bar with the simple line—"Come on, let's go fuck"—but tonight I oddly felt out of place here. I was glad when my drink came so I didn't have to respond to the flirty eyes all around me looking to make contact.

At the same time my drink came, a burly middle-aged man with a buzz cut took a seat cattycorner to me. With his straight-laced looks and unstylish black trench coat he stood out from the hip, well-dressed crowd. He didn't look like he belonged here, and as he kept his beady eyes locked on me, he made me feel even more uncomfortable than I already felt. An unsettling thought tore through me. Had Victor sent someone to spy on me?

I sipped my smooth, cold beverage and kept my head bowed down to avoid him. Only one person occupied my mind—Gloria—and I fought the urge to call her room and invite her down for a quick drink. To celebrate our working together. Our future. Truthfully, I just wanted to see her. Tug her braid. Brush my lips against hers. Taste her. Feel her heat. Hold her close. I was feeling greedy and needy.

Without warning, a warm wet sensation spread across the nape of neck. My head jerked up and I spun around. Vivien! Rage filled every bone of my body. What was with this sick bitch? She was stalking me. Setting my tumbler down, I clenched my fists by my sides as she licked her pouty lips. I swear I wanted to tear them off her face. Then, douse her with the remains of my vodka and set her on fire. That's much I loathed her. Narrowing my eyes, I met her lustful gaze.

"I thought I told you, Vivien, to never touch me again."

She shrugged a shoulder. "I guess I don't remember that."

"Well, I'm telling it to you again. Stay away from me."

It was if she had deaf ears. She toyed with my loose tie and squeezed my balls. "Well, doll boy, I was thinking with Gloria going back to LA tonight, you and I could go out for dinner and get reacquainted."

I'd spent the last several years in therapy figuring her out and then trying to forget her. Or at least, shoving her to the back of my mind. She was one of the last people I wanted to spend time with. Her and her father.

"I'm busy." My voice was icy and dismissive. "Will you please excuse me."

I reached for my wallet, but as I did, she flung her arms around me and smashed her lips onto mine. Gnawing at them, trying to force them open. Jesus fucking Christ. What was wrong with her? I wanted to throw her aside, but knew she'd throw some kind of tantrum that would draw more attention to us. The last thing I needed was to create a scene in front of my employees and our clientele—or that possible Victor spy whose eyes were still on me—leaving myself open for some kind of sexual harassment charge. The pyscho bitch was capable of anything. So I rode out her revolting kiss, my eyes wide open, my lips pinched tight, my mind counting the seconds until she released me. Finally, after a minute or so, she broke away. It felt like an eternity.

"Well, Jaime, have I changed your mind?"

My eyes blinked once. Twice. Then froze.

"Well?" she snapped impatiently.

I couldn't get my lips to move. Straight in my line of vision was Gloria. Her eyes locked on mine. Shock registered on her face.

Fuck. She'd seen everything.

CHAPTER 28

Gloria

When the elevator reached the lobby and the doors parted, my reverie ended and reality set in. I was going back to Los Angeles. Back to the hectic but solitary life I led. Kevin was flying back with me on the corporate jet while Vivien was staying behind to get some shopping in over the three day weekend ahead; Monday was President's Day and our office was closed.

Following the valet, who was wheeling my luggage to the hotel entrance, I passed by the bar. Friday night, happy hour. It was packed. "Undercover Lover" was playing in the background. I recognized the Kids in Glass Houses song because we'd once used it in a James Bond-themed Gloria's Secret Fashion Show. My eyes took in the boisterous crowd, and then they grew wide. I stopped dead in my tracks. My breath hiccupped. At the end of the bar, facing me was Jaime Zander. And all over him was Vivien Holden, one hand fisting his hair, the other cupping his ass, their mouths interlocked. My blood ran cold. I was right. He was into her. I was just another conquest. Another fuck he could add to his stable.

Jaime's eyes caught my mine, frozen with shock. He broke away from Vivien and sprinted my way. I rushed off, my steps quickening until I was running in my six-inch heels to the entrance of the hotel.

"Wait, Gloria!" I heard him shout.

My insides wrenched at the sound of his voice. I didn't look back. Screw him! The two words looped around my brain. How could he use me like that to win my account? How stupid could I be? Tears stung my eyes. Thank goodness, Kevin was waiting for me at the entrance.

"Come on, Kev, let's get of here." I hooked my arm in his and pushed him through the revolving glass door.

Outside the hotel, in the semi-circular driveway, Nigel was waiting for us with the Town Car. My bags had already been stowed away in the trunk. I hopped into the car, with Kevin following behind me. Nigel closed the door and returned to the car. "Lock the doors!" I yelled to my trusty driver.

Shit! There were at least six cars ahead of us. As we waited in line for the vehicles in front of us to leave, there was a loud rapping on the passenger door window. Jaime! Thank goodness the door was locked. My heart was in a frenzy, and tears stabbed at my eyes.

"Open up!" He pounded against the glass with his fist, and with his other hand, tried yanking open the door. His voice boomed through the tinted glass. I looked away.

"Don't touch the door," I barked at a baffled Kevin.

"Glorious, what's going—"

I cut him off. "I'll explain everything as soon as we get out of here."

He shot me a perplexed look.

Jaime was persistent. He pounded with such ferocity I thought his fist might break through the glass. "Roll down the window, Gloria. I need to talk to you."

I shot him an icy glare, facing him just long enough to let him see a tear escape my eyes.

"Gloria!" he shouted again.

I turned my head away and bit my lip, battling more tears. Finally, the car started to move. Jaime stayed with it. Jesus. Was he going to run down Park Avenue with us?

"Nigel, step on it!" I ordered.

"Yes, ma'am." He floored the gas pedal, leaving Jaime behind after one final, frustrated thrust of his fist on the glass pane. I heard him curse as we zoomed off. In no time, we were cruising down the wide city street. I spun my head around and could see Jaime still standing motionless on the corner of Fifty-Ninth and Park.

A golf-ball-sized lump swelled in my throat. Tears I'd been holding back streamed down my cheeks.

"Glorious, what's wrong?" asked Kevin, brushing them away.

"Everything. Fucking everything."

CHAPTER 29

Jaime

"Gloria," I shouted at the top of my lungs as I raced down Park Avenue, clinging to the car. It was futile. Breathless, I finally stopped when it sped away and made a sharp turn onto 59th Street. As it disappeared, I rubbed my knuckles. They stung like hell, but the pain didn't compete with the ache in my chest. I'd won Gloria's account, but I'd just lost her. Goddamn Vivien. She'd fucked up everything. I'd made a terrible mistake succumbing to her kiss.

The chill of the night air bit into me. Shivering, I hugged myself to stay warm. But something else was going on. The tremors grew violent. My blood heating in the bitter cold. The heart palps uncontrollable. The tightness in my chest suffocating. I hadn't experienced these sensations in ages. I knew what was happening. A panic attack. My hand shaky, I pulled out my cell phone from my back pocket. The phone shook in my hand. Thank fuck, I had his number on speed dial. My jittery index finger jabbed it. My heart hammered like a jackrabbit's as it rang and rang. My muscles clenched. Finally, my shrink picked up.

Dr. Harold Zimmer's office was located on upper Fifth Avenue not too far from The Walden. I was lucky his last appointment had canceled and he'd agreed to see me.

I'd been seeing my psychoanalyst for several years, having been introduced to him by one of my clients—Ari Golden, the head of one of the world's leading pharmaceutical companies. While developing a cancer-fighting drug, his company had inadvertently invented a miraculous youth-enhancing skin cream—Derma Doo—and thanks to my breakthrough advertising campaign—"Derma Doo. Life's too short. Be Beautiful"—the product had gone through the roof and made Ari billions.

Dr. Zimmer specialized in treating men—specifically helping them with self-esteem and relationship issues. He was instrumental in helping Ari, one of New York's most eligible bachelors, overcome his fear of commitment which led him to ultimately marrying a fabulous woman.

"Thanks for seeing me at such short notice," I began, sitting restlessly on the couch I normally occupied during our sessions.

"What's going on, Jaime?" asked my scholarly-looking shrink, sitting cross-legged on a club chair facing me.

I rubbed the back of neck where most my tension had settled though my chest still felt like a sledgehammer had been put to it.

"It's complicated."

My shrink chuckled. "Life is always complicated, Jaime."

"Tell me."

"Does it have to do with someone?"

"Yes. A woman."

My shrink smiled. "That's good. What's her name?"

"Gloria." Damn, I loved saying her name. Even in my agitated state, it took my breath away.

"Ah, like in that eighties song my wife loves. Tell me about her."

"She's a new client. But I feel something more for her."

"Specifically . . ."

"An attraction. She's different from other women I've been with."

Adjusting his horn rimmed glasses, Dr. Zimmer's gaze stayed on me. "How is she different?"

"Well, for one, she's tall and blond."

"So, physically not like your usual hook-ups."

I nodded. All my hook-ups were dark-haired and petite. My shrink had made me realize I gravitated to women who looked like my exotic mother. Women who were an outlet for my pent-up anger. It was easy to fuck and forget them— abandon them as my mother had done to me. Take my hurt out on them.

"Tell me more. How else is she different?"

"She's smart, powerful, and intriguing."

"Ah, so you're also attracted to her personality." He smiled. "Sounds like you've met your match."

Dr. Zimmer was smart as fuck. He could synthesize things readily. "Yeah. She also makes me laugh."

My shrink's smile widened. "That's excellent, Jaime. You've connected to her."

"In more ways than one."

My shrink raised a brow. "You've slept with her?"

I shook my head. "No. But I've been sexually intimate with her."

Dr. Zimmer knew about my kinky tendencies. I was relieved he didn't press for details.

"Did she enjoy it?"

"I think so." I paused. "She's the first woman I've ever wanted to please."

Dr. Zimmer clasped his hands with a clap. "That's a

major breakthrough."

He also knew that the only person I wanted to please was yours truly. Pleasing women was not high on my priority list. In fact, it wasn't on my list at all. I got what I needed from them and said adieu. Disposing of them like used Kleenex. I told Dr. Zimmer that Gloria was the first and only woman I'd ever wanted to spend quality time with. Without getting into the sexual details, I mentioned that I'd had dinner with her twice, both times me doing the asking.

"So you went out on dates with her."

Up until now, the word date didn't exist in my vocabulary. I fucked; I didn't date.

My shrink continued. "So, Jaime, are you going to see more of her socially?"

I let out a loud exasperated breath that did little to relieve my tension. "I'm not sure."

"Why is that?"

Taking another deep breath, I launched into the complicated details surrounding Gloria. How I'd courted her business and won it. And how in the process I'd discovered that Victor Holden and his daughter Vivien were involved with Gloria's Secret.

Dr. Zimmer knew everything about Victor and Vivien. They were as equally responsible for my fuckedupness as my mother. And my father. The reason I was here. The reason I couldn't have a normal relationship with a woman. The reason love eluded me.

Dr. Zimmer didn't frown upon mixing work with pleasure. However, upon hearing about Victor and Vivien's sudden reappearance in my life, he removed his glasses and pinched the bridge of his nose, deep in thought. Following a pensive hmm, a short silence transpired between us. The tick-tick-tick of the antique grandfather's clock that stood in the corner of his office clicked in my ears, making me astutely aware of the passing time. It was six forty-five. My session with my therapist would be over in fifteen minutes. Returning his glasses to his nose, he stroked his chin with this thumb.

"This *is* complicated, Jaime," he finally said.

Well, at least we saw eye to eye. But his assessment was hardly the salve I was looking for to soothe my malaise.

"Have you had any interactions with Victor?"

I didn't hold back and told him how Victor had paid a visit to my office and threatened me if I got involved with Gloria in any way.

"He's the one threatened by you. He doesn't like the tables turned."

I processed his words. For a long time, Victor had the upper hand and used it to quell me.

"And what about Vivien?"

I proceeded to tell Dr. Zimmer about Vivien's visit to my hotel room, not sparing any details.

He shook his head. "She hasn't changed. She's still a delusional sociopath. Your presence has rekindled her need to dominate and control you. She may be more of a threat than her father. You handled her well. With authority."

"But I didn't handle her well tonight."

My shrink cocked a brow. "What do you mean?"

"She hit on me again tonight at The Walden bar. She groped my genitals and then kissed me. Gloria saw everything and fled. That's why I'm here." Pausing, I bowed my head. "I fucked up."

"Jaime, look at me." My doctor's voice was soft but authoritative. Slowly, I lifted my head and met his compassionate gaze.

"Jaime, you didn't fuck up. It was a misunderstanding. Does Gloria know about your past with Victor and Vivien?"

I shook my head. "No. I was afraid it would have cost

me her account."

Dr. Zimmer's eyes stayed on me, his hands folded on his lap. "Jaime, the most important thing about any relationship, be it business or personal, is communication. Honesty and openness." He gave me a little time to process his words, then said with a warm smile, "Time is fleeting. Find Gloria and tell her the truth."

The grandfather's clock struck seven. My session was over. I had no time to waste.

Stepping out of Dr. Zimmer's building, I reached for my phone and speed dialed Ray to let him know I was jetting off to L.A. later tonight. Without questioning me, he offered to make arrangements to get my private plane ready. I thanked him and told him I'd text him when I landed. Slipping my phone back into my coat pocket, I walked briskly down Fifth. The temperature was dropping and I lifted the collar of my coat, wishing I'd worn a scarf. A shiver threaded through me, but not just because it was cold. I had the gut feeling I was being followed. Looking over my shoulder, I recognized the man on my trail immediately. It was the burly man who'd been watching me at The Walden bar earlier. My pulse in overdrive, I quickened my pace, breaking into a jog. Dodging the many pedestrians lining the street as well as cars and cabs. Not slowing down, I glanced over my shoulder again, and the fucker was still hot on my trail. He had some kind of communication device in his hand and was talking into it. Shit. I had to get away from him. On impulse, I turned the corner on Sixty-Sixth Street and as I did, I ran smack into a man who could be the twin brother of the man chasing me. Dazed, I stopped dead in my tracks as my pursuer joined us. One of them reached under his coat and I glimpsed a holster. Jesus. Was he going to pull out a gun? My heart thudded. Was Victor so insane that he was going to dispose of me? Shoot me in cold blood?

Instead, as I took what I thought was my last breath, he pulled out a shiny gold badge from his breast pocket.

"FBI. We'd like to talk to you."

CHAPTER 30

Gloria

By the time we arrived at Teterboro, the nearby New Jersey airport that catered to corporate jets and private celebrity planes, I'd spilled everything to Kevin. He had listened intently, only stopping me with a question or two. Few things shocked Kevin; today's events were among them.

"Shit! This is fucked. Maybe we should move forward with a different agency. We haven't signed a contract."

That wasn't an option. The ZAP! pitch was perfect. It would take weeks, maybe months to find another agency that could come up with a campaign that was as good—if that was even possible. And in the retail business, the longer you waited, the more likely your competition would jump in ahead of you.

"Listen, Glorious. He's on the East Coast; you're on the West. There's three thousand plus miles between the two of you. You never have to physically see him again. Everything can be done through emails, texts, and an occasional Skype. If someone has to oversee the shoot from our end, I can do that."

I sighed with relief. Kevin was my problem solver. He always had been and always would be. I gave him a hug. I loved him to pieces. We would always be there for each other.

"What about Vivien?" I asked.

"Don't worry about the little minx. I'll handle her."

By the time we arrived at the airport, I was feeling much better. Except for better and for worse, I couldn't get Jaime Zander out of my head.

I braced myself for takeoff. The Gloria's Secret corporate jet was next in line. My stomach bubbled with nerves. I squeezed Kevin's hand. I was petrified of flying, especially takeoffs and landings. Flying made me feel so out of control. My life was totally in the hands of others. The pilot's. And God's. Unfortunately, I spent a good part of my life up in the air, traveling frequently for business meetings around the world. You would think the more I flew, the easier it would get, but it didn't work that way.

Once the plane was up in the air and cruising smoothly, my pulse rate calmed down, and the butterflies in my stomach disappeared. A glass of champagne, served by one of the flight attendants, further relaxed me. By the time I finished it, I was sleepy and shifted my roomy pink leather chair into a reclining position.

"Wake me when we land in LA," I told Kevin who was watching an old episode of *Queer as Folk* on his iPad.

"Sure." He gave me a light peck on my cheek.

I closed my eyes, willing my mind to let go of Jaime Zander. The ache in my heart, however, lingered until sleep took over.

Six hours later, an announcement from our captain awakened me with a startle. It was time to return our chairs to an upright position as we were beginning our descent into Los Angeles. Kevin had dozed off too. We simultaneously lifted our chairs.

"Home sweet home," sighed Kevin, who loved sunny Los Angeles as much as I did. It was almost midnight on the West Coast. I gazed out the window at the myriad of twinkling lights below and smiled. Neither of us had known when we'd fled to the City of Angels how much we would fall in love with the sun-kissed weather, the Pacific Ocean, the Spanish architecture, the canyons and hills, and the colorful, multi-ethnic neighborhoods.

As the plane swooped down, my fear of flying once again took hold of me. My stomach fluttered and my chest tightened. Gripping my hand, Kevin comforted me. "Hold on, Glorious. We're almost there."

I breathed a deep sigh of relief as the plane touched down on the tarmac. We were safely home. Yes, at last! I immediately turned my cell phone back on.

There were a dozen calls waiting for me from a private number. When I saw the equal number of texts, I knew whom they were from. Jaime.

I read the first text.

Call me as soon as u land.

And then the second.

I can explain.

I didn't need to read the rest. Nor did I have to play his messages. The last thing I wanted was to hear his voice. My body tensed. Anguish propelled my rapid heartbeat.

As we pulled into the terminal, the phone rang again. Again a private number. I ignored it. The phone rang again.

"It's him." I gritted my teeth and looked at Kevin beseechingly. "Kev, will you answer it?"

Kevin clutched the phone and put it to his diamond-studded ear. A somber expression washed over his face. "Hold on, please." His long-lashed eyes took in mine. "Glorious, you need to take this call." He handed me the phone.

The phone shook in my trembling hand. I could feel my blood drain from me as I listened to a familiar voice on the other end.

It was Nurse Perez from the Cadbury House for Assisted Living. Madame Paulette was dead. She had died peacefully in her sleep.

My body froze over. I could only feel the scorching tears that poured down my face.

"It's Madame Paulette," I spluttered.

I needed to say no more. Kevin took me into his arms and let me cry on his shoulder. He knew what Madame had meant to me.

"Oh, Glorious, I'm so, so sorry," he soothed as I heaved against him.

The plane refueled. Without ever leaving the cabin, we did an about face, heading back to New York. Collecting myself, I told Kevin about Madame Paulette's wish to be buried next to her late husband in Paris.

"Glorious, I'll arrange for her body to be properly flown to Paris. I'm pretty sure Sandrine, our Paris store manager, is Jewish. I'll contact her to see if she can help with the funeral arrangements."

Thank goodness for my beloved Kevin. Indeed, Sandrine, a good friend, was Jewish. My mind was in a thick fog. What would I do without him?

"Do you want me to come to Paris with you?" he asked.

A ghost of a smile flickered on my face; Kevin was always there for me. But this time, I needed to be alone. As soon as he debarked the plane back in Jersey, I was flying solo to Paris.

CHAPTER 31

Gloria

I arrived in Paris on Saturday a little after eight p.m. I was exhausted, totally jetlagged. Though we fortunately didn't encounter any turbulence during the seven-hour flight from New York, the turbulent memories of the last twenty-four hours rocked my body and mind, making sleep impossible.

As soon as we touched down at Le Bourget airport, I got a text from Kevin. Madame Paulette's body was being flown to Paris, and Sandrine had managed to set up a Jewish burial service the next day, Sunday, at the cemetery where her husband Henri was buried. The driver Kevin had arranged met me on the tarmac and whisked me off in his limo to The InterContinental Hotel where I was staying. Like Madame Paulette, I loved Paris. As the Eiffel Tower came into view, a pang of sadness stabbed at my heart. This time, my love affair with the City of Light might end.

Bleary eyed, I checked into the hotel with just a couple of bags as I planned to head back to Los Angeles on Monday after Madame Paulette's funeral.

Having stayed at The InterContinental numerous times, I was treated like royalty, the staff working quickly to get me into my suite. All I wanted to do was snuggle under fluffy covers and sleep. I couldn't even see straight. As I followed the valet through the bustling opulent lobby to the elevators, a stocky man wearing a long black trench coat and wide-brimmed hat that hid his face brushed by me, almost knocking me over.

"Izvinite," he muttered gruffly without slowing down.

It was Russian for "excuse me." A chill ran through me at the thought of Boris Borofsky. I pivoted my head, but the rude man, whose back was now to me, was almost at the front entrance. I took a calming breath. I was tired. It couldn't be him. My mind was just playing tricks on me.

Five minutes later, I was in my beautiful suite, with its plush four-poster canopy bed and regal French furnishings. I quickly shed my clothing, my lingerie the last to go. I could still smell Jaime Zander on me. The memory of him ravaging me on his conference room table replayed in my head. And then the sight of him kissing Vivien kicked that memory out of the ballpark. A mixture of rage and self-loathing coursed through my veins. I shoved all of my undergarments into the wastebasket by the sink, and then hopped into the shower to wash away the memory of this deceitful man. No matter how hard I scrubbed, his face lingered in my mind.

I towel dried myself and readied myself for bed, slipping into Gloria's Secret iconic pink and white striped cotton PJs—made for sweet dreams. *Enfin!* I crawled into the luxurious duvet-covered bed and turned off the light. Unconsciously, I rubbed my fingers over my scar as tears leaked from my eyes. The words of my beloved Madame Paulette swirled around in my head. *It eez better to have loved and lost than never to have loved at all.* In my heart, I mourned the loss of my cherished mentor and scorned the loss of Jaime Zander. My heavy, teary eyes couldn't fight gravity. At last, sleep triumphed over sorrow, but sweet dreams were not to be had.

My wake-up call sounded at six forty-five the next morning. As in any hotel I stayed at, a subsequent knock at my door, signaling the arrival of my coffee, forced me out of bed. I was groggy, a victim of a restless toss and turn sleep and jetlag. After unlocking the door, a jovial mustached waiter set a tray with a pot of steaming coffee along with a pitcher of steamed milk on a small table. It was a welcomed blessing.

After draining the strong café au lait, my mind re-activated. I wasn't looking forward to the sad day ahead. A long, hot shower followed. Under the pounding water, I plotted what I was going to wear to Madame's burial. I wanted to look elegant and dignified; I owed her that.

Rifling through my neatly packed garment bag, I came upon the perfect black dress—an almost knee-length Dior with a scooped neckline and three-quarter length sleeves. It was one of my favorites and I was glad that I'd packed it. From my other suitcase, a piece of matching luggage, I pulled out my one-piece black lace merrywidow, designed with an underwire and adjustable garters, and the matching G-string panty. After donning the undergarments, I ferreted through the pocket of the suitcase for a pair of black silk seamed stockings. The ones I settled on were my lucky stockings—I took them everywhere I flew, believing their magical powers could protect me from danger, especially a fatal accident. They came from Paris. And dated back to the 1940s. Madame Paulette had bestowed them upon me on my eighteenth birthday—the first of many pairs she would send me in the years afterward. As I carefully rolled them up my legs, I heard her deep raspy voice. "Love *eez* like a fine pair of silk stockings, *ma chérie*. One snag and it can all unravel."

The image of Jaime Zander crept back into my mind. Grabbing my purse and overcoat, I slumped out of the room, tears threatening to fall.

The cemetery where Madame Paulette was being buried was located on the outskirts of Paris. Tombstones with both crosses and Stars of David dotted the verdant grounds; many dated back to the nineteenth century. A kindly looking rabbi, with a graying beard and skullcap, met me at the gravesite and introduced himself. Rabbi Rosoff. As he took my gloved hands in his, my eyes darted to the tombstone of Henri Lévy. My French was good enough to understand the epitaph beneath the etched Jewish star: "Noble hero and devoted husband of Paulette." Soon his beloved would be by his side again. A chill in the air shot through me.

"She was a special woman, beautiful both inside and out," the rabbi told me. He spoke perfect English. "I knew her well."

I was surprised the rabbi knew her and asked how. It turned out that Madame Paulette attended Shabbat services at his synagogue on Friday nights on her buying trips to Paris.

"She spoke highly about you. You were like a daughter to her."

"Merci," I said in French, tears welling in my eyes. From the corner of one of them, I saw a dozen or so men transporting her casket toward us. My breath caught in my throat.

"A *minyan* from our congregation," said the rabbi, knowing I wasn't Jewish. "They will help us bury her in her final resting place."

The men laid the casket on the grass beside the tombstone of Henri. It was made of pinewood and in the center was a carved Jewish star. It was pure understated elegance—just like her.

One of the men, who was carrying a shovel, began to dig into the earth. They took turns shoveling until a hole that was big and deep enough was made. Using a pulley system, they worked together to lower the casket into it. Then, as the rabbi prayed in Hebrew, each took a turn with the shovel, refilling the hole. I fought back tears as I watched the casket disappear from sight and the large hole fill in. Warm memories of our years together floated in my head along with our final day together. A member of the *minyan* offered me the shovel to cover her with the last mound of dirt. As I scooped up the soil and hurled it onto the grave, the dam holding back my tears burst. The rabbi's melodic Hebrew saturated my mind and soul. I recognized the prayer—the mourner's Kaddish. Madame would recite it once a year on the eve of Yom Kippur over the memorial candle that burnt for Henri through the night. The final words, *Oh say, Shalom, Amen,* echoed in my ears. Peace. Rivulets streamed down my face. Madame Paulette was gone . . . now, in her final resting place . . . reunited with the man she loved.

I squatted down and retrieved the bouquet of flowers I had brought along—long stemmed white roses—Madame's favorite blooms. I gently laid several on her grave and the remainder against the tombstone of her husband. *Au revoir*, *Madame*. May you rest in peace and with your true love.

I returned to the hotel, drained and exhausted. It was late afternoon.

Before heading up to my room for a much needed nap, I made a stop at the bar. Perhaps, a drink would quell the sorrow that filled my soul. Unable to find an empty table, I settled in at the crowded bar. A lively, international mix of beautiful people surrounded me.

Usually just a wine drinker, I ordered something stronger from the young, twinkly-eyed bartender. A vodka martini with extra olives. The very drink I'd ordered with Jaime at the Gloria's Secret after-party. The drink arrived quickly. The cold velvety liquid washed down my throat and was soothing. Just what I needed. The images of Madame Paulette and Jaime Zander faded. I amused myself by observing the eclectic mix of movers and shakers.

Halfway through my martini, I felt a warm breath on the nape of my neck. A familiar voice sent a chill spiraling down my spine.

"Why, Gloria. How uncanny! We meet again."

I spun around, almost knocking over the remains of my drink. Victor!

He was wearing one of his custom-tailored three-piece gray suits. In his hand was a tumbler filled with his favorite drink. Bourbon. I knew because I recognized the smell, emanating from both the glass and his breath.

He leaned in close to me. "So, Gloria, what brings you to Paris?"

"Personal business." He had no need to know. "What about you?"

"Business. Pure business. I'm meeting here with someone whose global organization could be a potential strategic partner. If the meeting is successful, I'll invite him to LA to meet you."

Dealmaker Victor was always looking for ways to expand Gloria's Secret. While it was not the only retailer in Victor's vast empire, it was his most profitable. The more money Gloria's Secret made, the more money Victor made.

He chugged his cocktail and ordered one more. "Can I

get you another drink?" he asked, pressing his thigh against mine.

He was making my skin crawl. I edged away from him and shook my head. "I'm fine, thank you." What I really wanted to say was: "Get lost, you prick."

As I began thinking of a way to excuse myself, he hovered next to me, nauseating me with his foul bourbon-and-tobacco-tainted breath. His steely eyes glared into mine. "So, Gloria, I understand from my daughter that you're hiring Jaime Zander and his agency ZAP! to take over advertising."

"Yes." I nodded.

His gunmetal eyes darkened. "I don't think that's a good idea. I want you to reconsider."

Still sober, I couldn't believe he was still mad at Jaime for outbidding him on Rihanna's diamond-studded underwear.

"I believe his advertising campaign will bring us to new heights," I retorted. This was the truth, regardless of how much Jaime's deceit had hurt me.

Victor's face pinched. "Let me tell you, Gloria. Nothing good will come from your relationship with that dilettante."

As much as I loathed Jaime, he was no amateur when it came to his trade. He was pure brilliance. It was time to stand up for him . . . and myself.

"Victor, you can control our shareholders, but you can't control my day-to-day decisions as CEO. Gloria's Secret is *my* company, and *I* make those decisions."

He smirked. "You're very sexy when you're defiant." He leaned in close to me, his tight lips descending onto mine.

I jerked away. *The pig!* I forced myself to stay diplomatic. "Good night, Victor. And good luck with your meeting. I'll keep you in the loop with regard to our new ad campaign. I think you'll like it."

I slammed my martini down on the bar counter, leaving Victor with the tab, and stalked off to my hotel room. I so needed to get some rest.

Once at the door to my suite, I rummaged through my purse for my key card. Where had I put it? My designer bag was so monstrous it could be anywhere. I kept digging. My fatigue made me all the more frustrated.

"I want you, Gloria."

The familiar drawl made me whirl around. Victor again! The TT in his eyes told me he was drunk, and in a breath, he was all over me, his hands groping and squeezing.

"Let go of me, Victor," I pleaded.

"No, darling. It's time you and I got to know each other better."

His muscular body pressed me against the hard slab of my door, and then his mouth crushed mine before I could say another word. Exhausted, I didn't have the strength to fend him off. The more I resisted, the harder he pressed. He wormed his repulsive tongue into my mouth and ground his stiff arousal against my middle. The groping and squeezing intensified. I writhed and wanted to scream. Desperately. But his mouth and body held me captive. Painfully, I submitted to his advances. I squeezed my eyes closed to shut out the ugly sight of him.

Then, suddenly, another familiar voice growled. "Get your fucking hands off her."

In a nano-second, Victor was sprawled over a bouquet of red roses on the carpeted floor. My eyes found my hero. Jaime Zander! He'd come to my rescue. My rapid heartbeat didn't know whether to slow down or speed up. My emotions were in turmoil.

Victor crawled to his knees. He shot Jaime a glaring look, his eyes filled with cold fury. "Be careful, Zander. Don't fuck with *me*. You were always a problem child. And you still are."

Victor's words rippled through me. He had known Jaime since he was a boy?

CHAPTER 32

Jaime

Fate. Had I not been intercepted by the two FBI agents, I would have ended up in Los Angeles and then had to fly halfway around the world to get to Paris. My phone call with Ray saved me from that unnecessary trip. Gloria's PR guy Kevin had unexpectedly returned to The Walden and asked Ray if he was free for a late dinner where he informed my protégé that Gloria had detoured to Paris for personal reasons.

My eyes lingered on the sack of shit sprawled on the floor. Timing was everything. Had I arrived a minute later, I may not have been able to protect Gloria. God only knows what the bastard would have done to her. I forced myself to shut down my imagination. Right now, all that mattered was that I was here. And as much as I wanted to break every bone in the motherfucker's body, I needed him alive. *If* I was going to bring him down. I had twenty-four hours to decide.

Not moving a muscle, I watched as the bastard collected himself and stood up. He plucked out a thorn from his expensive suit jacket. And tossed it at me.

"Get the hell out of here, Victor," I barked.

"I'll be watching your every move," growled my nemesis, snarling at me like a rabid dog. "And yours too, Gloria." Red with rage, he stomped on the flowers I'd bought for her on the way to the hotel, crushing the delicate buds. He then staggered down the hall to the elevators and disappeared.

Gloria stared down at the tattered roses. Once beautiful, they were now in ruin. Tears filled her eyes. Her fragility touched something deep inside me.

"Are you okay?" I asked, my voice soft.

Wordlessly, she nodded. She seemed distraught.

I placed my hands on her shoulders, drawing her into me. She felt as fragile as she looked. My angel.

"I'm sorry about the flowers," she whispered through her tears.

"Don't be. I'll buy you three dozen more."

Her watering eyes lifted to mine. "Jaime, what are you doing here?"

I fisted her braid and traced her exquisite face with the wispy ends. Then heaved a breath. "I owe you an explanation. What you saw with Vivien is not what you think."

Her brows arched, her eyes clouded with doubt. "What do you mean?"

She had the right to distrust me. She'd seen what she'd seen and the kiss between Vivien and me probably seemed real. Gently, I cupped her face in my hands and tilted up her head. Our eyes locked, and on my next breath, my lips consumed hers with a deep, passionate, genuine kiss. Instead of resisting me, her body grew slack and she moaned into it. I think the release was mutual. After all that had transpired today and the long trip, it felt so good. So fucking good.

"Come on, angel," I murmured, finally breaking away. "Let's get the hell out of this place. We need to talk."

Then she did something that practically broke me. She began to sob. A loud heaving sob with an ocean of tears.

"Come here, you," I said softly, drawing her against my chest.

I let her cry into me.

Silently, I just held her.

CHAPTER 33

Gloria

Twenty minutes later, we were on the Left Bank in a small but elegant hotel on the Boulevard Saint-Germain that Jaime had stayed at before. Soaking in a deep, claw foot tub with champagne flutes on a tray table, an arm's reach away, I was seated between his long muscular legs, my backside to him. The hot, sudsy bath was just what my body and soul craved. The tension that spread from my head to my toes began to melt away as Jaime bathed me. His touch was gentle. Reverent. Circling my breasts with the sponge in one hand, he moved my braid to the side with the other and nuzzled the back of my neck. A soft sigh escaped my lips as arousal kindled in my core, my need for him seeping under my skin. Nibbling my earlobes, he breathed into an ear, "We need to talk, my angel, but first . . ."

"First what?" I murmured as I felt his own arousal meet mine.

"First this." His voice trailed off as he lifted my hips and inserted his rock hard cock into me, inch by delicious inch. The fullness of him inside me made me moan with pleasure.

"Oh, Gloria, you feel so fucking good. Work with me. Trust me." He slowly slid his shaft back down and when he pushed it back up, I met his thrust, clenching him, enhancing the pleasure for both of us. He let out a deep virile groan.

"Yes, Gloria, yes."

He was different with me this time. The strokes were smooth and measured, and his soft lips pressed all over the nape of my neck and upper back. The only restraints were his hands, which gripped my hips. Actually, they were more like anchors than restraints, holding me up and helping me ride him as his glorious cock worked me up and down.

He breathed against me. "Play with yourself. It'll make it even better for you." His voice was dominant yet tender.

Still gripping a hip and not missing a stroke, he placed my right hand on the soft folds between my inner thighs. His hand stayed on top of mine as he guided it up and down along the sensitive tissue. No stranger to masturbation, I quickly found my clit and circled my fingers around it. His hand returned to my hip and he intensified the grinding between my legs. He was right. Right as usual. My backbone arched as the intense pleasure I was giving myself mingled with the extreme pleasure he was giving me. Whimpers spilled from my lips. Oh, God! I wanted to come!

"Don't come yet," instructed Jaime, a hint of his controlling behavior creeping into his husky voice. "I want to enjoy this for as long as I can."

"Please," I panted out, not knowing how much longer I could hold on. The waves of ecstasy had begun to crest, the inevitable not far away. Craving my moment of release, I dug the fingernails of my free hand into his thigh as I tried to restrain myself.

"Now, angel," he finally said. "Fall apart for me."

On cue, my whole body shook as I combusted with a sob around his pulsating cock. His own orgasm came seconds later with a roar of my name. My head fell back against his taut chest. I could feel it rise and fall, the movements slowing as his breathing stilled. His heartbeat sang in my ears like a love song. He wrapped a brawny arm around my shoulder, coiling my damp braid around his hand, and nuzzled the side of my sensitive neck. His other hand caressed my quivering clit. Bliss. Pure bliss. I don't know how long we stayed in that position when I heard him say, "Gloria, turn around. Face me. We need to talk."

So relaxed, all I wanted to do was stay curled up in his arms and close my eyes. But he was right. We needed to talk, and he had traveled far to have a serious conversation. There were so many burning questions that needed answers. I shifted my body so that my longs legs were spread over his, and we were facing each other. His expression was intense, his lips pressed tight, and his blue eyes piercing. He looked anxious. I'd never seen this side of him. My heart pounded with anticipation. Maybe I wasn't going to like what I was about to hear.

I inwardly shuddered.

CHAPTER 34

Jaime

The hot bath was just what I needed after this long, crazy-ass day.

Gloria was like an elixir. Magical. Transformative. How fucking good it felt to be inside her tight cunt. Taking my time. Savoring every deep, determined stroke. Getting off on the pleasure I was giving her. Lost in her. It was so different from the way I'd fucked her before. In fact, fucked anyone before. It wasn't fucking at all. Though I'd never loved a woman, I'd made love to her. That I knew.

When her orgasm crashed through her, I followed, shouting her name, with a release that transcended time and place. Otherworldly. I swear I'd left this planet and rocketed to outer space because shooting stars soared behind my eyes.

I wanted to stay in this trance-like state. I wanted to make it last. Partly, because it felt so damn good. Partly, because I dreaded telling her about the past. Shifting her so that she faced me, my chest constricted as I braced myself for the inevitable. The reason I'd followed her to Paris. I swallowed hard. Where should I begin? This was not a story I could fit into a slick thirty-second commercial.

As I pondered where to start, Gloria gave me an opening. The expression on her face was piqued with both curiosity and apprehension. "How did you know I was here in Paris?"

I brushed a wisp of her hair off her forehead. "Gloria, you should know this about me by now. Where there's a will, there's a way. I had to see you."

"You didn't answer my question." Her voice sharpened and grew edgy.

"I found out from your PR guy. Are you here on business?"

"Personal business. A dear friend of mine passed away."

Her voice was hesitant and she chewed her lip as a wistful expression washed over her face. I extended my condolences. She was holding back, but I decided not pursue it. In retrospect, I should have when she spit out her next question.

"Are you fucking Vivien?"

Every muscle in my body tensed. Her eyes held me fiercely, waiting for an answer. I sucked in a gulp of air between my teeth and then blew it out.

"Vivien is my stepsister."

Her eyes grew as wide as saucers. Her jaw dropped to her chest. I could almost see the shockwaves coursing through her body in living color.

"Victor Holden is your father?"

"No, my stepfather. My mother was his second wife."

With that, I launched into my sorry-ass life story. Gloria listened intently, only stopping me a few times to ask a question or make a comment.

Over the next twenty minutes, she learned that my mother, a raven-haired nymph named Delilah, married my real father, Payton Anthony Zander, a struggling artist, when she found out that she was pregnant with his child. A painter's model, they had met when the young beauty had posed for him. For my father, it was love at first sight. Stunning eighteen-year-old Delilah was the muse and lover he'd always dreamt about. The child only added to his infatuation. Nine months later I was born. Adored by my father; unwanted by my mother.

Unbeknownst to my father, my beautiful, money-hungry mother was an opportunist. She'd agreed to marry him, not because he'd fathered her child, but because he had the potential to become a breakout painter in the league of Jackson Pollack. She longed for a life of riches and glamour. And he was the gateway. Except life didn't turn out as she'd hoped.

Living in a rat-infested loft in Venice Beach, California, my parents struggled to make ends meet; years went by. My father remained convinced that each painting would be his first masterpiece, his ticket to fame and fortune. My mother grew angry and frustrated with his delusions and resented me because I was just another mouth to feed. Excess baggage that got in the way.

"Did she spend time with you?" asked Gloria, compassion written all over her face. Her deep-seated concern was making it easy to open up to her.

I shook my head. "She was hardly ever there. It was my dad that took care of me. Made me meals. Took me to school. Helped me with my homework. He took me everywhere and he taught me how to draw."

I told Gloria that I had no clue how my mother spent her days, but somehow she always came home with a new dress or pair of shoes. Looking back, she was probably being paid for sexual favors, but my infatuated, idealist father was blindsided. He looked the other way, always believing my mother was there for him. When I was twelve-years-old, she took on a temporary job as the assistant to a mega-wealthy CEO, a recent divorcé.

"Let me guess," interrupted Gloria. "Victor."

Yes, Victor Holden. Her sensual beauty, at the age of

thirty, was still irresistible. Their relationship blossomed into something more permanent, both professionally and personally. Six months later, Delilah Zander was the next Mrs. Victor Holden. And I, now thirteen, was living under the roof of their Beverly Hills mansion along with Victor's daughter from his first marriage—Vivien.

"How did your father react?" asked Gloria.

"My father was devastated. He never stopped loving my mother. We were his whole world."

My mouth dry, I took a break to sip some champagne. Gloria followed suit, eager to hear more.

"Why didn't your father fight for custody of you? Even joint-custody?"

I took another sip of the bubbling liquid and set the glass back onto the tray table next to the tub. Pain filled my next breath. "He didn't have a chance. He was stone-broke and stoned-out. And within no time, he graduated from weed to heroin. I used to watch him shoot up."

"Oh, Jaime. I'm so sorry."

I paused, then fast-forwarded "Three months after my mother married Victor, my father took his life. He shot himself."

Gasping, Gloria clasped one hand to her mouth, the other to her chest over her scar. "Oh my God," she rasped, her face paling.

"I was the one who found him." I tried to blink away the horrific memory, but it only became more vibrant. More alive. Able to see the blood pouring from the hole in my father's head as if it were only yesterday, I gulped down my pain and paused.

CHAPTER 35

Gloria

"Oh my God," I heard myself repeat, my voice just above a whisper. A bolt of pain blasted through my valves as I relived my own gunshot. As it pierced my soul, I jolted with a shudder. My thumb rubbed the scar it had left behind as the memory faded.

Gently, Jaime cupped my face between his hands. "Gloria, are you okay?"

Hesitantly, I nodded, my watering eyes not letting go of him. I now understood what made Jaime Zander who he was. Why he needed money, power, and control. He was afraid of falling into a dark abyss in the footsteps of his poor, struggling father. By controlling women and shunning commitment, he could avoid being hurt the way his father had been by his mother. I also understood why he hated Victor Holden. Victor had destroyed his parents' marriage and brought his father to the ultimate jumping off point of despair.

"Do you still miss your father?" I asked softly.

"Yeah, a lot. Even with his downfalls. He was loving. Creative. Fun. He taught me to open my eyes and see the world. To use my imagination. I was a lot like him." A poignant pause. "And still am."

The look on Jaime's face grew melancholic. Perhaps, in

his mind, he was traveling back in time. Reliving nostalgic memories with his beloved father. The good *and* the bad.

A pang of sadness shot through me. It wasn't hard for me to imagine how difficult it was for a beautiful, confused thirteen-year-old boy to lose his father, the person he loved the most in the world. Kevin, in a way, had gone through that tragic journey with his homophobic father; a different kind of loss, but nonetheless the loss of a cherished parent.

I gently brushed my hand along the side of his face, relishing the soft layer of unshaven stubble. "I'm so sorry about your loss."

Jaime quirked a ghost of a smile. "My father's always been my inspiration. A day doesn't go by without thinking about him."

I now saw Jaime differently. Behind the confident, cocky façade was a sensitive, wounded soul. With my own narcissistic, negligent mother and broken childhood, there was a new, profound connection between us that transcended the physical. I circled his face lightly with my fingertips. Though I already knew the answer, I asked, "Do you blame Victor for destroying your father?"

Jaime stiffened, his eyes blazing with fury. "Yes." He paused. *"And* for almost destroying me."

My eyes widened. "What do you mean?"

"He abused me."

The web of fine scars along his back flickered in my head. He was being very candid, so I dared to ask him, "Did Victor physically hurt you?"

Jaime's blue eyes narrowed and his lips pinched "The son of a bitch beat me. I would beg him to stop, but instead he always picked another target, never once missing his bull's eye."

"Didn't your mother try to stop him?" My eyes stayed on him as he scrunched his face. The pain was palpable.

"She was clueless. Usually passed out in a drunken stupor."

"Jesus." My heart wrenched for this virile but tormented man as my loathing for Victor consumed me. A mixture of rage and sorrow coursed through my veins. I had the burning urge to run my lips over every one of Jaime's scars. I'd read once that scars tell you the hurt is over. That you've healed. That was pure bullshit. They always reminded you of the past and the pain. My own above my heart never stopped.

Jaime continued. "Victor hated me. I was just something in the way. And I was not his blood . . . unlike Vivien who he adored."

Vivien. The mention of her name made me cringe. "How old was Vivien when you moved to Victor's house?" I asked.

"Twelve going on twenty."

I did the math in my head. That meant she was older than the twenty-nine years she claimed to be; in fact, we were probably the same age. *The lying bitch!*

"How did you and Vivien get along?"

"Vivien was a manipulative, spoiled brat who had a crush on me. I was a vulnerable, insecure, fucked-up kid. One night when she was fifteen, she raided her father's liquor cabinet and got drunk."

Uncertain of what was coming next, I braced myself.

"She seduced me."

My chest tightening, I inhaled air through my nose. "Do you still fuck her?"

On my next strangled breath, Jaime gripped my shoulders. His piercing eyes held me as fiercely. "Gloria, listen to me. I *never* fucked her."

Blinking, I tried to make sense of his words.

"I resisted. Pushed her off me. But she's never stopped trying. What you saw at the bar was another one of her manipulative attempts to get me into bed. I was trying to ward her off without creating too much of a scene when you passed by." His gaze softened. "Gloria, I need you to believe me. Do you?"

I nodded. Deep inside, I knew he was telling the truth. He'd come so far.

"I need to hear words."

"Yes, I believe you." I lowered my head, suddenly feeling bad that I'd mistrusted him. "I'm sorry I ran off." My voice was small.

Jaime tilted up my chin and gazed into my eyes. "Angel, you don't have to apologize. You had no idea." He paused. "There's something else you need to know. Vivien's not my type. I could never be with her. She's a dominatrix."

The news of Vivien's sexuality didn't surprise me, given her brazen personality and fashion sense. In my mind, I could easily imagine her in a black leather corset, fishnet stockings, and thigh-high leather boots, wielding a whip. *On Jaime?*

"There's more, Gloria. That night she tried to fuck me she left the door to my bedroom wide open. Victor saw us."

I held my breath as Jaime continued.

"Victor was livid. Then he went into a rampage when Vivien twisted things and pretended that I was raping her."

"Jesus." The manipulative bitch.

"He almost beat me to death . . . with his riding crop."

"The scars on your back?" I asked softly, at last running my fingers across them.

"Yeah."

I wanted to ask more, but the mental exhaustion we shared shut me down. Jaime toyed with my wet braid. "You understand now why I can't work with her on the account. She's a force, however, that must be reckoned with. She's potentially dangerous and destructive."

I processed his words. The situation was complicated. I was going to have to figure out a way to keep Jaime away from Vivien. And also from Victor. While I didn't have a clear-cut solution, I told him we'd make things work. Whatever it took.

An afterthought flew into my head. I knew that Victor was now single and never talked about Jaime's mother. I recalled Jaime telling me he'd inherited a lot of money from her. Had she died?

"What happened to your mother?" I asked.

"Five years after Victor married my mother, he had an affair with a young starlet and asked for a divorce. My mother was more angry than heartbroken, and in the end, went for a large settlement that included a mansion in Bel Air. No longer the beauty she used to be, she resorted more and more to alcohol and sedatives. Driving under the influence, she died the day she turned thirty-five—one day after their divorce—in a head-on collision on the canyon road that led to our house."

So, in a way, Victor had destroyed Jaime's mother's life as well. Jaime's tragic past tugged at my heartstrings. I felt connected to him in a way that I could never have imagined. He was a tortured soul just like me. Deprived of maternal love. And that of a father who adored him. I had just one last question.

I looked him straight in the eye. "Jaime, why did you wait so long to tell me all this?" So many complicated conflicts of interest that could have been avoided had I known about his toxic connection to Victor and Vivien.

He did that swirly thing with my braid again and then tickled my lips with the ends. "Because . . ." His voice trailed off.

"Because why?" I asked softly, his intense gaze arousing me.

"Because I wanted to work with you, Gloria. From the minute I read about you online, I was drawn to you. Your success, your drive, your own need for control. And when I met you in the elevator, I was so taken by your beauty, feistiness, and independence. The need to control you consumed me. You're different from all the women I've been with. You're brilliant, intoxicating, and infuriating. You inspire and excite me, and sometimes you even make me lose control." He tugged hard at my braid and shot me a wry smile. "And because, Ms. Long . . . I'm crazy about you."

"Mr. Zander, *you* make me crazy!" *Crazy in love?* I wasn't sure because I really didn't know first hand what that meant. Feeling tingles everywhere? Shortness of breath? Fiery desire? Jealousy? Emptiness when I wasn't with him? That's what my book heroines felt. And I felt all those things too.

I laughed. A nervous laugh. For sure, some kind of defense mechanism. Then, a silence between us ensued. A long stretch that was strewn with unspoken words. A silence that glued us together. Only the sparks in the air were palpable.

Growing serious, Jaime finally broke the quiet. "So, Gloria would you have worked with me had you known about my past? My relationship with Victor and Vivien?"

I chewed down on my lip. Confession: I wasn't sure. But now, what relevance did that have? I was too involved with this intoxicating man on every level to back away. I eschewed his question.

"Mr. Zander, I would only work with the very best." I eyed him earnestly. "You know that about me."

"Come here, you," Jaime breathed out, a smile widening on his face. His eyes glinted with a mix of lust and desire I'd never seen before. Wrapping his arms around me, he hauled me into him and our bodies touched. My breasts skimming his chest, my bent legs hugging his hips. Our hearts colliding. I expected him to drive his cock into me, but instead he pressed his forehead against mine.

"Gloria, Gloria, Gloria," he repeated, each mention of my name growing softer and softer. Like a prayer.

"I swear on my life I'll never let anyone hurt you." His voice was almost inaudible as his fingers at once flicked my clit and penetrated my body.

My arms circled his chiseled body, embracing the scars that lined his back. Our breathing grew shallow and he moaned my name yet again. As this beautiful, controlling, complex man brought me to yet another earth-shattering climax, I was too distracted to think of all the complications he was bringing into my life.

CHAPTER 36

Gloria

Jaime was still on East Coast time, and I truthfully didn't know what time zone I was in. I just knew I was zoned out. Emotionally and physically.

After room service, a light supper consisting of scrumptious cheese-filled crepes and another bottle of champagne, I could barely keep my eyes open though my companion seemed indefatigable. Yawning, I convinced him to call it a night. Ready for a good night's sleep, Jaime was clad in loose blue pajama bottoms that hung sexily low on his narrow hips, and me in a polka dot baby doll that he'd picked out.

"Which bed?" asked Jaime, admiring his choice of my sleepwear, though I felt him mentally undressing me. "The client gets to pick."

Typical of European boutique hotels, the charmingly furnished floral room had two double beds. I went for the one on the right closest to the French doors opening to the terrace. He followed me under the covers and snuggled close to my scantily clad body, wrapping an arm around me. The warmth of his flesh heated mine.

Despite how delicious it felt, I rolled over to my side and propped myself up on an elbow. My eyes soaked in his face. His hooded blue eyes, his lush lips, manly straight nose, and the strong angles of his stubble-laced jaw. God, he was gorgeous any way you looked at him. I dusted the tip of my braid across his dimpled chin, fighting off my incendiary desire to dip my tongue into the kissable indent.

"Mr. Zander, what I meant is . . . this is my bed. You sleep in the other one. Client's wishes." While he'd fucked me senseless, sleeping with him in the same bed was strangely something I wasn't ready for. It felt wrong. Even more so, it scared me.

His head resting on the mountain of fluffy pillows, he turned to look at me and cocked an eyebrow. "Gloria, you've got to be fucking kidding. I flew all the way to Paris to be with you, and you don't want to sleep with me?"

With a surge of unexpected energy, I sat up and folded my arms across my chest. The way his eyes bored into mine was making this difficult. "No," I said before changing my mind. "Go!" I aimed my pointer finger at the other bed.

Mr. Cocky and Beautiful shot me that maddening smirk. "So, Ms. Long, before I unfortunately have to leave, can you tell me if I should put this room on my list of client expenses?"

"Stop procrastinating!" I playfully hit his bare chest with one of the pillows. When I thought about it more, I shouldn't have been so frivolous. I was going to have to be extra careful working with Jaime, with his ruthless stepfather, Victor Holden, watching our every move with his vicious daughter on the sidelines.

"And should I bill time for this?" In a breath, Jaime rolled on top of me, flattening me on the mattress. He smashed his lips against mine with a fierce kiss that all but melted me, and then slipped his hand beneath my lace-trimmed bottoms. He fingered his way to my clit, quickly setting me on fire. I groaned.

"You don't really want me to leave," he breathed into

my ear.

Confession: No, I didn't. Flames licked my clit as his fingers circled my bud vigorously, bringing me closer to imploding with each rotation. I fisted his silky hair and moaned, "Don't stop."

"Don't worry," he replied with a devilish grin.

With a hot breath of relief, I could feel his cock hardening and elongating, growing thicker and more heated by the second. My body was desperate for him. Consumed with feverish desire, I moved one hand to the waistband of his pajama bottom and fumbled with the drawstring to loosen it.

"Good girl, Gloria." Pleased, he raised his torso just slightly, enabling me to lower his bottoms. My hand skimmed his rock-hard ass. *What an ass!*

"Lift up!" he ordered.

I did as bid, and he pulled down my baby doll bottoms as far as they would go. "I should have just torn them off you," he mumbled under his breath as my feet wiggled out of them.

With a powerful thrust of his knees, he spread my legs wide and then plunged his hot, pulsing cock into me, burying it deeper and deeper. A loud, satisfied sigh met his penetration.

"Jesus, angel, you're so wet and ready for me." He anchored his hands on the mattress to support himself and began to pump in and out of me. I pulled at his hair as my body bucked with his. Up and down. Perfectly in sync.

"So. Do. You. Still. Want. Me. In. The. Other. Bed?" he grunted with each determined bang.

"No!" I gasped. He was hitting my G-spot repeatedly. Oh, God! I was falling apart at the seams. With ecstasy.

A triumphant smile splayed on his face. "That's what I thought."

He picked up his pace with each long, hard stroke. Moving my hands, I gripped his buns of steel, pressing them forward with his thrusts, though, trust me, assistance was the last thing he needed. I just needed something solid to hold on to—to keep me grounded. Rocking with him, I squeezed my eyes shut. Sparks shot through me—everywhere—as my body prepared to burst into flames with out-of-this-world pleasure. *Oh, God!* I was not going to last much longer.

His voice pierced me. "Gloria, open your eyes. I want you to watch me come."

I did as he asked and drank in the intensity that lusted on his sweat-laced face. His half-moon eyes sucked me in and his luscious lips parted with pants of desire. His pulsating cock let me know he was on the verge.

"Now!" he shouted. He let out a loud savage sound from deep inside him and arched his back, throwing back his head. We climaxed together. His cock exploded while my core lit up like a disco with strobing bright lights. The song "Gloria" played in my head. *Oh, oh, oh, calling Gloria.*

"Gloria, that was fucking amazing."

Yes, it was. Fucking. Amazing.

Catching his breath, he sunk his head into the thick fold of my cleavage. I wrapped one arm around his sweat-drenched body and threaded the fingers of the other through his damp, tousled locks. Closing my eyes, I hummed the melody of "Gloria." Except all the voices in my head were calling his name.

We were too wound up to go to sleep. Too wound up with each other.

Repositioned on my back, my head resting on his bare, rugged chest and my legs tangled with his, I asked him something that had been on my mind ever since I'd first met him. "Mr. Zander, are you into BDSM?"

He chuckled. "No, angel. My shrink says I'm a just a creative control freak with kinky tendencies."

Semantics.

"Do you get off on physically hurting women?" My heartbeat accelerated going into this dangerous territory. Given that his mother had destroyed his beloved father, the psychologist in me thought it was likely though he'd never physically harmed me.

"It's not my thing." He planted a tender kiss on my cheek. "Besides, angel, you're like the lace you wear. Beautiful and fragile, easily torn. I could never hurt you."

Inwardly, I heaved a sigh of relief. I'd already had enough emotional and physical pain in my life. The lace analogy struck a deep chord inside me.

He played with my braid. "So I assume after that mind-blowing fuck it's okay for me to sleep with you." A statement not a question.

"Don't assume anything." *Mr. Presumptuous!* I had to show him that I had some power. That he couldn't always fuck me into submission.

We had a stare-off. His intense denim blues and cocky half smile were wearing me down. God, he was sexy and beautiful! Every nerve was buzzing. I wanted him all over me again. *And again.* Finally, before I caved in, I said, "If you don't leave this bed, I will."

"You're a tough client." With a roll of his eyes, he climbed out of the bed and nestled into the other one to my left. He turned off the overhead light between us.

"Sweet dreams, Ms. Long."

"Sweet dreams, Mr. Zander," I parroted before drifting off.

I'm running through a black tunnel. I can see nothing in front of me, nothing behind me. My legs propel me as fast as they can; my lungs burn. My heavy breaths and footsteps pierce the darkness. I can't let him find me. I can't! Suddenly, footsteps thunder behind me. I steal a glance backward; I see nothing, but the footsteps are getting louder and faster; they're gaining on me. I try to run faster, but my legs won't let me.

"Nobody steals from Boris Borofsky!" The accented voice booms behind me. "You will pay!"

"No!" I scream silently. I must escape. Oh God, where is the light? Where is the end? Will I always be on the run?

A deafening blast echoes in the endless chamber of darkness. And then another. A bolt of white light scorches through my body. Red-hot liquid streams down my flesh. I keep running. I must keep running! I can never stop running! Oh the pain!

Screaming, I bolted to an upright position. The hot liquid in my dream was now a rush of cold sweat, and it was pouring out of every crevice of my quaking body. Two strong arms wrapped around my drenched torso and pulled me against a slab of warm, rippled flesh.

"Gloria, what is it? Are you okay?" Jaime's deep, velvety voice filtered into my ears. I let myself sink into him, shuddering against his manly, hard chest. His warmth blanketed me.

I took several deep, calming breaths just like my shrink instructed me to do after one of these mind-shattering dreams. Words, however, stayed trapped in my throat.

Still holding me, Jaime smoothed my damp, matted hair.

"It's okay, angel. I've got you. Why are you shaking?"

I moistened my parched palate with my tongue and found my voice. "It was just a bad dream." *My forever nightmare.*

"Do you want to tell me about it?" His voice was soft and full of compassion.

"I can't." At least right then, I couldn't. I wasn't ready to confide in this man—to tell him my secret. Though he had shared his scars, mine was still my cross to bear alone—with the exceptions of Kevin, who had lived it, and Madame Paulette, who had taken it to her grave.

"Come on, let's go back to sleep." He gently lowered me to the bed, and tucked me back in like a child. He kissed me lightly on the lips before lowering himself next to me.

"I don't think this is a good idea," I whispered.

His beautiful agile fingers traced my face. "Gloria, I'm not going to ravage you. I'm just going to hold you. You need me. Now roll over."

I did as he asked and felt my body cocooned in his. He draped his arms around me, one hand brushing across my scar. My body softened against his as his heartbeat soothed my soul. For the first time in my life, I truly felt safe. There were so many things this gorgeous man could do to me. And needing him right now was one of them.

"Gloria, you've got to learn to trust me. Even with your secrets." He gently kissed my head. "Now, sleep, my angel. I've got a big day planned for us tomorrow."

Spooned in the safe harbor of his arms, I couldn't battle the weight of my heavy eyelids. Before I could tell him that I was heading back to Los Angeles first thing in the morning, sleep took hold of me.

CHAPTER 37

Jaime

S leep claimed Gloria quickly. I, in contrast, had insomnia. As I held her against me, my arm draped over her, all my senses were activated. The taste of her lingered on my tongue, and I could hear her soft breathing, smell her essence, feel her heart beat in my palm, and glimpse her exquisite profile from the corner of my eye. Illuminated by the sliver of light that filtered into the room, she now looked so peaceful. Like the angel she was.

This had been a day of many firsts. The first time I'd pursued a woman, traveling halfway around the world to find her. The first time I'd ever bathed a woman. The first time I'd ever opened up to a woman—or anyone for that matter except my shrink—about my past. And the first time I was spending the night with a woman in bed. Because I wanted to.

But it went beyond these milestones. And the sex. There was a current between us, an electric spark that stemmed from so much more than chemistry or lust. A powerful, emotional connection that surged from some place deep inside me. Emotions I'd never felt before.

This was the first time I'd ever cared about a woman.

I wanted to be there for her.

Protect her.

Whatever the cost. Even if it meant putting my life on the line.

I hugged her closer to me, eliciting a contented *mmm*. Below on the street, the sounds of Paris nightlife droned in my ears. Still unable to sleep, I slid out of the bed and headed to the small balcony off our bedroom. Quietly, I opened the French doors and slipped outside, standing bare chested in the cold air on the small wrought iron terrace. The chill of the air against my skin felt good and brought me clarity.

I took in the twinkling lights, the lit up Eiffel tower in the distance, as well as the sight and sound of young lovers frolicking on the street below. Listening to their laughter. Spying on their kisses. Smiling at their youth.

Though I was no longer a smoker, something I gave up in my twenties, I craved a cigarette. To inhale and exhale. And blow out rings of gray in the air. Suppressing my urge, I replayed the earlier events of today in my head. Chasing after Gloria. Being stopped in my tracks by the Feds. My clandestine meeting. All that was said. What I needed to do. Had fate brought me to Victor and Paris and allowed me to save Gloria from the unscrupulous bastard? Was this all meant to be?

They had presented a game plan. A risky one. One that could blow up in my face and cost Gloria her business. And totally blow apart my relationship with her on every level. Professional and personal.

Then, there was the other side, I could make it work.

No risk no gain. A blast of cold air blew through me. Right then and there, I made my decision. *Les jeux sont faits.* The die was cast. I'd contact them in the morning and confirm they could count on me.

The chill ran through me and I hugged myself to fend it off. Or maybe to embrace it. Revenge is a dish best served cold.

Then, I headed back inside, closing the doors behind me.

Gloria murmured my name, and at the sight of the beautiful woman in my bed who needed me as much as I needed her, I stood by my decision. It was a complex game I had to play. Made more complicated by the fact she still didn't trust me. And despite the game player I was, I wasn't sure of my next move. There was one unsettling question.

Who in the end would be the pawn?

As I crawled back into bed, cradling Gloria again in my arms, I shoved this unknown to the back of my mind and focused only on the what is.

Gloria, Paris, and me.

CHAPTER 38

Gloria

I woke up in the morning in the same position I'd fallen asleep. Blinking one sleepy eye open after the other, I glanced at the alarm clock on the night stand—6:05 a.m.—and then cranked my neck to look at the man who was holding me. He was still sound asleep, soft rhythmic breaths emanating from his perfect, parted lips. Wisps of his tousled hair tumbled onto his forehead and a thicker layer of stubble laced his face. God, he was beautiful in the morning.

And the first man I'd ever spent the night with.

Resisting the urge to run my fingers over his fine features, I carefully rolled away from him, hoping not to wake him.

He stirred. "Gloria," he moaned, sexy morning gravel in his voice. He stirred again, but to my relief, his eyes remained shut. A dreamy smile played across his peaceful face. I wondered—could he be dreaming about me?

I tiptoed over to the luggage rack, where my suitcase was sitting. Rifling through the contents, I found something comfortable to wear on my long flight back to Los Angeles—a pair of pink sweats and a matching hoodie. I decided to forego underwear. All I wanted to feel was the softness of the fleece against my skin. And the memory of Jaime Zander's touch everywhere.

I lifted off my baby doll top, stepped out of the matching bikini bottoms, and then folded them neatly into my suitcase. Mementos of our night. As I reached for the sweats, a breath of hot air descended on my neck and two powerful arms cinched my waist. His bare silky chest brushed against my back. He was up.

"Where do you think you're going, Ms. Long?" Jaime purred. His velvety lips nuzzled the uber-sensitive spot on my neck just below my ear. My skin prickled all over.

I squirmed, trying to break loose of his grip. "I'm going back to LA. My plane departs this morning."

He tightened his grip with one hand, and tugged my disheveled braid with the other. "You're not going any-where. We're in Paris. I have the whole day planned, and maybe a special treat in store for you this evening."

Special treat? The words sent a flood of goosebumps to my skin. I was intrigued and tempted, but I stuck to my guns.

"Really, I've got to get back. I've been out of my office for more than a week."

"Bullshit. Your office is closed today. It's President's Day."

He was right. *Think, Gloria, think*. Except it was hard to think with this sex god nibbling at my earlobes. A bolt of unexpected erotic pleasure zapped me. I was heating up.

"I've got a lot of paperwork to do and emails to catch up on," I stammered.

"Me too," he breathed into my ear. "We can get things done here. Plus, we can get a head start on your ad cam-paign."

I had to get used to the idea that this impossible man and I would be working together. The obstacles ahead—salacious Victor and his predatory daughter Vivien—flew into my head, sending a chill down my spine. And I still wasn't sure how I was going to manage our physical relationship or my emotions. Feeling me tense up, Jaime massaged my upper back.

"Let me think about it," I managed as he pressed his lips to my shoulder blades and trailed them down my spine with deliciously ticklish flutter kisses.

"Angel, don't overthink because there's nothing to think about."

I closed my eyes, my mind filled only with the sweet sensation of his kisses. Oh, God! I was melting into him. My body slackening with pleasure, it took all I had to stay on track.

"Let go of me. I need to get dressed," I pleaded.

He let out a loud, exaggerated sigh. "Oh, Gloria, must I?"

Still clutching me with one arm, he leaned over me and dug his spare hand into my suitcase. He rummaged through my neatly folded garments.

"What the hell are you doing?" I quipped.

"Security check. Looking for a dangerous weapon."

What!?

"Bingo!" he exclaimed as he pulled out one of my sheer silk stockings. "You're under arrest."

"Huh?"

Before I could get my mouth to close, he yanked my arms behind my back with such force a painful pull ripped across my shoulder blades. Then with one hand, he gripped both my wrists.

"What are you doing, you crazy asshole?" I cried out, trying impossibly to free myself.

"You're going to pay, my sweetness, for calling me that."

I swallowed hard, still writhing.

With his spare hand, he began binding my hands together with the stocking. I felt him tie a tight knot. I couldn't even wiggle my fingers. They were bound together so tightly I was sure my circulation had been cut off.

"Untie me, you bastard! You can't do this to me." I wheeled around. A diabolical smirk played on his gorgeous face. Damn him! He could.

"I'm going to call security," I threatened.

Jaime bent over with laughter. "Oh, so you're going to dial the room phone with your nose?" He lightly flicked the tip of my nose with his thumb. "And then you're going to unlock the door with that talented mouth of yours and let Mr. Security see you tied up and naked?" He playfully traced the outline of my lips.

I screwed up my face.

"You're so cute when you do that."

I was so fuming mad I could scream, but before I could get a sound out, my cell phone rang from inside my handbag.

"I need to get that. It could be some kind of emergency."

The ringing stopped. And then it picked up again.

"Mr. Zander, would you be kind enough to retrieve my phone, press answer, and then put it to my ear."

"Say please."

"Please," I grumbled. "It's in the zipper compartment of my purse."

With a wicked grin, he did as I asked. My monstrous bag was parked on the dresser across from the beds. My eyes stayed fixed on him as he strode over to it, soaking in his broad shoulders, rippled back, and boyishly narrow hips. His beauty made his canvas of scars almost invisible.

He found the phone easily and headed back to me with it in his hand. It kept ringing.

He hovered over me. "Tell whoever it is you're tied up."

That was a fact.

I gazed at the screen. It was Kevin.

Jaime pressed answer and then held the phone to my ear.

"Hi, Kev. Is everything okay?" My voice faltered.

"More than okay. I'm just checking up on you. You sound strange. Are you okay?"

"Yeah. I'm just a little tied up at the moment." *Did I really just say that?*

Jaime rewarded me with a chaste kiss on top of my head. Kev continued.

"Did everything go smoothly with Madame Paulette's funeral?"

"Yes. It was a beautiful service. Thanks so much for helping."

"Say good-bye," Jaime breathed against my neck, his lips skimming my sensitive skin. He simultaneously draped his free arm over my shoulder, crossing my chest until he was coddling my breasts. He began to massage them. A delicious chill shimmied down my spine, erasing the sad memory of my beloved mentor and friend.

"When are you coming back?" asked Kevin.

"Um, uh, tomorrow. I'm going to stay in Paris an extra day."

Jaime rewarded me this time with a squeeze of each nipple. They instantly grew into pointed crowns as he twirled them between his forefingers and thumbs. My temperature was rising. He tweaked them again, the heat between my legs making it almost impossible to talk. I moaned into the phone; Kevin heard it.

"Is Jaime there?"

I gulped. I couldn't hide anything from Kevin.

"Yes."

"A YES right back at you! I know all about Vivien hitting on him. He's a good guy. Paris is the City of Love. You should let him fuck your brains out."

Kev never held back. Never. "I'm thinking about it."

"Oh, Glorious, I wish you could see me. I'm doing a

happy dance."

I could actually picture Kevin doing a little jig. Not wanting to dwell on Jaime, I changed the subject. "And what about you?"

"I'm still in New York . . ."

"With . . ."

"Ray. He's the one who told me about Vivien. Oh, and he's fucking amazing."

I mentally jolted. Kevin and Ray were getting it on? While I was thrilled for my best friend in the world, this entangled business relationship was growing more complicated and crazier by the minute. Maybe I should end it.

Jaime nibbled my earlobe. "Say good-bye," he breathed again. "And then say hello to this." He dragged his thick erection along my backside. His heat penetrated my skin, sending embers to the pit of my stomach. Wetness pooled between my legs. Oh God. He was making me lose control again.

"Kev, I've got to go," I stammered.

Kevin let out a laugh. "Don't let me keep you from sightseeing."

The only sightseeing in my near future was the monument between Jaime's legs.

As we exchanged good-byes, Jaime tossed the phone across the room into my open handbag. "Now, spread your legs and bend over," he ordered.

I did as he asked, pressing my head to the soft mattress. My hands remained tied up behind me. They were beginning to go numb.

"I'll be right back. Don't move." He strode off.

Cranking my neck, I sneaked a peek behind me and saw that he was rummaging through my luggage again. Now what? My eyes grew wide as he retrieved a half-used jar of our bestselling Gloria's Secret moisturizer. Unscrewing the top, he dipped his hand inside, scooping out a generous dollop of the cream with his fingers. Then, I watched as he spread the thick cream all over his thick cock, stroking it as if he were playing with himself. Making himself hard. And so big. Shocked by the enormity of his organ, I turned my head to face the bed as he made his way back to me.

"Good girl, Gloria," he beamed, having no clue I'd watched his actions.

The pleasing scent of the coconut cream drifted up my nose as he stood behind me. On my next inhale, Mr. Impossible clutched my butt cheeks and then kneaded them. "This must be the finest view in all of Paris," he purred. "You've got one magnificent ass."

Before I could say a word, he rubbed the head of his thick, coated shaft up and down the crack of my butt. Though I didn't feel much sensation, it was strangely erotic. A hand moved between my thighs, his fingers finding their way to my aching clit. He stroked my sensitive folds and then rubbed circles around my nub. Now, that I felt.

"Mmm. You're so wet for me, angel."

A muffled moan escaped my throat as he continued his ministrations.

"I'm going to fuck your beautiful ass. Have you ever been fucked this way before?"

"No," I managed with a shake of my head.

"Good. You're going to love it."

He rubbed his rigid cock along my wet folds. It didn't stay there long—just long enough to bathe in my hot juices. His fingers released my clit, and the next thing I knew his hands, one of them warm and wet, were spreading my ass cheeks apart. I felt his hot crown nudging at my opening. I wasn't sure about this. With my head still pressed against the bed, I squeezed my eyes shut. His cock was so insanely big. A battle between fear and desire warred between my legs.

Every muscle in my body tensed.

"Relax, Gloria. This may hurt at first, but once I'm inside you're going to wish I never left."

I took a deep breath, preparing myself for his invasion.

He penetrated me and I winced. Then, slowly he began to fill me, sliding his lubricated cock straight to my center. I clenched my weeping pussy. It hurt like hell, but not as much as I thought it would. I kept on taking deep breaths as he stretched me, his warm hands splayed on my hips to hold me steady. When I began to relax, the pain morphed into tortuous pleasure. The fullness of his slick length inside my virgin hole sent a blast of erotic sensations through my body that I wasn't expecting.

"Jesus. You're so hot and tight. Are you okay?"

I simply nodded into the bed. My brain had forgotten how to send words to my voice box. All I could think about was him dominating me this way.

He caressed my ass. "Good, angel. Keep breathing." He slowly withdrew and then pushed forward, again slow and deep. I groaned, growing fonder of the snugness. His pelvic bones slammed against me as he repeated the movement and picked up his pace. Moaning, I found myself rocking back and forth with his thrusts, each one more intense. Each one more divine. The burning fire inside me was making me delirious. I was loving it.

"This will make it even more pleasurable." His fingers moved back to my throbbing clit, and he began to rub it vigorously. A scream escaped my throat. His other hand clutched my left butt cheek, still steadying me as he dragged his length up and down my tender hole.

"Oh, angel," he groaned, his breathing harsh. "You feel fucking incredible. So wet and hot everywhere. How does it feel for you?"

I was totally losing it. The hot tingles between my legs

mingled with the fiery friction of his thrusts. The insane pressure inside me was building like a rockslide. He was doing it again—sending me over a cliff. Making me lose control.

"I'm going to come!" I cried out.

"Not yet!" he growled.

Oh, God. I was so close to the edge. How was I going to hang on? And then a new mind-blowing sensation blew through me. Two slick fingers plunged into my other opening and began sliding up and down, hitting my hot spot again and again. He was finger fucking and butt fucking me in tandem. I began to whimper. I thought I would pass out right on the bed. *Oh, please let me come*!

As I raced toward orgasm, Jaime continued to work me on both ends. His panting accelerated with his relentless thrusts. My body was convulsing. I could hold on no longer. The pressure was so intense I was actually seeing stars.

"Please!" I pleaded, lifting my head from the bed and twisting it so that I could see his face. His expression was sexy and savage. His tousled hair fell into his hooded eyes; sweat beads dusted his skin, and his parted mouth curved in a dangerous pout. His lustful eyes met mine. Filled with fire and determination.

"Now, Gloria. Fall apart, now!" he commanded.

I screamed as everything inside me broke loose. Waves of ecstasy wracked my body, spasm after spasm. He shoved his two fingers and his cock deep inside me one more time, and then with a roar, he climaxed violently inside me. Hot cum seeped into my backside while juices seeped out the depths of my core. His intense vibrations collided with mine. With one more thrust, this one softer, he finished off his orgasm and made me come with fury once again. *Holy fuck!*

I buried my head back into the bed as he eased out of me. He was right yet again. I was bereft. I missed his fullness already.

On my next harsh breath, he untied my hands, and after wiggling my fingers to bring back sensation, I just let my arms hang lose by the sides of my legs; I couldn't walk if you paid me. As I hung like a rag doll, Jaime ran his warm velvety tongue down my spine and then back up, sending a rush of goosebumps to my already prickling skin.

He gave my ass a playful slap. "You're free to go back to LA now, angel."

I wasn't going anywhere.

Paris was for lovers.

CHAPTER 39

Jaime

That was just for starters. I knew she wasn't going anywhere without me. After a delicious, hot shower during which I fucked her once more against the wall, I ordered room service. Scrumptious flakey croissants and steaming café au lait that we savored around a small round table. Both of us wearing fluffy terry cloth robes that came with the room, I told her what I'd planned for the day. It was going to be a leisurely day of strolling around Paris and taking in a few sights and museums. And of course, a stop for lunch and a glass of wine at a neighborhood bistro.

Sipping her frothy coffee, Gloria piped in. "I can't do lunch."

I cocked a brow. "You have other plans?" *What the fuck?*

Taking another sip, she nodded. Before jealousy reared its ugly head, she informed me that she wanted to head over to her Paris flagship store on the Champs-Elysées. "I want to see how things are going and above all personally thank the store manager Sandrine, for helping me with my friend's funeral arrangements by taking her out for a bite."

While I was relieved she wasn't seeing another man, I felt snubbed. It shocked me how possessive I'd become of her in such a short time. Maybe fucking someone you genuinely cared about and wanted to be with did that to you. To rile her up a little, I told her I had personal stuff to take care of, too, including seeing a client.

"You have a client in Paris?" she asked, her voice a mixture of surprise and suspicion.

"Angel, I have clients all over the world." Grinning, I bit into my almond croissant. "Emmanuel happens to be one of my favorite."

"Emmanuelle?" Gloria's eyes grew round, her brows lifting. "What does *she* look like?"

I inwardly chuckled. Gloria had a jealous streak, too, and it turned me on. Beneath the table, my cock stirred as I played right into her false assumption. "Seriously, what does it matter?"

She tore off a piece of her butter croissant and shoved it into her mouth. Her brows creased as she slowly chewed it and then swallowed. "You're right. It doesn't matter."

HA! I knew how to get to her. She was totally flustered. All hot and bothered and she was doing a lousy job pretending she wasn't. My dick grew harder.

With a smug smirk, I flicked a crumb of the croissant off her bottom lip. "What are you planning to wear today?"

"Seriously, what does it matter?" Her sarcastic tone parroted my earlier words.

Adding another sugar cube to my coffee, I feigned innocence and shrugged one shoulder. "I was just curious."

"Fine." Her lips twisted. "Black leggings and a heavy cashmere sweater. I want to be comfortable."

"Sounds perfect, Ms. Matchy-matchy Girl."

Polishing off my croissant, I stood up and ambled back to her open suitcase. Neatly arranged was a treasure trove of scanty lace bras and bikinis. A saucy smile that she couldn't see played on my face as I examined each and every piece of the sexy lingerie.

"What the hell are doing?" Her voice was shrill.

I looked over my shoulder. "What does it look like? I'm choosing your underwear."

"No way." Reddening with rage, she leaped up from her chair and stomped over to me. Snatching the matching leopard-print bra and thong out of my hands, she flung them back into the suitcase. Stifling laughter, I held my hands up in surrender as if I were being arrested.

"Come on, Gloria. Call it research. I'm getting a really good feel for the Gloria's Secret line . . . and for the woman behind it."

Wrinkling her nose, she looked me straight in the eye. "And what does your research tell you about me?"

I nuzzled her sensitive neck. The sensation forced her head to loll and her eyelids to lower. My dick hard as stone, I began to slide her robe down her shoulders.

"Well, Mr. Zander . . ."

Her skin seared my fingertips as I slipped the robe off her, letting it puddle on the floor. I purred in her ear. "That you're dripping with desire."

Her breath hitched, and as I tweaked them, her nipples flexed. I was right. She was desperate for me.

"And I'm going to prove my theory."

In one swift move, I scooped her up in my arms and tossed her onto the bed. Disrobing, I crashed upon her with my weight, and in an instant, my cock was inside her, pounding her without mercy. Effortlessly. My tempo accelerating with each thrust because just as I'd predicted, she was soaking wet. My climax was building with the force of an avalanche. I couldn't believe how fast she could make me come. With one final bang, I exploded inside her as she juddered around me.

"Holy fuck!" we moaned in unison.

Our sweat-slicked, heaving bodies stayed still in that

position for several long minutes, allowing our breathing to calm down.

"Paris awaits us, angel," I said brightly after smacking her lips with a hot, impetuous kiss.

"Have you decided on what undies I should wear?" she asked coyly, threading her fingers through my mussed hair.

"Yeah . . . none."

Her jaw slackened.

"I want to imagine you just the way you are all day long."

CHAPTER 40

Gloria

We spent the day meandering through Paris, staying close to the Left Bank. Neither of us wanted to risk the chance of running into Victor, who never strayed from the Right Bank and would likely take his business meeting at The InterContinental. The weather, like in New York, was surprisingly mild for this time of year. Global warming, I supposed. I couldn't complain, however, about the pleasant temperature and sunny sky.

We took in several of the famous Rive Gauche monuments—The Panthéon, The Sorbonne, Notre Dame to name a few. To be honest, I had never really gone sightseeing in Paris before. My trips, always rushed, were strictly for business—be it to catch a fashion show, explore new trends, or visit the Champs-Elysées store. Having this god-like tour guide beside me added to both the beauty and my enjoyment of the City of Light. As we strolled along the Seine, arm in arm, en route to The Louvre, I couldn't help noticing how many female heads he turned. I stole a glance at his face and could understand why. His profile with its strong dimpled chin, manly straight nose, and thick-lashed eyes arrestingly gorgeous. He still hadn't shaven—the thicker than usual layer of stubble making him even sexier. My heart fluttered. No man had ever had this effect on me. He had made me fall apart. And now, I was falling for him. In just one week, this man had captured me, both physically and emotionally. He was in my bloodstream, bringing me to new levels of sensuality and self-awareness I'd never known. Unable to get enough of him, I was worried about working with him professionally. The uncertainty of the future and the challenges ahead sent a shiver skittering down my spine. I had to admit—I was afraid of getting hurt, and the threat that both Victor and Vivien posed didn't help. I wished I could share everything with Madame Paulette. She'd know what to do. Her last words to me swirled around in my head. "It *eez* better to have loved . . ." I still wasn't sure what I felt. *Just enjoy the moment, Gloria*, I told myself, taking a deep breath as we approached the majestic Louvre.

Experiencing The Louvre with Jaime was something else and not just because every female tourist from eighteen to eighty had eyes for him as if he were some rare Greek statue. As we glided from one gallery of paintings to another, Jaime, who was truly more beautiful than any of the museum's god-like male sculptures, came alive like I'd never seen before. His blue eyes glistened, and his voice was animated as he explained the significance and details of each masterpiece.

"How do you know so much about art?" I asked him, in awe of his knowledge. It actually turned me on, but I wasn't going to share that with him.

"My father." His voice was coated with melancholy. "Though he never fulfilled his dream of coming to Paris, he took me to museums in Los Angeles and had tons of art books that he shared with me. He would play games with me—make me guess the name of a painter or race with him to find a particular painting. Or show me tricks."

"What kind of tricks?" I asked as we stood before the *Mona Lisa.*

"Look at the *Mona Lisa's* eyes. They'll follow yours."

I gazed at the painting and shifted my eyes to the right. Sure enough, the iconic beauty's eyes followed mine. "Wow! That's incredible!"

We continued to study the hypnotic painting.

"Who were your father's favorite painters?" I asked.

Jaime smiled wistfully. "He admired so many, but his favorite was Van Gogh."

"Why Van Gogh?"

"I think he connected to his tortured life . . . his inner demons."

The paintings I'd seen in both his office space and hotel suite flashed into my head. They had actually reminded me a lot of Van Gogh's work, with their vivid colors and turbulent brush strokes.

Seeking confirmation, I queried, "Those paintings in your office and at the hotel . . . did your father paint them?"

Jaime's smile widened. Pride washed over his face. "Yes. I'm glad you noticed them. When he died, I secretly gathered all his paintings and hid them in storage until I could display them. One day, when I have time, I'm going to exhibit them. I want my father to have the glory he deserved."

"They're pretty amazing."

"You're pretty amazing, Ms. Long."

Gripping my shoulders, he spun me around and crushed his beautifully etched lips onto mine with a bruising, passionate kiss. A moan escaped my throat as he deepened the kiss with his velvety tongue. Oh, God, he tasted divine! Our tongues danced, swirling together in figure eights. Tingles shot down my body, from my head to my toes. I swear if we weren't in a public place, I would have let this masterpiece of a man fuck me right here and now and let the *Mona Lisa* watch with her magical eyes.

After a quick espresso at a nearby café and another long, delicious tongue-driven kiss, Jaime and I went our separate ways. Him to visit that mysterious client, who I still didn't trust, and me to visit the Gloria's Secret store on the busy Champs-Elysées.

I was happy to see that our first Paris store was bustling with customers. I took special satisfaction in knowing that even Parisian women were gobbling up our reasonably priced American-made lingerie when they had the most exquisite underwear in the world at their fingertips. I found Sandrine quickly. Dressed in head to toe black with the exception of a colorful silk scarf knotted around her neck, the slim, spiky-haired woman epitomized French chic. She was showing a young attractive salesgirl how to re-stack bikinis and bras after they had been mussed up by customers. I found it so annoying that customers were often such slobs, with no sympathy for the low-paid, hard-working sales assistants who had to clean up after their rummaging.

Sandrine spotted me immediately and ran over to me with open arms. We exchanged a typically French double cheek embrace.

"*Ça va?*" she asked.

"*Ça va bien.*" I replied. "*Merci beaucoup* for helping me with Madame Paulette's burial."

"*Pas de problème.* I'm so sorry for your loss." Like many Europeans, Sandrine spoke perfect English though she liked to throw in a little French. I, in turn, could conduct a conversation with her in French, thanks to Madame

Paulette's tutelage.

Sandrine was one of my favorite and most respected store managers. She was bright, organized, and always one step ahead. She ran the store with both a smile and an iron fist. Recently, at the age of thirty-two, she had become engaged to a successful, handsome doctor.

"Do you have a little time? I'd love to take you out for lunch to thank you for helping me and to celebrate your engagement."

"For you, I always have *zee* time," she said brightly.

We ended up going to a lively café that was a few doors down from the store. Over champagne and salads, we caught up on business and then moved on to personal stuff. She was getting married in April—it was going to be a big Jewish wedding at her family's country home in Provence.

"My *maman eez* driving me crazy!" she sighed. "Everything she loves, I detest. Can you imagine . . . she wants jars of butterflies on every table that *zee* guests will set free after we say our vows!"

I laughed lightly. "At least you have a mother who cares about you," I countered. A wistful expression fell over me. Sandrine was one of the few people, other than Kevin and Madame Paulette, who knew about my crack whore mother.

She twitched a guilty smile. "You are right. She means well." She sipped her champagne. "I hope you will come."

I let her know I wouldn't miss it for the world. A big smile spread across her face.

"What about you, Gloria? *Eez* there anyone new in your life?"

Blushing, I shook my head and said, "Not really."

"Gloria, I don't believe you. Your face gives *eet* away. Spill *zee* beans as you Americans say."

Draining my champagne, I broke down and told her all about Jaime—including the complications with Victor and

Vivien, whom she openly despised.

"Mon dieu! This *eez* heavy. But I would have given my tongue to *zee* cat to see Vivien's expression when she saw you and Jaime kissing at *zee* restaurant. *La putain!"*

I couldn't stop laughing. She'd just called Vivien a whore! Like Kevin, Sandrine could be so brutally honest. And a bit wicked. That's why I adored her.

She munched on some greens. "So what does Monsieur Zahn-deur look like?"

The way she breathily said his name with her French accent sent me over the moon. I described Jaime to her, from head to toe, as if he were a painting in The Louvre. The words came so easily. In my mind, he was a work of art.

"He sounds like a hottie!"

I giggled. Usually the word "hottie" made me cringe, but the way Sandrine said it—HAH-tee—was charming. My cheeks heated.

My delightful French friend and colleague took another sip of her champagne. "Gloria, are you in love with him?"

"I've only known him for a week."

"You didn't answer my question."

A loud sigh escaped my lungs.

"Ah, Gloria, you are! You are! *Mazel tov!"*

I remembered Madame Paulette once telling me that sometimes *l'amour* slinks up to you like a cat; other times it attacks you like a lion. Jaime Zander was a sexy beast who had all but devoured me. I could no longer deny my feelings. Yes, I was hopelessly, helplessly head over heels in love with him.

My heart began to roar at the very thought of him touching me. Longing and lust surged through my body. I grasped my friend's French manicured hand and murmured, "Sandrine, what should I do?"

"It *eez* simple. Don't let him go."

I smiled back. It never ceased to amaze me how wise French women were.

"But don't tell him you love him until he tells *eet* to you." More words of wisdom.

We finished our salads and the check came. As we hugged good-bye, my sage friend whispered into my ear, "I'll see the future Monsieur and Madame Zahn-deur at my wedding."

CHAPTER 41

Jaime

The left-bank restaurant where I was meeting Emmanu-el—or Mani as he was known to everyone—was not far from the Louvre or his office on the Rue de Rivoli. It felt good to walk in the unseasonably warm Paris air, and I loosened the scarf around my neck as I did. Taking brisk steps, I was glad I wasn't stuck in the insane Paris traffic. Seriously, it made being stuck in Manhattan traffic feel like a drive in the country. Well, not quite, but at least New Yorkers stayed in lanes, and with the no honking law, cabs were no longer as disruptive as they used to be.

Approaching the bistro, I spotted my friend seated at a table outside. I broke into a jog and when we met, he rose and we gave each other man hugs. Like me, the hefty, jovial man was wearing a leather jacket, jeans, and a scarf. A bright smile beamed on his bearded face and his chocolate brown eyes twinkled.

"*Bonjour, mon ami,*" he piped as we patted each other's backs. "*Ça va?*"

"I'm great. What about you?"

"*Fantastique.* Are you okay with eating outdoors? The weather is *magnifique* so I thought we'd take advan-*teege.*"

"Fine with me," I replied, taking the seat opposite his.

Over apératives, we caught up on business. We were

both thriving. Thanks to my sexy, cutting-edge advertising campaign for the French Bureau of Tourism—"Come to the country that put the OOH in Ooh La La"—I'd turned things around for Emanuel whose country had been hit hard by recent waves of terrorism. French tourism was now at an all time high. Fifty-percent higher than the year before at this time, and this year's first quarter numbers were looking to exceed all records.

Mani ordered a bottle of Bordeaux and we both ordered the plat du jour. The wine came quickly and Mani proposed a toast to our success. Clinking our glasses, we each took a long sip of the velvety rich wine. I was familiar with this Bordeaux, but somehow in Paris it tasted so much better. Coincidentally, it was the wine I'd ordered at my dinner with Gloria at Rafael's in New York. Though Mani and I talked business, I kept thinking about her as our main courses arrived. Two steaks au poivre with *frites.*

"How is your wife?" I asked, changing the subject as I dipped one of the skinny fries into the tasty garlic mayonnaise accompaniment.

"Formidable!" We are expecting a third child in September."

He and his lovely wife Françoise already had two kids. A year and a half apart, age seven and five. Amélie and Antoine. I congratulated him and then apologized for not bringing his family souvenirs from New York. They especially liked sports memorabilia like Yankee caps and anything iconic like an Empire State Building keychain.

"It was a spur of the moment trip," I added, cutting into my juicy medium rare steak.

My companion laughed his hearty laugh as I swallowed the tender morsel of meat. *"Pas de problème.* My wife and children have so much stuff we may need to buy a bigger apartment. What do you say in English? Rat packs?"

"Pack rats." My turn to laugh. One of the things I loved about Mani was his sense of humor. He was one of my favorite clients and one of the easiest to work with because of his open mind and big heart. I couldn't say the same about some of my new clients in Japan who had difficulty communicating and rarely cracked a smile.

Mani grabbed a fry. "So, what about you, *mon ami*. What brings you to the City of Love?"

Taking a long sip of my rich wine, I felt myself flush, my body heat. As I set my goblet down, I felt Mani's knowing eyes on me.

"Ah, there *eez* a woman!"

"Yeah." Taking another sip of the wine, I felt my blood heat further and my heartbeat quicken.

"She lives here in Paris?"

"No, she lives in LA."

"You came together on a vacation?"

"No. She came to Paris for personal reasons. I followed her here and surprised her."

"Vraiment?"

"Yeah, really." I felt as sheepish as I sounded. Mani, who considered himself an expert on the subject of love, knew of my history with women. My disposable hooks-ups. He was forever telling me that I needed to find a special woman, settle down, and make beautiful babies.

His face brightened. "She must be very special."

"She is." I didn't go into details about how intriguing and sexy I found Gloria.

"So tell me, what *eez* her name?"

"Gloria." Just saying her name took my breath away. Transported me. I felt my cock flex beneath the table.

"Gloria," my companion repeated, making her name sound even more breathtaking with his French accent. "That *eez* a beautiful name."

I nibbled on another French fry. "Mani, what did you mean when you told me that the real way to a woman's G-spot is through her heart?"

He grinned. "It *eez* simple, *mon ami*. While *zee* sex *eez* important, you must romance her to win her."

All ears, I cocked my head. "You mean like send her flowers and give her jewelry?"

"Not exactly. To woo her, you must personalize them."

My brows lifted. "What do you mean by that?"

"Don't just give her a dozen red roses. A dime a dozen, *n'est-ce pas?* Give her flowers that will—how do you say *eet?*—blow her away. Ones that she favors. And the jewelry should be unique to her—speak to her soul."

I digested his words. Romancing Gloria wasn't going to be easy. Why should I be surprised? Everything about her was a challenge.

"And when you give her these kinds of gifts they must be presented in a very special way. A way she will never forget."

We both cut back into our mouthwatering steaks and drank more wine. By the end of the lunch, I was feeling very sated and very relaxed. And very excited. Mani had shared the name of one of the best florists in Paris as well as that of a nearby antique store that specialized in one-of-a-kind vintage jewelry. The question was: what kind of flowers would appeal to Gloria? As I drained my wine, a thought came to me. Only one person seemed to know her well. On my way to the antique shop, I would text *him*.

The check came. Mani reached for it first. Despite my protest, he insisted on paying for lunch.

"Mon plaisir." He smiled broadly as he slipped his credit card into the bill holder. "And I have something else for you to surprise your Gloria. To make your night in the City of Light unforgettable."

Waiting for our server to return, I listened intently as Mani explained what he had in mind. My eyes lit up like lanterns.

"Holy shit! You would do that for me. Seriously?"

"Seriously." Mani repeated one of my overused words, his accented voice playfully mocking mine.

"But—"

"But nothing, *mon ami*. I owe you. My country owes you. For you, anything in the world I can do."

One hour later, I knew Gloria's preference in flowers and in my pocket was something that spoke to the two of us the minute I set eyes on it in the antique shop. I couldn't wait to give it to her. I began to whistle "Gloria" as I headed back to the hotel, a lightness in my gait from both the wine and drunk desire.

Paris, I decided, was the most beautiful city in the world.

And tonight, if things went to plan, it would be unforgettable.

CHAPTER 42

Gloria

When I got back to our hotel room, I gasped. Dozens of Asiatic lilies and long-stemmed roses in shades of pink, arranged in myriad crystal vases, awaited me. My favorite flowers! How did he know? My heart melted. Mr. Zander was true to his word and a romantic.

I dipped my nose into one of the bouquets and inhaled deeply. The scent was divine. Intoxicating just like him. Any jealousy I harbored over his lunch date evaporated like vapor.

"Hey."

At the sound of his voice, I straightened up and caught sight of him stepping out of the bathroom. He was wearing nothing but a white towel wrapped around his hips. My eyes zeroed in on the deep pelvic V that cut into his body and then traveled up over his washboard abs and toned pecs. God, he was gorgeous! My gaze met his, and my breath hitched.

"They're beautiful!"

"My biceps?"

The egomaniac! I scrunched my nose.

"No, the flowers."

"Thanks." He cocked a bashful smile as though the flowers were an embarrassing afterthought. Our eyes stayed locked on one another. Silence. My pussy was throbbing, my heart pounding. I wanted to be lost in him. Neither of us moved. The seconds felt like hours.

"Come here, you," he said at last, and in a heartbeat, I was in his arms. We were at each other as if an apocalypse was dawning. Kissing, groping, stroking, licking. He lifted my sweater over my head, unable to get it off fast enough. Panting, I kicked off my ballet flats and said good-bye to my leggings. The towel fell off his torso, and we were fused together, flesh to flesh. With his mouth locked on mine, he walked me backward until I was sandwiched between him and a wall.

"Wrap your legs around me, angel," he said, lifting me off my feet.

Our eyes level, I did as he asked, looping my long legs around his waist and my arms around his neck. He gripped my ass to support me. Between my thighs, I felt his hot cock line up with my opening. "Gloria, you don't know how badly I've wanted to have you like this."

"Shut up and fuck me." I couldn't believe my own words. I was begging for him.

"I'm going to give it to you hard."

Oh, yes!

"Promise me you'll scream my name like it's the only word you know."

"Girl Scout's honor!" I rasped even though I'd never been one.

Satisfied, he slammed into me with a powerful thrust, pushing me into the wall with the force of his body. We both cried out with carnal pleasure. As he got into a rhythm, he latched his hungry lips back onto mine, and I moved my hands to his face, cupping it in my palms. Our kiss deepened, our tongues locking together in an erotic dance. We moaned and groaned into each other's mouths.

I squeezed my legs tighter around him as he picked up his pace. My breasts skimmed his chest, and my clit was pressed tight against his pubic bone, making the sensation of every deep thrust so much more intense. I was a sweaty, whimpering bundle of bliss on the verge of a major orgasm.

"Angel, I can't fucking get enough of you," he breathed against my mouth.

And I couldn't get enough of him. The words, "I love you" were on the tip of my tongue, but I bit down on it to hold them back. Sandrine was right. He had to say them first. I drank in his sexy, heated face, longing for those three little words to form on his lips.

"Does this feel good?" he asked instead, his breathing harsh. "Is it hard enough for you?"

"Yes!" I gasped. I was losing all control, a breath away from detonating.

"Good," he grunted out.

"Please make me come. Please!"

He smiled fiendishly. "Angel, hold on. I'm going to take you to the moon."

A squeeze of my clit, and that's all it took. I screamed his name until my voice was hoarse as a barrage of fireworks exploded inside me. With another deep thrust, his orgasm chased mine and he came long and hard, my name spilling from his lips. I could feel his hot release pouring down my already drenched thighs. He rested his glistening forehead on mine, our heated breaths mingling. I stroked his damp hair.

"Jesus, Gloria. That was even better than I imagined," he rasped, his voice as raw as mine.

Confession: Wall banging was something I'd fantasized about, too, ever since he'd mentioned it in his conference room. It had exceeded my expectations too. It was like a thrill ride—the kind you had to hold on to tightly or you might fall off. The experience was in a word: mind-blowing.

I wanted more. More of him.

As if he read my mind again, he breathed against my ear. "I'm not done with you, Ms. Long."

Shrouded in his scent, his breath, his touch, I reflected on this shift in power. Being dominated by a man was something new for me—unchartered territory. This man was insatiable. We fucked again in the shower and then he carried me to our bed, nuzzling my neck.

I loved it. And I loved him. Only one question weighed on my heart: Did he love me?

As he brought me to orgasm once again, I yearned to hear them. The three little magic words. Basking in each other's juices, we held each other as I awaited his declaration.

It never came.

Disappointment shot through my veins like a depressant. But Sandrine's other words echoed in my head like an antidote.

Don't let him go.

No. I couldn't let him go.

And I held him tighter. The unknown blanketing us like something on loan.

CHAPTER 43

Jaime

If buying Gloria her favorite flowers—thanks to a tip from her PR guy—was all it took to get to her heart, tonight was going to be a good, good night. The combination of the fragrant lilies and roses was like an intoxicating drug. Or maybe I was just addicted to her. Still semi-erect after our amazing wall bang, it took me no time to get hard as nails again. We fucked our brains out one more time in the shower, bringing each other to another round of mind-shattering orgasms. Actually, she had three. This gorgeous woman was as insatiable as I was. When it came to control, she had none.

"What's that your holding?" she asked as she sat on the edge of the bed towel drying her waist-length hair.

"A surprise." Carrying the large, beautifully wrapped box, which I'd hidden in the closet, I headed her way and then set it down on her lap.

She looked up at me. "For me?"

I jutted my chin. "Open it."

My gaze stayed on her as she carefully ripped off the bow and paper and then lifted off the lid of the shiny white box. Her eyes lit up at the contents inside.

"Oh my God, Jaime. This is stunning!" she beamed as she unfolded the garment.

Indeed it was. I'd spotted the dress in the window of a high-end boutique a few doors down from the antique store where I'd scored big time thanks to Mani. It had called Gloria's name. Though maybe in retrospect, it called my name when it came to this evening's plans.

Standing up, Gloria held the dress up against her. It was a bit reminiscent of the blue dress she'd worn on our dinner date in New York, but fancier. And bright red. The haltered top was beaded with ruby sequins, and the flowy chiffon skirt was long in the back and knee-length in the front. I knew Gloria's size—and taste—and knew it would look perfect on her. Best of all, it was perfect for what I had in mind later.

"I want you to wear this dress tonight, angel. With those red lace undergarments I saw in your bag and that red lipstick you have." In my mind, I was already fantasizing helping her into it, adjusting it so that her gorgeous tits fell perfectly in the halter neckline and then zipping it up as my lips trailed kisses up her arms to that sensitive part of her neck which I would kiss and lick while I slipped my hand under the skirt, sweeping away those scanty little panties so I could finger her clit until she was squirming and begging for me to make her come. Oh, the pleasure I would give her! Just the thought of it sent my cock into a tither. If she looked down, she would for sure see the bulge beneath my robe.

"What are the plans for tonight?" she asked, still admiring the dress.

"Dinner and a surprise."

"What kind of surprise?" she asked inquisitively, glancing up at me.

"Come on, it wouldn't be a surprise if I told you." She made one of her adorable scrunched up faces, and as turned on as I was, I told her we needed to get some rest. We needed to conserve every bit of energy for tonight.

Still focused on tonight's plans, she didn't thank me for the dress. As I cuddled her in my arms under the bed covers, I gave her a chaste kiss on the top of her head and laughed to myself.

She'd be thanking me later. That was for sure.

CHAPTER 44

Gloria

The restaurant Jaime took me to was an intimate neighborhood bistro, walking distance from the hotel. With its candlelit, red-checkered tablecloth tables and funky local art on the walls, it was definitely not the kind of restaurant where you'd find Victor Holden. Chances were he was holding court with his business associate and some high-priced female escorts at some posh club on the Right Bank.

We sat side by side like true Parisians along a red leather banquet. His thigh brushed against mine and our shoulders touched. When he turned to speak or look at me, his warm breath grazed my flesh. He smelled delicious and looked as sexy as sin. He was clad in all black—elegantly tailored wool slacks and a soft cashmere sweater that clung to his prominent biceps and showed off his broad, chiseled chest. Mr. Beautiful and Continental! I was wearing the new red dress he'd bought me. He had insisted I wear it along with my hair down and red lipstick. The least I could do was oblige.

"Mr. Zander, I meant to thank you for this beautiful dress," I said humbly after a sip of the expensive Côtes du Rhône wine he'd ordered. "You really shouldn't have. There was no need. I can afford to buy my own designer clothing."

Setting down his half-full goblet, he turned to me and

smiled.

"Ms. Long, it gave me great pleasure to buy it for you. And it makes you very surprise-worthy."

A shiver zigzagged down my spine. He still hadn't given me a clue about the surprise he had planned. Though I was sure it had to do with lifting up the skirt of my dress and doing some very naughty things. My nerve endings buzzed at the thought of the possibilities. While the dish in front of me, a delicate poisson au beurre, looked delectable, I had a hard time eating it when I knew this breathtaking man was totally eye-fucking me. His smoldering blue eyes burnt into mine. I squirmed, my panties soaked from desire while my cheeks flushed with embarrassment.

He smirked at me, knowing damn well he was affecting me. I kept waiting for him to make a move. The surprise. My gaze drank in his searing eyes and that sexy, slightly parted mouth that was longing for a taste of me. My body was crackling all over with anticipation. Seated so intimately close to each other, a kiss was just inches away. And that was just for starters.

I finally managed a bite of my fish. It was delicious. Jaime watched as I savored the flavorful, buttery fillet.

"So where did you learn to fuck, Gloria?" he asked before I could swallow.

I almost gagged. I was certainly not prepared for that conversation game changer.

Genetics. My mother was a crack whore.

"I've been around," I managed after regaining my composure and feeling assured I wouldn't regurgitate my food. We turned in tandem to face one another.

He cocked a brow. "What does that mean?"

"I fucked a lot of guys when I moved to LA."

"Anyone serious?"

"No just a bunch of fucks." Heartless fucks—none of

which had ever given me an orgasm. Not even a clitoral one. It was a just stupid phase I went through to keep my mind off the heinous crime I'd committed back East. My secret. Once Gloria's Secret took off, I had little time or interest in any kind of sexual relationship.

"What about that PR guy of yours?"

"You mean, Kevin?"

"Yeah. He's very good-looking, and it seems like he's really into you."

"He happens to be my best friend. He also happens to be gay." *And he's fucking your assistant Ray.*

A wry smile flickered on his face. "Good. That's what I thought. I don't want to share you with anyone." He sipped his wine. "And what about that boyfriend you were visiting in New York?"

Huh? My brows furrowing, I had no idea whom he was talking about, but then I remembered. The one I made up. I thought he'd seen right through my pathetic white lie, but maybe he'd given it second thought. *Score one for me.*

I took a long swig of my wine to keep him in suspense.

He tugged at my hair. His face tensed. "Well . . ."

Okay, enough torture. "You don't have to worry about him."

"Good." His face relaxed a bit. "You know, I'm very possessive. If I ever see you with him, I'll knock his teeth out and make it so he'll never be able to put his mouth to yours ever."

"You won't have to," I reassured him, both intimidated and turned on by his fierce jealous streak. After another morsel of fish, I asked, "And what about you, Mr. Zander? It's only fair that I get some more insight into your social life."

He grinned. "You mean, sex life." A statement, not a question.

"Semantics." I wrinkled my nose at him, knowing that turned him on.

"Let's put it this way. I've probably fucked every model in your Gloria's Secret catalogue."

I almost choked again. Why should I be surprised?

"But just like you, they were only mindless fucks."

That wasn't good enough. "That could pose another major conflict of interest." Jealousy scorched through me, thinking that whomever we cast in the new advertising campaign might be someone he'd fucked. Or wanted to fuck. I inwardly shuddered at the thought of being just another conquest . . . the latest entry on his find-feel-fuck-and-forget list.

With a roguish glint in his eyes, Mr. God's Gift to Models twisted a lock of my loose hair around his index finger. "Don't worry, Gloria. I plan to use fresh talent. In fact, I'm convinced that *you* should be the star."

What?

His eyes traveled from my face to my cleavage and stayed there. "My creative instincts tell me it just feels right."

My forehead creased. "I don't get it."

"Think about it, angel. A beautiful, sexy CEO selling what she believes in. It would be breakthrough. And trust me, a camera couldn't take a bad shot of you. We'll just have to airbrush that scar of yours that you won't tell me about."

That did it. Before I could ingest another bite of the fish, I glanced down at my chest and choked. Feeling myself turn red, I immediately reached for my sparkling water and gulped it down.

"Are you okay?" asked a concerned Jaime.

"I'll be right back." Still choking, I excused myself to go to the restroom where I splashed some cold water on my face to calm down. Wherever I went my secret followed me.

"Do you want me to take you back to the hotel?" Jaime asked when I returned five minutes later.

"No. I'm fine."

"Are you sure? You still look flushed."

"I'm just not sure about me being in the ad campaign."

Jaime looked relieved. "Trust me, you'll change your mind." He leaned into me and planted a chaste kiss on my forehead, his first physical advance thus far. I felt myself trembling, still reeling from his obsession with my scar and his sexploits. I also wondered if this kiss would lead to my surprise. Any form of sex in this small intimate restaurant made my nerves sizzle.

To my relief, his advances stopped with the kiss. He continued to talk business, focusing on the timeline and logistics of the shoot. I half-listened, too wrapped up with my newfound insecurities. Feelings never entered the conversation. I was glad when the check came and reached for it.

"Remember, I still owe you a dinner."

He grabbed the check out of my hand. "No, Gloria. Let me pay. I'll charge it back to your account as I would call this strictly a business dinner."

"Fine." I flung the word at him as he dug into a pocket for his credit card and slapped it onto the table.

A few minutes later, our waiter returned with the paid bill. Jaime had obviously tipped him well because he had brought us our outerwear that we'd left with the coat-check. Rising, Jaime shrugged on his leather bomber jacket; it was one he wore when I first met him. One look at him in it made him once again totally irresistible. He adjusted my shawl over my shoulders, reverently lifting up my blanket of hair as he did. I put my doubts aside. By his actions—oh, those flowers!—and the amount of time he spent with me, I had to believe I was different from the others. He even said I was.

He kissed a sensitive spot on the side of my neck, bringing me into the moment. "So, Ms. Long, are you ready for your surprise?"

Ten minutes later, I was huddled next to him in his limo, blindfolded with a dense piece of black lace, heading to an unknown destination.

"Where are we going?" I asked nervously, brushing against his soft leather jacket as the limo made a sharp turn.

"That, my angel, *is* the surprise."

CHAPTER 45

Jaime

In the limo, I reflected on the evening thus far. I wasn't sure how well it was going. If I were sharing it in a session with Dr. Zimmer, he'd probably say I'd resorted to my defense mechanisms. Asking Gloria about her former lovers wasn't exactly romantic and the conversation made her uneasy. Put her on the defensive. Again I got the feeling she was hiding something. More specifically, something about someone. Maybe she still had feelings for that dude in New York that she was denying. Or maybe it was an abusive relationship she wanted to forget. One that had something to do with the scar on her chest.

My boasting about my sexual conquests didn't help. I didn't need my shrink to tell me it was another form of putting up barriers. Hearing about them made Gloria visibly upset. I certainly wasn't getting an "A" in the romance department. "A" for asshole was more like it. And when I got carried away, mixing business with pleasure, I'm sure my grade dropped to an "F." "F" for fuck-up. I'd freaked her out.

What made things more unsettling is that I noticed someone at the bar checking out Gloria. Yes, it was a fact that stunning Gloria turned heads everywhere we went in Paris—both men and women were awestruck by her mesmerizing beauty—but this was different. He was studying her as if he knew her. He didn't seem like her type or American for that matter. Fifty-ish, he was short and stocky, wearing a long dark trench coat and broad rimmed fedora that obscured his face. I could glean that his skin was a ghostly white marred by odd scars on either side of his plump lips, his nose bulbous as if had been broken several times, and his eyes eerily pinkish. I thought he might be albino, but it was difficult to tell in the dim lighting. But for sure, there was something in his translucent eyes that glinted with recognition—or at least curiosity—at the sight of my beautiful companion. Every time he caught me staring at him, he jerked his head around and went back to draining his expensive vodka. He'd ordered an entire bottle of Beluga.

Just as I was about to ask Gloria if she knew him, he shot around again while she excused herself to go to the restroom. As she headed to the back of the restaurant, the man's squinty eyes followed her while mine darted back and forth between them to make sure Gloria was safe. Then, his menacing gaze locked on me.

Another thought leapfrogged into my head. Maybe he was watching me. That he was some fucking goon that Victor had put on my trail after last night's encounter. Though it was unlikely my stepfather knew where I was staying, it wasn't impossible. Men like him had ways. And had people.

And then another thought. *They* were following me. The Feds. Checking up on me to see if I was really their man. Their next to last words to me circled my head. "We need you to get close to her . . . Even if you have to fuck the truth out of her."

With so much at stake—everything to win, everything to lose—my chest tightened. The man's unyielding stare grated at me. I had the urge to confront him, but before I could, he slapped a few hundred Euros on the bar counter, adjusted the collar of his coat, and got up from his seat. His head stayed low as he flew through the bistro like a phantom. Halfway to the entrance of the small restaurant, he slipped out his cell phone from a pocket and put it to his ear. My eyes stayed on him as he snarled, cursing loudly in a Slavic language I didn't understand. Serbian? Russian? Polish? Clearly agitated by the phone call or from too much vodka, he swung open the door to the bistro and stormed out. When Gloria returned, I asked for the check and paid it despite her protests.

Now as we drove along the Seine, my thoughts were still focused on the suspicious freak when Gloria cut into them.

"Where are we going??" Her tenuous voice sounded in my ears and brought my attention back to the moment. To *my* game plan.

"It's a surprise, my angel." After glancing behind us to make sure we weren't being followed, I whisked out my first surprise from my jacket pocket. A black lace blindfold. Before Gloria had a chance to protest, it was secured around her eyes.

"Jaime, what the hell are you doing?" she snapped.

"What does it look like? I'm blindfolding you. Get used to it."

Her body tensed; her face scrunched. But she was being a good girl. My angel.

I looked back one more time to make sure we weren't being followed. For sure we weren't and then facing forward, my eyes took in our destination ahead of us.

"Jaime, are we almost there?" asked Gloria again, her voice impetuous.

She couldn't see it, but I smiled. And my eyes lit up.

"Yeah. We're here."

I shoved all my second-guessing and suspicions to the

back of mind. Mental reset. Things were about to turn around. Literally.

Yup. Tonight was going to be a good, good night.

CHAPTER 46

Gloria

A short fifteen minutes later, I found myself traipsing across what my other senses told me was a pebbly path in my six-inch stilettos. Except for the crunching sounds of our footsteps and sirens in the distance, the balmy Paris air was silent. Frustration and anticipation accompanied my unsteady steps. I wished I could see where Mr. Surprise was taking me.

"Why did you have to blindfold me?" I asked, clutching his arm for balance.

"Gloria, shame on you. You should know the answer to that already. To learn to trust me."

My eyes rolled under the blindfold. Distracted, one of my sharp heels caught in the gravel. I stumbled, but he caught me. "Are you taking me to some private underground sex club?" I asked nervously.

Jaime laughed heartily. "Close but no cigar. It's definitely private, but underground is the last word I'd use to describe it."

Frustration mounted. Beneath my lace blindfold, my nose scrunched. "Are we there yet?" I asked, silently berating myself for sounding like a whiny six-year-old on a road trip.

"Patience has its virtues, Ms. Long," he replied, picking

up our pace to my chagrin.

Several steps later, I could hear music. A familiar song, one of Madame Paulette's favorites. "Toi et Moi" sung by Charles Aznavour.

"*Bonsoir,* Monsieur Zander. I have been looking forward to seeing you again."

A Frenchman's deep, jovial voice sounded in my ears. We must be at our destination, I thought.

"*Bonsoir*, Claude. Are we set to go?"

"*Oui, monsieur*. Up, up, and away. You and *zee* beautiful *mademoiselle* can board *tout de suite.*"

My stomach bunched up with nerves. Was he taking me on a private plane? Or on a helicopter? Or a hot air balloon? Flying in an airplane was bad enough, but a chopper? That flimsy whirling flying machine? Even worse . . . a hot air balloon that could hit a power line and explode in mid air. I bit down on my lip. Oh, God. Is that what he had in store?

"I'm afraid of flying!" I gasped. My hand grew cold and clammy in his.

Jaime yanked me unceremoniously away; I assumed, in the direction of the aircraft. I resisted, clumsily tripping a couple of times in my heels along the way.

"Relax, Gloria. You're going to be flying all right but not the kind you have in mind." He led the way. "Watch your head and your step."

Too late. Instead of ducking, I banged my head hard as I climbed over some mysterious threshold. I let out a loud "OW."

"Are you okay?" asked Jaime. There was humor in his voice, like he was holding back laughter. *Insensitive jerk!*

"Yes," I grumbled, rubbing the already forming bump with my free hand. I hesitantly took a few more steps.

"Sit," he commanded, pressing down on my shoulders.

I slowly lowered my butt to a hard, lightly cushioned

surface and then explored my surroundings with both hands like a blind person, tapping, touching, and absorbing everything around me. I was sitting on some kind of bench, surrounded by glass. Was I in some kind of elevator? Enough with the blindfold! But when I raised my hands to my head, Jaime grasped them midway and stopped me. He was definitely sitting across from me.

"Uh, uh, uh," he chided playfully. "Don't make me tie you up. I've got another lace binding right here in my pocket. It'll only take me seconds to wrap it around those lovely hands of yours."

"Sorry," I said meekly. *Asshole!*

"Promise you won't undo the blindfold?" He squeezed my hands so tight I yelped.

"Promise." Why did I continue to submit to his little sadistic power games? The answer was simple: I was still crazy in love with him.

"Enjoy your ride," said Claude.

I heard two gliding doors slide closed. *Clink!*

"Where are we going?" I asked anxiously.

"You'll see soon enough." Despite the blindfold, I could picture the smirk on his smug face.

Suddenly, we jerked. I jolted. And then swoop! My stomach fluttered. We were going up! Up and around! I gulped. The butterflies inside me multiplied as we rose higher and higher. The spinning sensation was familiar. Brighton Beach memories. I had an idea of where I was. My heart began to race, and sweat seeped out of my pores. I was having a panic attack.

Sixty long seconds later, the spinning came to a halt. Jaime yanked off my blindfold.

"Open your eyes, Gloria," he commanded.

I flicked my eyes open and gasped. I was suspended high in the air, seated opposite a very smug Jaime Zander.

My heart pitter-pattered. Oh my God! I was trapped in a cabin with this gorgeous god on Paris's famed Ferris wheel, the Grande Roue. At a standstill at the very apex—as high as the wheel could go.

I was at a loss for words. A combination of terror, outrage, and pure awe consumed me. Surrounded by glass on all sides, I took in the twinkling lights of Paris—The City of Light—below. The view took my breath away.

I finally found my voice. "How did you manage this?"

Jaime's lush mouth curled into a proud, cocky smile. "A client. He's the head of the French Tourism Bureau. The advertising campaign I created for him last year resulted in a fifty percent spike in tourism. He was beholden to me and told me he owed me. And *voilà,* Mademoiselle Long, here we are."

The cabin suddenly rocked. I let out a frightened gasp. Jaime clasped my hands in his. "Relax, Gloria. This is going to be fun. The thrill ride of your life."

"I don't do well with Ferris wheels," I stammered. Like airplanes and high-speed elevators, they were one of those things that made me feel out of control. When I was a teenager living close to Brooklyn's Coney Island, I had once ridden the amusement park's famed Ferris wheel, and it had gotten stuck, leaving me helplessly trapped in the swinging open-air carriage on the top. The memory of that dreadful experience made me tremble.

Jaime squeezed my hands. "Take a deep breath, angel. You're going to do just fine with me. What do you think of the view?"

Inhaling, I pressed my face against a glass pane. It's spectacular," I managed, my eyes lingering on the lit up Eiffel Tower.

"No, Gloria. I meant this view."

My gaze jumped back to his beautiful face and followed

his eyes as they led me to his crotch.

My eyes almost popped out of their sockets as another tower of steel sprung into view. Jaime's monumental cock!

"Well . . .?"

"It's spectacular," I repeated with a stutter as tingles mixed with the flood between my legs. My inner muscles clenched and my blood pounded in my ears.

"Good. I want you to enjoy it." A broad, saucy grin spread across his face. He gestured with his long forefinger. "Come here, you."

My legs jelly, I hesitantly stood up and staggered over to him, bending so as not to bang my head again. Thank goodness, the cabin had stopped rocking.

My heartbeat quickened. I knew what was next. "Do you want me to suck you?"

Sure of his response, I lowered myself to my knees. But before they could hit the floor, he yanked me upright by my hair.

"Not this time, angel."

I stared at him blankly.

"Sit on me!" A command.

In a breath, he lifted up my chiffon dress and—*Slash!*—tore off my lacy red bikinis. All that remained was the matching lace garter and attached sheer silk stockings. I was very exposed. A finger slid across my wet folds, igniting sparks of pleasure. He sucked on it and then ran it across the wide rim of his erection.

"Perfect!" Planting his manly hands firmly on my waist, he positioned me exactly where he wanted me to be, straddling his rock-hard thighs and . . .

Impaled on his giant cock! I moaned as his hot cock, that magnificent tower, speared into me, filling me to the hilt. Oh. My. God.

His denim eyes, now fiery and fierce, burned into mine.

His hot breath heated my already flaming face.

"Aren't you going to tie me up?" I immediately regretted my words. I wasn't thinking straight.

"Hey, angel, no need; there's no place to go . . . except down on me." He lifted me up a few inches by my hips and dragged his hard throbbing cock down my wet tunnel. He immediately bucked back up me, so deep I yelped.

"And besides, you'll need your hands. Hold on to my shoulders."

I slapped my palms onto them, curling my fingers around the bone-hard edges. A gasp escaped my throat as he lifted me again.

"Now, ride me, angel! Hard!"

I crashed down on his slick thickness, then immediately lifted my hips and descended hard on him again. We instantly got into a rhythm. Up and down. Up and down. I loved every thrust. Now, this was a thrill ride! I kept pace with him as he bucked harder and faster. My breasts brushed up and down his leather jacket, the friction causing heat waves. Beneath the delicate lace of my bra, I could feel my nipples swelling and hardening. His eyes grew hooded, his breathing ragged. I was riding him to heaven. I chewed my lip to hold back whimpers.

He bit my upper lip, and my mouth parted from the delicious pain.

"It's okay to scream," he said, his voice low. "No one's going to hear you up here except me."

Suddenly, the wheel started spinning again. He gripped my hips tighter, for sure bruising my skin, as I clung to his shoulders, still riding him. We were descending to earth but I was ascending skyward to an out of this world orgasm. My head was spinning and I couldn't help screaming. The whirling dervish of sensations that swirled inside me was bringing me to the edge. Let me rephrase . . . this was one *extreme* thrill ride.

"I need to come!" I pleaded, hot tears now trickling down my cheeks. Even my aching thighs were crying out for relief.

"Not yet." He could barely manage the two words, his breathing so ragged.

Ruthlessly, relentlessly, he continued pounding me as I posted and met his every thrust. This man had no mercy. His face contorted and moans filled the cabin. The intense pressure inside me was building. Building so fast I thought I'd implode. I squeezed my eyes shut.

"Gloria, open your eyes. Now!"

I forced them open.

"Don't take them off the Eiffel Tower."

A heartbeat away from coming, I focused my gaze on the Paris landmark. My mouth dropped open, forming a big O, as the monumental tower burst into a shower of scintillating white light. At that very moment, my own shower of titillating sparks burst inside me, zapping every inch of my being.

"Oh my God, oh my God, oh my God," I screamed over and over as the sparks kept flying.

"Gloria, now watch me light up." He turned my head away from the window to face him.

My eyes met his for a brief second. His face distorted with tortuous rapture as he rammed into me one more time.

"Oh my God," I shrieked again as his electrifying explosion met mine fast and furious with a roar of my name. I collapsed onto his chest, dazed and totally awed that this sex god had so skillfully managed to orchestrate our orgasms with the Eiffel Tower's own orgasmic spectacle of lights.

"Jesus, angel," he groaned, his voice hoarse, and his still flickering dick going nowhere. "That was so fucking amazing."

I responded with the only three words I seemed to know. "Oh. My. God."

He lifted me off his chest with a fistful of my hair and held me in his gaze. "My turn to enjoy the view. You're so beautiful after a good fuck." His pouted lips latched onto mine, sucking and gnawing until my mouth parted and met his tongue, stroke for stroke. My hands left his shoulders and cupped his beautiful face. The touch of the stubble along his jawline brought feeling back to my nearly numb, stiff fingers. Though my eyes were closed, I could still see and feel the sparks inside me. His cock, still pulsing, didn't budge. We were totally lost in one another.

A scraping thud brought us back to reality. The spinning wheel came to a halt. We were at last back on the ground although my mind and body were still spinning wildly somewhere in space. Jaime slowly withdrew his tongue, and then his slick, swollen cock, tucking it inside his slacks. After zipping up his fly, he helped straighten my dress so it covered my legs in a lady-like way. My shredded bikinis crumpled down by my ankles were now part of French history.

I was still in a daze, sitting on his lap with my arms clasped around his neck, when the cabin doors automatically slid open. My heart jumped. Claude!

"One more spin?" he asked. The mischievous twinkle in his dark eyes clued me in that he knew what had gone down up there. I flushed with embarrassment, acutely aware of the wetness between my legs.

Jaime winked at the robust, mustached man. "Take it away, Claude."

My heart leapt into my throat. Holy shit! He was going to fuck my brains out again and send me orbiting back into space? I tensed up.

"Are you going to—?"

He cut me off with a fierce kiss that made me melt.

Pulling away, he shot me a wry smile and twirled a clump of my hair. He hadn't done that for a while.

"Gloria, I overestimate you and you underestimate me. Do you really think a creative guy like me would do the same thing twice?"

I screwed up my face. "Well, to be honest—"

He cut me off again. "To be honest, I just want to hold you this time around." He coaxed me to sink my head against his warm, tight chest. I sighed as I sunk into him. The sweet musky smell of his leather jacket wafted up my nose. I closed my eyes to the song of our heartbeats thrumming together. *Heaven!*

When we got to the top, the cabin began to rock again. Blissfully, I just let myself rock with him, swathed by the warmth of his body. The rise and fall of his chest and the sound of his soft breathing lulled me into a trance-like state. I felt so safe when I should have felt so scared. I'd lost track of time when he nuzzled my neck, bringing awareness back into me.

"Gloria," he whispered into my ear. "I have another surprise for you."

Another surprise? What now? He never ceased to amaze me. Slowly, I lifted my head from his chest and met his gaze. His eyes were twinkling like the lights below us. He circled my lips with his index finger and then dug his hand into a pocket of his jacket. He whipped out a small red velvet box and held it in his palm. "Open it, Gloria," he ordered. "It'll turn you on."

A mixture of curiosity and anticipation coursed through me as I took the box from him. What could be inside? A butt plug? A nipple clamp? A clit ring? I was familiar with all of these little sex toys from our research for our new product line but knew nothing about them personally. With jittery fingers, I flicked it open. I gasped in shock and my heart skipped a beat. Glaring in my eyes was a magnificent platinum ring with two entwined, heart-shaped diamonds. They sparkled like the stars surrounding us. I couldn't get my mouth to close.

"Do you know what this is?" asked my companion, his eyes burning into mine.

My heart was slamming so hard against my chest I thought it would leap out. "Jaime, are you asking me to marry you?"

SEX, LUST & LINGERIE

The steamy, explosive CONCLUSION to *Sex, Lies & Lingerie* and Book 2 in *USA Today* Bestselling Author Nelle L'Amour's *Secrets and Lies* series.

> "5-Stars. Ms. L'Amour wraps up this riveting story with lots of drama, action, and intense passion that'll have you on the edge of your seat until the very last page!"
>
> —Maria Loves Book Book Blog

Jaime:
She's on her knees.

Gloria Long.

Just for me.

I'm the man who rules her. I'm the man who owns her. I'm the man who can make her or break her.

But our time together is threatened by my deceit. And a demon I must destroy.

All shit is about to break loose.

And in the end I may lose her.

Gloria:
Why didn't I resist him?

Because he was too strong, too determined, too beautiful.

He made me fall apart. And fall for him.

I could have had it all. But I won't.

My dark, horrific secret is about to cost me everything I've worked for. And the man I love.

My world is about to be shattered. And so is my heart.

*NOTE: NO cliffhanger.

FOLLOW NELLE!

Please be sure to sign up for my mailing list and follow me on Amazon, BookBub, and my Facebook Reader Group to be the first to know about my new releases, sales, and giveaways.

Newsletter:
nellelamour.com/newsletter

Facebook Reader Group Nelle's Belles
facebook.com/groups/1943750875863015

Amazon Author Page:
amazon.com/Nelle-LAmour/e/B00ATHR0LQ

BookBub:
bookbub.com/authors/nelle-l-amour

Website:
www.nellelamour.com

Instagram:
instagram.com/nellelamourauthor

Email:
nellelamour@gmail.com

ABOUT THE AUTHOR

Nelle L'Amour is a *NEW YORK TIMES* and *USA TODAY* Bestselling Author who lives in Los Angeles with her Prince Charming-ish husband, twin college-aged princesses, and a bevy of royal pain-in-the-butt pets. A former executive in the entertainment industry with a prestigious Humanitus Award to her credit, she gave up playing with Barbies a long time ago but still enjoys playing with toys with her husband. While she writes in her PJs, she loves to get dressed up and pretend she's Hollywood royalty. She writes juicy stories with characters that will make you both laugh and cry and stay in your heart forever.

BOOKS BY NELLE L'AMOUR

Secrets and Lies
Sex, Lies & Lingerie
Sex, Lust & Lingerie
Sex, Love & Lingerie

Unforgettable
Unforgettable Book 1
Unforgettable Book 2
Unforgettable Book 3

THAT MAN Series
THAT MAN 1
THAT MAN 2
THAT MAN 3
THAT MAN 4
THAT MAN 5
THAT MAN 6

Alpha Billionaire Duet
TRAINWRECK 1
TRAINWRECK 2

Love Duet
Undying Love
Endless Love

A Standalone Romantic Comedy
Baby Daddy

An OTT Insta-love Standalone
The Big O

Standalone Second Chance Romance
Remember Me

A Romance Compilation
Naughty Nelle

Printed in Great Britain
by Amazon